A SIMPLE KISS

The lines of misery on Jon's face touched Emma's heart. It seemed grossly unfair that he should be subjected to such pain after all that he had endured. Wanting to lend some sort of comfort, she stepped forward. But the toe of her wet boot caught on the uneven ground and she tripped.

She reached out a hand blindly for support and Jon expertly caught her by the waist. With a startled cry, Emma instinctively threw her arms around his neck to keep herself from tumbling to the ground.

They turned their heads at precisely the same moment, bumping noses. Emma squeaked in surprise, but there was an even greater shock to come when the viscount angled his head and kissed her lips . . .

Books by Adrienne Basso

HIS WICKED EMBRACE

HIS NOBLE PROMISE

TO WED A VISCOUNT

TO PROTECT AN HEIRESS

TO TEMPT A ROGUE

THE WEDDING DECEPTION

THE CHRISTMAS HEIRESS

HIGHLAND VAMPIRE

HOW TO ENJOY A SCANDAL

NATURE OF THE BEAST

THE CHRISTMAS COUNTESS

HOW TO SEDUCE A SINNER

A LITTLE BIT SINFUL

'TIS THE SEASON TO BE SINFUL

INTIMATE BETRAYAL

NOTORIOUS DECEPTION

SWEET SENSATIONS

A NIGHT TO REMEMBER

HOW TO BE A SCOTTISH MISTRESS

BRIDE OF A SCOTTISH WARRIOR

THE HIGHLANDER WHO LOVED ME

NO OTHER HIGHLANDER

THE BRIDE CHOOSES A HIGHLANDER

EVERY BIT A ROGUE

Published by Kensington Publishing Corporation

EVERY BIT
A ROGUE

ADRIENNE
BASSO

ZEBRA BOOKS
KENSINGTON PUBLISHING CORP.
www.kensingtonbooks.com

*With love and thanks to my incredible family,
dear friends and faithful readers
who have encouraged and supported me
throughout the years*

Chapter One

English Countryside, 1824

The bride was late. Not modestly late, not traditionally late, not coyly late.

Alarmingly late.

Scandalously late.

Unforgivably late.

The slight spring breeze that had earlier drifted through the small, crowded chapel had ceased. The guests, growing warm and impatient, began fidgeting in their seats. Those who had previously turned around to discreetly glance at the church doors, were now openly staring and the murmurs of conversations speculating as to what, exactly, was keeping the bride had begun to swell in volume.

"Can you see anything, Carter?" Lady Dorothea Grayson, Marchioness of Atwood, asked. Her husband dutifully angled his shoulder, raised his chin, and stole a quick look at the open church doors.

"Or hear anything?" her older sister, Gwendolyn Barrington, added as she extracted a fan from her reticule and began vigorously waving it in front of her face.

"Not a blessed thing to be seen or heard," Carter replied. As he was taller than most men, the marquess had an unobstructed view, so there was no need to be as vulgar as some of the other guests and so obviously crane his neck.

Sitting quietly between her two sisters, Gwendolyn and Dorothea, Miss Emma Ellingham lifted her head and glanced about the chapel, noting for the first time that something was amiss. She had been woolgathering, caught so intently in her own thoughts that until now she had shut out her surroundings.

It was an understandable circumstance. She had been invited to the wedding merely as a courtesy out of respect for her brother-in-law Carter Grayson, the Marquess of Atwood, heir to the Dukedom of Hansborough. Carter and her sister Dorothea were the groom's neighbors, and since Emma was currently living with them, it would have been considered impolite to exclude her.

Emma had only briefly met the groom, Viscount Kendall, in passing last month and had never once laid eyes upon the bride. Apparently, from what she could now glean, there was a chance she might never be afforded that opportunity.

"Brides, especially younger ones, can suffer from extreme nerves on their wedding day," Emma said, hastily adding, "or so I've been told. Perhaps the poor girl needs a few extra moments to steady herself before the ceremony. I believe you mentioned that she was only nineteen years of age, Dorothea?"

"I did." Dorothea cocked an eyebrow at Emma. "I'm surprised that you remembered. Actually, I had assumed that you weren't even listening to me when I told you."

Emma blushed. Dorothea and Carter had been nothing but kind to her since she had left Gwen's household and come to live with them last month. Emma appreciated their warm hospitality and efforts to include her in all things, but frankly she found the many intricacies of their social life exhausting. Especially given her ever-present, lingering melancholy.

No matter how hard she tried, Emma had been unable to get past her current preoccupation with her future. Specifically, what she was going to do with herself now that her artistic muse, the one thing that had sustained her for all of her twenty-two years, appeared to have vanished.

Who was she, if not an artist? What could she possibly do with herself, with her life, if she did not paint? The question was terrifying to contemplate, even more so when no reasonable answer was to be found.

Her artistic talent had been obvious from a young age, but since she was female, it had never been encouraged. Growing up, art lessons had been beyond her family's financial circumstances, especially after her parents had died, but despite the lack of formal training, Emma's skills had continued to grow.

Her oldest sister Gwendolyn's marriage to the wealthy Jason Barrington seven years ago had changed everything. Suddenly, there were art lessons with the finest instructors, along with encouragement and admiration for her work. 'Twas glorious and humbling and wonderful.

Then two months ago—unexpectedly, inexplicably—her passion and inspiration for her art deserted her. And it seemed the harder she tried to get it back, the further it slipped away, leaving her puzzled and fearful.

Emma sighed and looked again around the church, the muttering crowd and the nervous groom, acknowledging that she wasn't the only one facing an uncertain future.

"What precisely is the etiquette for this sort of thing?" Gwendolyn wanted to know.

Gwen's husband, Jason Barrington, crossed his arms and sighed. "I suppose we must wait until the groom decides he has had enough."

Carter removed a gold pocket watch from the vest of his patterned silk waistcoat. "The bride is nearly an hour late. I highly doubt the chit is going to make an appearance. Kendall must have come to that realization already."

"Ah, but according to Mr. Pope, hope springs eternal," Emma interjected, quoting the famous poet. "We might be here for an indeterminable amount of time."

"Oh, dear." Gwen sighed heavily and increased the already rapid speed of her fan.

"Our discomfort is nothing compared to the agony that poor Lord Kendall must be feeling," Dorothea said with a sympathetic sigh. "'Tis common knowledge that he has a great affection for his fiancée and holds her in the highest regard and esteem. The scandal of being jilted will only add another layer of pain to his heartbreak. Especially since he is such a levelheaded, responsible, proper sort of fellow. Truly above reproach."

"In other words, dull," Jason interjected wryly.

"Don't be unkind," Gwen scolded, rapping her husband's knuckles with the base of her fan. "Not all men are cut out to be daring, dashing rogues like you, my love."

"Alas, Barrington is a rogue no longer. He's been thoroughly domesticated by years of marriage to you, Gwen," Carter joked.

Jason furrowed his brow. "I could say the same of you, Atwood, but I've too much breeding to mention it."

The two men exchanged an exaggerated glare before breaking into roguish grins.

Emma shook her head, marveling at how much alike her two brothers-in-law could be at times. An odd occurrence, given that her sisters were very different women. Gwen was sensible, practical, and selfless while Dorothea was fanciful, unconventional the majority of the time, and kind.

There was no denying that marriage had brought them both great happiness and joy, along with a love that was deep and true. Could marriage do the same for her? Was it the lack of a partner that kept her tossing and turning at night, dissatisfied with seemingly everything in her life?

Emma sighed deeply. Nay. The man she loved, with her whole heart and full spirit, was married to another. Sebastian Dodd, Viscount Benton, Earl of Tinsdale, had captured her devotion within minutes of their first meeting. He was dark and brooding, complicated and witty and handsome to a fault.

Yet beneath the roguish exterior beat the heart of a sensitive man. For years it seemed as though she was the only one who saw it—or rather, she was the only one Sebastian felt safe revealing his true self to.

She had fallen in love with him when she was sixteen and though she was considerably younger than he, Sebastian had always treated her as an adult. He made her feel special, important, alive. He teased her, confided in her, listened to and valued her opinions, and when she had finally gained the courage to confess her love, he claimed that he loved her too—in a very different way. As one would love a younger sister, a boon companion, the closest of friends.

Not passionately—as she had loved him. Not as a man loved a woman. As Jason loved Gwen. As Carter loved Dorothea.

As, based on the green tinge of his complexion and the bleak, worried eyes of Viscount Kendall, today's groom loved his prospective bride.

A noisy scuffle at the back of the church broke through Emma's gloomy memories. Following the lead of the other guests in the chapel, she shifted in the pew and stared at the heavy oak doors, which were now shut. Then, suddenly, they swung open with a resounding thud, the harsh sound reverberating to the wooden rafters.

It appeared that the bride had finally arrived.

Jon Burwell, Viscount Kendall, tugged at his pristine white cravat, attempting to ease the tightness that encircled his neck. His valet, Gilmore, had fussed for nearly fifteen minutes this morning, insisting that his lordship needed to look perfect on this most auspicious occasion. For once Jon had allowed it, willing to accept the fashionable discomfort in exchange for pleasing his soon-to-be wife.

Above all, he wanted to make Dianna proud when she beheld her groom. He wanted her to know that he was willing to make the small—as well as the grand—

gestures in order to assure her happiness. The love he felt for her was all encompassing, so deep that often he felt unable to adequately express it in words.

Instead he relied on actions to demonstrate his utter devotion. Personally, he would have preferred a simple, family affair, but Dianna had wanted a large church wedding with a noble guest list. Jon had acquiesced.

She asked for their wedding breakfast to be held in the ballroom of his manor house, as it was far grander than her father's home, and Jon was quick to agree. The long list of dishes she requested to be served put a sour expression on his cook's face as well as a sizable dent in Jon's wallet, but any unpleasantness was well worth enduring if it made Dianna happy.

His enchanting bride-to-be had begged to visit dozens of European cities on an extended wedding trip, and Jon had worked tirelessly making the arrangements. He planned their route thoughtfully, booking the finest accommodations available and hiring the most luxurious modes of transportation he could find to take them from one place to the next.

This trip would put a strain on his finances, but he had tightened his estate and household budgets and limited or even eliminated a variety of other personal expenses to accommodate Dianna's wishes.

And he had done it all with joy and eagerness.

Not everyone, however, approved of his actions. A few of his friends had warned him that he was being far too indulgent and his mother had sputtered with outrage each time she learned of Dianna's latest request.

It all came to a head yesterday morning when his mother saw the wedding cake Dianna had chosen—a multi-tiered confection that required the services of a French pastry chef to carefully construct. Stammering with indignity, Jon's mother had pronounced it a vulgar monstrosity, and the height of poor taste. He had silenced her objections with a stern warning to keep her opinions to herself, which in turn had set off a torrent of tears.

His mother's reaction made Jon feel like a brute, yet there was no help for it. He would not tolerate any criticism of his future wife, even from the mother that he adored. His greatest hope was that the two women he loved most in the world would someday share a more congenial relationship, and perhaps in time, that a bond would form.

One could only hope. And perhaps pray.

Jon's heart skipped a beat when he heard the commotion at the church doors. *At last!* He sniffed, swallowing the lump that had settled in his throat and insisted that he had not truly been worried. He should have known that Dianna would insist upon making a grand, dramatic entrance.

The minx.

Jon pulled his hand away from his cravat, straightened his spine, and lifted his chin. With a rapidly beating pulse, he waited anxiously for the organ to swell with the majestic music announcing the arrival—at long last—of the bride.

Alas, the pipes remained eerily quiet and Jon soon realized why. 'Twas not a vision of feminine beauty and grace that strode down the aisle toward him, but rather a red-faced, heavy-breathing gentleman.

Hector Winthrope, Dianna's older brother.

Hector literally ran down the aisle, seemingly unaware of the many eyes that followed him. The wave of chattering voices abruptly ceased when he reached Jon and an almost obscene quiet descended upon the church.

"Have you left Dianna in the carriage?" Jon asked, frowning with worry.

"Lord, no!" Hector exclaimed, thrusting the parchment dangling from his hand at Jon. "Read it. This note explains all. Well, rather, it states why she isn't here. In truth, I fear it explains nothing."

Jon accepted the letter, quickly scanning its contents. He recognized the handwriting instantly. The long, delicate swirls and slightly tilted lines could only have been written by Dianna.

> *Dear Jon,*
>   *Despite the admiration and regard I feel for you, I realize that I cannot marry you, as it would be a mistake that would eventually lead to grief for both of us. I crave more from this life and rejoice that I have found it with another man. I know that I do not have the right to ask for your forgiveness, but I pray that in time you will come to acknowledge that this is best for both of us.*
>
> > *Your Dianna*

"She's run off," Hector interrupted impatiently in a loud whisper. "With that scoundrel Dickenson."

Jon's head shifted. He returned his gaze to the note in his hand, but was unable to comprehend the written words.

Run off? What the devil?

"Did you see her?" Jon inquired anxiously. "Speak with her?"

"Nay. She knew better than to tell me this atrocious

news herself, knowing that I would have prevented it."
Hector clenched his fists. "When the chambermaid
delivered the breakfast tray, she discovered Dianna's
empty bedchamber. My sister must have left sometime
in the early morning hours, though the servants all
claim they neither saw nor heard anything unusual."

"What about Dianna's maid?"

Hector shook his head. "She insisted, between sobs,
that she knew nothing. I sacked her on the spot, of
course, and sent her packing. Without a reference."

Putting a hand to his pounding head, Jon stood
motionless as he tried to sort through the myriad of
unanswered questions that swirled relentlessly through
his mind.

"Dianna was quiet, almost subdued when I last saw
her yesterday morning," he muttered. "I assumed it
was due to nervous excitement."

Flustered, Hector puffed out his cheeks. "She was
no doubt planning her escape. How could she be such
a reckless fool? Who knows if Dickenson will even
marry her? She has ruined herself and brought dis-
grace upon our family name and honor. My dear
mother has taken to her bed, prostrate with grief. How
will we ever survive this scandal?"

How indeed?

A sinking feeling descended over Jon as shock and
disbelief mingled in his head. It felt as though he had
taken a hard punch to his gut. His breathing grew
uneven; his chest hurt.

Dianna had left him. Left him! Why? To satisfy a
desperate need for *more in her life.* More what?

She had promised to be his wife. His partner, his
helpmate, the mother of his children. He adored her.
He indulged her. He loved her—unconditionally.

Wasn't that enough?

The rising tide of inquisitive chatter brought Jon's attention back to the calamity of the moment and the wedding that would now not take place. The reverend approached, his eyes filled with puzzlement. Jon crumpled the note in his fist and turned away, his jumbled thoughts momentarily distracted by the too tight, bright scarlet waistcoat Hector wore over a belly that was far too soft for a man of his years.

Hector was squeezed into the garment like a giant sausage. There was no doubt that if one of the gold buttons were to become dislodged, it could prove to be a formidable weapon, hurtling across the church like a lead ball shot from a pistol. Potentially wounding or maiming one of the guests.

Yet another scandal to add to the one already brewing?

"How may I be of assistance, my lord?" the reverend asked.

"There will be no wedding this morning." Jon spoke calmly, yet he could feel himself growing clammy and queasy. His palms began to sweat and his tongue felt oddly oversized and thick. "I must make the announcement."

"Please, allow me." The reverend placed his hand on Jon's shoulder.

Though meant to be comforting, it made Jon feel even worse, for it made the moment all too real. *She truly isn't coming. She will not marry me.*

Jon drew in a shaky breath and then another. It seemed his carefully constructed, well-ordered life had just spun into total chaos.

Though she barely knew the viscount, Emma felt a tightening in her chest and she did her best not to send a pitying look toward the jilted groom. Instead, she allowed her compassion to shine through in her expression, hoping that somehow he would feel it among the snide glances and unkind remarks.

Society thrived upon appearance. Being left at the altar hinted at all manner of juicy scandal and impropriety. Judging by the bits of conversations around her that she could hear, Emma knew that speculation as to what the viscount had done to cause his own humiliation was running rampant.

Poor man.

"Such a horrible turn of events," Gwen said sadly.

"The vultures are already circling in search of any sordid and salacious details," Carter remarked.

"I'm sorry to say that I'm not surprised," Dorothea added. "I fear the interest, speculation, and gossip will continue until a fresh scandal occurs."

"Did you think it was wise of the reverend to invite the guests back to the manor house for a meal?" Jason questioned. "I suspect the very last thing Kendall wants—or needs—is to face this crowd."

"I imagine the viscount's mother, Lady Sybil, insisted upon it," Dorothea said. "'Twas well-known that no expense was spared on the wedding breakfast and a considerable amount of food has been prepared. Perhaps if she feeds this ravenous crowd, they will speak more kindly of her son."

"Don't count upon it," Gwen muttered.

"Well, we must be the exception to this ill-bred rabble. The viscount deserves to be surrounded by concerned and supportive friends," Dorothea stated.

Carter nodded. "We shall stay and do all that we can. Agreed?"

Everyone nodded and dutifully filed out of the

pew. Emma glanced over at Gwen, wondering if her sister was remembering the hurt and humiliation of the scandal she had suffered years ago. It had made her something of a recluse, until Jason had entered their lives.

Thankfully, he was not a man to be easily intimidated by society and its tireless rules. Jason scoffed at convention and had doggedly pursued Gwen until she had agreed to be his wife.

Emma and the rest of the family exited the church and the first thing they saw was the viscount's open carriage, festooned with ribbons and flowers. The driver and footman, dressed in their finest livery, stood attentively around the convenience, keeping the curious group of locals at a distance.

"Oh, Lord." Emma blanched. "It appears Lord Kendall's coachman has not been informed of the canceled wedding. He and the footmen are clearly waiting for the newly married couple to arrive."

"I'll take care of it," Carter offered.

"Ask the villagers to disperse too," Dorothea suggested. "Then once the coach is stripped of its bridal finery, offer to ride in the carriage with the viscount. No doubt he'll feel foolish going alone."

Carter nodded.

"I'll accompany you," Jason offered. "It will look odd having two men in the wedding carriage."

The men departed and Emma caught sight of the viscount's mother, Lady Sybil. Dressed in a gown of fine yellow satin, draped in luscious pearls and sporting a wide-brimmed hat with the tallest group of ostrich plumes Emma had ever seen, Lady Sybil stood alone, rigidly waiting for her coach, her hands clasped tightly in front of her.

"Dorothea—" Emma began.

"I see her," Dorothea interrupted. "Ladies, shall we?"

Gwen and Emma nodded and they all stepped forward. In the blink of an eye, the three Ellingham sisters had formed a protective circle around the viscountess.

Though she said nothing, Lady Sybil appeared to welcome their company. She held her head high as she was assisted into her coach by a footman, then motioned for Gwen, Dorothea, and Emma to follow.

The short journey to the manor house began in steely silence broken only when suddenly Lady Sybil spoke.

"Well, isn't this a fine mess! Left at the altar in front of everyone! This confirms my worst opinions of the girl. Honestly, I never approved of the match. I found Dianna Winthrope to be a thoroughly disagreeable female, a vain, pea-witted, giddy flirt.

"Jon always defended her, insisting that I was being too critical. She was young and enthusiastic and he claimed that it gave him pleasure to spoil her." Lady Sybil huffed, her distaste evident. "Yet even my dislike could not have predicted Dianna was capable of an act so heinous, so hurtful, so utterly cowardly. To leave Jon standing at the altar . . ."

With a sniff of pure disgust, Lady Sybil turned her head, looked out the window and sighed. Emma exchanged glances with her sisters, unable to formulate an appropriate or comforting retort.

"My Jon is the most loving and amiable of men, a model of propriety and restraint," Lady Sybil continued. "Why, I can scarce recall hearing him raise his voice in anger, no matter how vexed. 'Twas child's play for that odious chit to take advantage of him, encouraging him to enact the most undisciplined, free-spending habits while planning this wedding. An affair she lacked the decency to attend. Or at least call off days ago and spare Jon such a public humiliation."

"That would have been the kinder way to handle this situation," Dorothea agreed.

Lady Sybil frowned. "I fear that kindness is something Dianna Winthrope neither subscribes to nor understands."

Emma blinked. Apparently, Lady Sybil was not one to mince words.

"We are all very sorry for the pain that your son— and you—have been forced to endure," Emma said quietly.

"Yes," Gwen quickly agreed. "I hope that in some small way our support provides some comfort."

Lady Sybil's hand flew out and grasped Gwen's in gratitude. "I appreciate your kindness and understanding. I fear there are others who will find delight in my poor Jon's misfortune."

The three Ellingham sisters all nodded in sympathetic agreement.

"You must try to put them out of your mind," Dorothea said firmly. "Their opinions are of no consequence."

Lady Sybil sighed. "You are right, my dear. The scandal will eventually fade, and another take its place. Jon and I will simply have to find the courage and fortitude to withstand the gossip and become adept at hiding our true feelings from those who will relish our suffering."

The women fell silent. Emma glanced at her sisters.

"'Tis Dianna who will bear the brunt of the *ton*'s censure," Emma remarked.

"Yes, if she dares to ever show her face again, she will be a pariah among polite society," Dorothea agreed.

"Oh, she will not return until all of this has died down," Lady Sybil predicted. "And when she does, then a true reckoning for her actions on this day will occur."

Chapter Two

In a peaceful and private corner of his mother's solarium, Jon stretched his legs, crossed his ankles, and leaned his head against the cushioned chair. Appreciating the quiet solitude he had discovered among the lavish foliage and comfortable, elegant furnishings, he understood why his mother always referred to this place as her refuge from the world.

If only he could stay here indefinitely. Jon sighed. This most extraordinary, most unpleasant day was finally drawing to a close. At last. The majority of the wedding guests—nay, he could not correctly refer to them as wedding guests, could he, since there had been no wedding—were gone. And he had no wish to engage in conversation with those who remained.

Far more people than he expected had returned to the manor house, and despite the bizarre situation, many appeared to enjoy themselves as they ate heartily of the lavish meal that would have been his wedding breakfast and drank innumerable bottles of champagne, wine, and spirits.

Somehow he had managed to be stoic and dignified while he circulated among them, accepting their words of sincere—and more often than not insincere—sympathy with a solemn expression.

Though encouraged to do otherwise, Jon had refused to put any food or drink in his own stomach while among them, fearing the contents would be unable to remain. 'Twould be yet another scandal to add to the original: jilted Viscount Kendall tosses up his accounts at what should have been his wedding feast.

The gossips would certainly embrace that tidbit.

Yet as he retreated to the privacy of the solarium, he admitted that he was in desperate need of a drink, and hastily grabbed the first bottle of spirits he could find. As he now lifted the champagne bottle and downed the last of its contents, Jon realized why he had never liked the stuff—too many damn bubbles. Yet he swallowed anyway.

Though the past few hours had been a waking nightmare, Jon felt a momentary twinge of panic over his guests' departure. Their presence had provided a distraction, albeit an unwelcome one; now he was forced to relive the almost surreal events of the morning and face the reality of his circumstance.

Dianna, the woman to whom he had given his whole heart, would never be his wife.

Why? What had gone wrong? She had never expressed any doubts or hesitation about their impending marriage. Indeed, she had accepted his proposal—and the diamond and sapphire ring he had chosen—with a squeal of joy and a kiss of passion.

Yet on the morning that he had anticipated to be among the happiest of his life, she had fled with another man. A man she believed could give her what Jon lacked.

One, according to her cryptic note, that she believed

would provide her with the *more* that she craved. *More?* Jon's fists clenched and he struggled to contain the need to strike out, to pummel something, anything, in hopes of releasing his frustration.

Though she was a local girl, Jon had not taken much notice of Dianna until he danced with her at her coming-out ball in London. By the end of that evening, he was smitten. She was young and vibrant and full of life, with a winning smile and a way of pursing her lips that made him long to kiss them.

She had a quick wit, an inquisitive mind, and a gift for charming conversation. He had courted her for several months, always dancing with her first and last at the balls, escorted her to parties and musical soirées, took her for carriage rides in Hyde Park, ices at Gunter's, and gifted her with flowers and sweets.

Jon wasn't exactly certain when he knew that the strong affection he felt for Dianna had blossomed into love, but once he realized it, he embraced it fully. Every word he exchanged with her, each gesture between them, held more meaning. His kisses had more ardor, his caresses more fervor. And she appeared to enjoy it all.

Why, then, had she left him?

The rejection stung like a physical blow, a cut deep enough to make his chest burn and ache, his head pound and his mind swirl with endless questions.

How would he survive this agony?

The sound of footsteps approaching interrupted Jon's painful thoughts. He opened his eyes and watched a slender woman of medium height enter the room. Though the solarium was constructed of glass walls and boasted a pointed, tapered glass ceiling, the gray afternoon skies made the room dim and shadowy.

She wandered slowly among the thick green foliage

and flowering plants, running her fingers delicately over the long shiny leaves. As she drew nearer, Jon thought she looked vaguely familiar, but he could neither place how he knew her nor her name.

Through the leaves he watched her wind down the path, hoping she would find her way out before he was discovered. Alas, she turned a corner and then another and suddenly stood before him. Her breath hitched in startled surprise when she saw him, a delicate hand reaching for her throat.

"Gracious, Lord Kendall, you surprised me!"

Her voice was pleasant, lower pitched than most females' and oddly soothing.

"I beg your pardon." His brow lifted and his expression turned quizzical. "And you are . . . ?"

"Emma," she responded, then blushed slightly, no doubt over the intimacy of using her first name. "Or rather, Miss Ellingham."

The name tripped off her tongue in the most lyrical fashion. He tested it silently on his own lips, then grinned. "Emma Ellingham?"

Her blush deepened. "Yes, it's dreadful, I know. My father was so disappointed to have a third daughter instead of a son, he voiced no opinion on the matter. I was told my birth was long and difficult and I fear my mother was truly exhausted and not in possession of her full faculties when she named me."

"Apparently." Jon slowly rose to his feet, as good manners dictated he stand when in the presence of a lady. "Forgive me for being so direct, Miss Ellingham, but it has been a rather long day and I'm tired. What exactly do you want?"

She didn't blush with coy, maidenly innocence. Instead, she nodded, as though she agreed with his need to forgo polite conversation and get to the matter at hand.

"Actually, Lady Sybil asked me to search for you. You have been gone for quite some time and she is concerned."

"My mother, for all her practical nature, can be rather dramatic at times. I'm sure she expects that I am prostrate with grief and so under the hatches that I can barely stand."

Miss Ellingham blushed with just enough color in her cheeks to let him know that he had hit upon the truth.

"Lady Sybil is concerned," Miss Ellingham repeated.

Jon nodded. "You may report to her that I have skin thick enough not to care what others think of my failed nuptials, am relatively sober, and only mildly despondent."

The last was a lie, as Jon had been most despondent while contemplating how he was going to live the rest of his life without Dianna at his side, but he had too much breeding and pride to let anyone see it.

"Forgive my boldness, Lord Kendall, but in my opinion you have handled today with a considerable amount of tact and decorum," she said. "Far better than most, I would say."

"Thank you," he replied, believing she was sincere. "I suspect most expected me to be frozen with embarrassment."

She shrugged. "Perhaps. I hope that you took pride in disappointing them."

"Ah, yes. 'Tis my greatest accomplishment for the day. Well, that and being able to keep up a steady stream of comments about the weather. Most of the women feared broaching any other topic besides the climate when speaking with me today." Jon creased his brow. "Though I confess that is preferable to some of the other advice I was offered. I am heartily sick of listening to an exhausting number of sympathetic clichés from my guests on how fate has saved me from a most disastrous marriage."

"People mean well," she said. "Yet I must agree that it can be difficult to remember that, when they speak such utter nonsense."

Jon nodded. "Precisely. I was told, by no less than three different gentlemen, that I have ducked in the nick of time and avoided being struck by a bullet."

The corners of her mouth lifted sarcastically. "A sage commentary. No doubt the men in question are married?"

"I believe they are."

"Hmmm." She pursed her lips knowingly.

The gesture brought a spot of color to her cheeks and made her eyes seem enormous. They were a lovely shade of blue, like a cloudless sky on a warm summer day.

"Another fellow told me that I must travel to London and join in the endless round of parties, indulge in drinking, gambling, flirting with the unmarried women, and dally with the widows and unhappily married females," he blurted out.

"Do you find that appealing?" she asked.

"No," he admitted sadly, almost wishing he did. Such behavior could numb his mind, if only temporarily. It would never mend his heart.

She nodded approvingly. "I must agree that sort of behavior is unlikely to bring you any solace."

She spoke with the calm authority of personal experience and he wondered how she might have gained it. She wasn't a recently-out-of-the-schoolroom girl in her first blush of youth, but she was hardly old. He judged her age to be a few years older than Dianna and several years younger than his own of twenty-eight.

Then he realized by society's standards she could be considered old for a woman, and as an unmarried female she was squarely on the path of becoming a spinster. A most unsavory fate.

Jon straightened his shoulders. "Now that we have agreed that I shall not fall into the depths of depravity, I suppose I should return so that my mother can assure herself of my well-being."

As he stepped forward his foot collided with the empty champagne bottle. It skidded, spinning wildly as it glided across the slate floor, coming to rest at Miss Ellingham's feet.

"Yours?" she asked, raising her brow. "The bottle is empty. I presume it was full when you brought it in here?"

"'Twas only champagne," he said defensively. "I'm not drunk."

"I know." She glanced down at the empty bottle. "Yet there is no harm in waiting a few more minutes before returning."

Jon rubbed his forehead, then nodded in agreement. He was a tad light-headed, and any excuse to avoid returning immediately was welcome. He looked through the foliage out the window. The wind was starting to swirl. No doubt the rain would soon follow.

He and Miss Ellingham didn't speak for several moments. It was a comfortable silence, devoid of awkward glances, soothing in its simplicity.

"Are many guests still here?" Jon asked.

"A few. My brother-in-law, the Marquess of Atwood, and I are among those who remain. We would have departed with my sisters when they left a half hour ago, but your mother asked me to look for you . . ."

Miss Ellingham's voice trailed off. Jon nodded. They should return. He was sober—well, sober enough to face the few nobles that remained and keep his wits about him.

"I cannot imagine the comments and opinions about me that have circulated among my guests," Jon remarked, acknowledging to himself that he was curious. "What did you hear?"

She lowered her chin demurely. "Gossip has never been an interest of mine, my lord."

"Nor mine," he answered. "But I find that I am curious. Indulge me. Please."

She chewed her bottom lip meditatively for a moment. "Many are in agreement that Lady Dianna's actions have been extremely foolish." Miss Ellingham cleared her throat. "One woman even suggested that she was insane."

His brow lifted. "Yes, I suppose for some people throwing over a viscount for an untitled gentleman is the height of madness."

"Apparently that kind of behavior is only mildly frowned upon if one does it for what is considered to be an acceptable reason," she said.

"Like landing a marquess instead of a viscount?" he quipped.

Emma eyed him mischievously. "Or even better— a duke."

"Ah, yes," Jon agreed, feeling the tension in his shoulders relax for the first time in hours.

Her mouth turned up in a subtle grin. "Forgive me. I do not mean to make light of the situation."

Jon shrugged, easing more of his natural restraint. For some incomprehensible reason he felt comfortable in Miss Ellingham's presence, even though she was a stranger. Or maybe because of it?

She had a kindness about her that struck him as genuine, and he appreciated how she held her gaze steadily upon him when they spoke. She did not appear to view him as a pathetic, misfortunate creature as so many others had today.

Still, Jon cautioned himself to tread carefully. Given the disastrous circumstance with Dianna, it was apparent that his instincts about females could be dreadfully wrong.

The viscount gained her side and Emma found herself craning her neck to look at him. Watching him from a distance in the chapel she had not realized that his shoulders were quite so broad, his jaw so chiseled, his eyes so dark.

Catching herself gawking at the poor man, Emma shifted her gaze and focused her attention on his elaborately tied cravat. It soon captured her genuine attention, and her artist's eye appreciated the intricate folds that reflected the light and shadow of the cloth.

The rest of his attire was tasteful and elegant, yet far more conservative. She wondered if he had made the more fashionable effort on his cravat for his bride's sake.

How unfortunate that she was not here to witness it.

Lord Kendall turned to Emma, offering her his arm. "Shall we return, Miss Ellingham?"

"Yes." She placed her gloved hand lightly on his forearm. It felt like iron beneath her fingers, clearly betraying his inner tension. "I'm sorry that I am forcing you to return."

He shrugged. "You need not be. This situation was not of your making."

"Nor yours," she muttered beneath her breath.

The corners of his mouth rose ever so slightly. "Are you trying to make me feel better, Miss Ellingham?"

"I would never be so bold or impertinent, my lord," she replied, feeling a burst of delight at being able to lighten his mood, if only for a moment. "I am merely being honest."

"Thank you," he said simply.

As they walked through the solarium, Emma unobtrusively studied him. Being someone who valued privacy, she had felt bad disturbing his peaceful solitude. He had received a shocking blow this morning that he was struggling to make sense of, to understand. The last thing he needed was an intrusion from a stranger, even if she was acting on behalf of his mother.

Under the circumstances it would have been perfectly understandable if he had been terse and ungracious toward her, even downright rude.

But he had not.

She admired that kind of inner strength and fortitude. It showed character and resilience. Traits he would need in the coming weeks and months.

His steps were slow and deliberate, his expression pensive as they swept into the ballroom. The remaining guests stopped what they were doing to stare at them. Emma felt the hair at the nape of her neck start to rise when she realized they were gawking. She drew in a sharp breath and quickly glanced at the viscount.

His face was stony, his lips pressed tightly together, but his shoulders were straight and square and his head held high. Emma was surprised to see there were more people than she originally thought who had not yet departed. She was hoping, for the viscount's sake, that only a few would be in the ballroom.

Lady Sybil crossed the room to meet them. The viscount bowed and greeted his mother graciously, no doubt attempting to assure her that he was not brooding. His mother favored him with a wan smile and placed her hand on his arm, running a soothing hand over it as though he were a lad.

Apparently, Lady Sybil was not fooled by her son's show of bravado.

The viscount attempted to smile at his mother, but something lurking in the depths of his eyes revealed the intensity of his pain. The sight caused an ache in Emma's chest, though she had no idea why his feelings should affect her so strongly. She barely knew the man.

Then again, the idea of anyone suffering was difficult for her to witness without experiencing some form of empathy. A stark reminder of her own heartbreak, perhaps?

Emma felt a presence at her elbow. She turned and discovered her brother-in-law Carter at her side, his handsome face marred by an expression of faint disapproval.

"I cannot fathom why so many people are lingering. 'Tis most inconsiderate. I think the biggest kindness we can offer Kendall and Lady Sybil is to shame the rest of this rabble into departing," the marquess declared.

Emma nodded in agreement.

Lady Sybil tilted her head. "I—rather, we—would be grateful if you could somehow accomplish such a feat, Lord Atwood."

"Consider it done."

Lady Sybil let out a small sigh of relief. "I always said that you had a sensible head on your shoulders. Got it from your father, I believe."

"I'll be certain to mention that to the duke the next time I see him," Carter replied.

Then, true to his word, Carter began circulating among the crowd, dipping his head and speaking in a low voice. Before long, Lord Kendall's very proper butler was ushering the last of the guests out the front door.

"Most impressive. Thank you, Atwood."

Viscount Kendall offered Carter his hand and the two men shook hands in farewell. Then with a polite bow in Emma's direction, Lord Kendall quit the room.

"We'll show ourselves out," Carter told a clearly exhausted Lady Sybil, who was leaning heavily on the back of a brocade chair.

"Wait!" The older woman moved forward and gave Carter a swift hug, then embraced Emma, pressing her cheek briefly against hers. "I will not soon forget your kindness today, nor that of your sisters."

"My one regret is that it was needed," Emma replied. "Please send word when you are ready to receive visitors and Dorothea and I will come to see you."

Lady Sybil smiled.

Carter's carriage was waiting when they stepped out onto the portico. Emma accepted the footman's assistance as she ascended into the vehicle and settled herself on the forward-facing seat.

Sitting with her back to the horses sometimes caused a queasy stomach, and though it was a short ride home she had no wish to test fate. They had already experienced far too much drama for one day.

"Thank you for staying and helping," Carter said as the carriage drove through the open wrought-iron gates. "Dorothea did not wish to abandon Lady Sybil in her hour of distress, but it was obvious that my wife was tiring. The only reason Dorothea finally agreed to go home was because you offered to stay."

"I'm glad that Gwen and I were finally able to

convince her to go. The only thing that worked was reminding Dorothea that a woman in her condition needed to be thinking of her health and the precious bundle she carried."

The marquess coughed loudly and color seeped into his cheeks. Was that a blush? From her powerful, aristocratic brother-in-law?

Hiding her smile, Emma glanced down at her lap.

"Yes, well, I should have surmised that Dorothea would share this news with her sisters, even though the doctor warned her it is still early stages and the possibility of complications exists."

Emma's head jerked upward at the thread of deep concern edging Carter's voice. "Dorothea has told us she is feeling wonderful, in fact even better than with her other pregnancies. Both Philip and Nicole were healthy babies and remain so as they have grown older. There's no reason not to expect the same outcome this time."

Carter smiled. "'Tis true my son and daughter are rarely ill, even with a cold. However, 'tis not the babe's health that worries me, but Dorothea's. She was a younger woman when they were born. Philip is six and Nicole will soon be five."

"Dorothea is still a young woman!" Emma insisted, yet she did understand Carter's point.

Much to the disappointment of Dorothea and Carter, there had been no other pregnancies since Nicole's birth five years ago. Her sister confessed that she had nearly given up hope that she would ever bring another child into this world, making this pregnancy all the more surprising and joyful.

"Nevertheless, we must watch Dorothea carefully and make certain she does not overtax her strength," Carter said solemnly. "'Tis another reason that I am so

pleased that you have decided to stay with us. I know
that I can count on your assistance."

"The promise of another child means everything to
my sister," Emma said. "She will be sensible."

A flash of lightning illuminated the sky, followed
swiftly by a loud crack of thunder. Emma and Carter
exchanged a look.

"We shouldn't be surprised this day is ending in a
storm," Carter quipped, as a blast of wet mist blew in
through the open window.

"It has been rather horrid," Emma agreed as she
pulled the hood of her cloak over her head to avoid
getting her face wet. "Poor Viscount Kendall. I still
don't understand how any woman with a conscience
could act so cruelly toward a man she had agreed to
marry."

"I don't know Dianna Winthrope very well, however
I suppose 'tis possible that she will come to her senses,
regret her actions, and return here one day, full of
apologies and regret," Carter speculated.

"To what end?" Emma questioned. "I cannot think
that any man would be kindly disposed toward a woman
who rejected him in a most humiliating, public way."

For some reason the idea of Dianna returning disturbed Emma. She believed in forgiveness, but seeing
Viscount Kendall's raw pain made an impression on
her that was not easily forgotten.

Carter shrugged. "I have long given up trying to
understand the oddities of male and female relation-
ships. 'Tis challenge enough keeping myself in your
sister's good graces."

"Keeps you on a short lead, does she?" Emma
teased, knowing that was far from the truth. Dorothea

loved her husband deeply and he returned that love and affection tenfold.

Theirs was a marriage of equals, the type of relationship Emma would have wanted if she could have married the man she loved.

Carter burst out laughing. "I do believe that you, Emma, are the boldest of the three Ellingham sisters. And that, indeed, is certainly an extraordinary accomplishment."

Chapter Three

The following spring

A persistent whimpering broke through the calm of the nursery. Emma, seated in a cozy chair near the open window, glanced down at the chubby babe on her lap. Harold James Joseph Grayson squirmed and fussed, arching his back as the whimpers emanating from the back of his throat grew louder.

Emma grasped the infant under his arms and lifted her four-month-old nephew close to her face, gently pressing her nose against his. "What's wrong, little man? Don't you like me anymore? I believed that we had become the best of friends during our daily afternoon visits."

Harold grew quiet and smiled briefly at the sound of her voice, but then his features scrunched with distress and he let out another whimper. Emma held him tightly as he kicked his legs and shoved a closed fist into his mouth.

"Oh, goodness, he looks just like Carter when he makes that face," Dorothea said with a laugh.

"A most unflattering observation," Emma said. "Yet true."

Still laughing, Dorothea reached out and took her son. "He must be hungry."

With a sigh of motherly wisdom, Dorothea expertly cradled her son in one arm and opened her bodice with the opposite hand. She put the squalling infant to her breast and he instantly quieted, his noisy suckles of contentment filling the nursery.

Fascinated, Emma watched her sister and wondered what it would feel like to do the same. To birth a child, to nourish, love, care for, and cherish this miraculous life you created. It must be an extraordinary feeling.

Though he had his own nurse, an affectionate middle-aged widow who had also cared for Philip and Nicole when they were infants, Dorothea often tended to the babe's needs herself.

"Cousin Agatha would be scandalized if she saw you now," Emma teased, referring to one of their very proper, distant relations.

Dorothea smiled. "Well, it never took much to bring on her vapors and start a lecture on the importance of a woman maintaining appropriate behavior under any circumstances. A marchioness nursing her own child—unthinkable!"

"Unfashionable," Emma added, proud that her sister had the will to follow her heart and do what she believed was best for her children, no matter what others thought.

"What I do in the privacy of my own home is of no concern to others," Dorothea stated firmly.

"Except me," Carter declared as he walked into the room. He leaned down and placed a gentle kiss on Dorothea's brow, then ruffled the few silky strands of hair on the babe's head. "And I approve of all that you do, my love. How is my youngest son today?"

"Hungry." Dorothea grinned. "As usual."

"Hmm." Carter leaned closer to his wife. "I find myself a bit envious of young Harold," he said in a low, seductive tone.

Dorothea blushed. Emma felt the heat bloom in her own cheeks and was glad she couldn't hear the rest of their whispered conversation, since it was slowly turning her sister's face a most impressive shade of red.

"Shouldn't you be meeting with the estate agent?" Dorothea asked breathlessly.

Carter straightened. "Actually, there are several ledgers awaiting me in my study that require my attention. Though I can assure you, there are other places I would much prefer to . . ."

Emma didn't catch the last of the sentence and though it seemed impossible, Dorothea's face grew even redder.

"You had best be on your way, Carter," Dorothea squeaked. She cleared her throat several times after her husband left, refusing to meet Emma's eye.

For a brief instant, Emma felt the urge to pick up a pencil or piece of chalk and begin sketching, intrigued with the notion of capturing her sister's flustered, blushing expression. But as usual, the moment passed as swiftly as it came.

Emma sighed softly. Her art remained an elusive, frustrating creature, impossible to seize. It saddened her, even scared her, but she had finally succeeded in pushing the loss of her artistic fire and passion into a dark corner of her mind. Obsessing over it had not been the solution—it had only made her more miserable.

Instead, she had spent the past year analyzing her life and with steely determination succeeded in concentrating only on the positive.

She liked living with Dorothea and Carter. They treated her with kindness and respect, never once making her feel as though she was a burden or intruding in their lives.

She was a valued member of their family and was grateful for the love and generosity they bestowed upon her. Her nephew Philip and niece Nicole were a joy to be around. They were sweet, inquisitive, and high-spirited children and never failed to make Emma laugh.

She had a beautiful, safe place to live, a generous allowance, and a family that cared about her. She was, in truth, a most fortunate woman.

Even though Dorothea insisted it wasn't necessary, several months ago Emma had started giving Philip and Nicole drawing lessons. It was an excellent indoor activity for this lively pair during the cold winter months, and the lessons continued now that the weather had begun to warm.

Emma enjoyed the time she spent with the children and the lessons afforded her a small connection to her former self, prompting her to pick up a sketchbook and paints twice a week.

It was far from the frantic, driven passion that had ruled her life for so many years. Yet it was better this way, she told herself. Sensible, measured, practical.

And frightfully dull.

"I received another letter from Gwen this morning," Dorothea said. "I do hope that you will consider going to London in a few weeks for the Season. Gwen and Jason are keen to have you with them. It would be a stimulating change from the quiet of the country."

"The Season? Surely you are joking."

"I'm perfectly serious. You are a social creature, Emma, and we have a limited society here. You barely saw anyone when I was in confinement before Christmas. In the past you always enjoyed the balls and parties and musical evenings in Town.

"It would be fun for you to meet some new people. Who knows, resuming your weekly trips to the art museum might inspire you to pick up your brushes again."

"Meet new people? You mean eligible men, I presume? Gracious, Dorothea, you are about as subtle as a cavalry charge," Emma said affectionately.

"I don't have the time or energy for tact," Dorothea said with a smile. "Besides, you are my sister. There is no need to walk upon eggshells in our conversations."

"I am well aware that there are some who find my life pitiable. Unmarried at my age and well on my way to spinsterhood. Disgraceful."

"Hardly." Dorothea lifted the babe from her breast and propped the infant on her shoulder. She rubbed his back soothingly until he let loose with a loud belch. "I only want your happiness, Emma."

"I know. But I don't need a husband for that, Dorothea," Emma said gently.

"Who said anything about a husband?" Dorothea protested, her eyes widening in mock innocence. Then, looking earnest, she leaned forward. "I know you feel that marriage should not be the ultimate achievement of your life, but doesn't it at least deserve some consideration?"

Emma winced, ignoring the distressing memories that so swiftly welled up inside her. She had never spoken of her love for Sebastian to either of her sisters—to anyone, actually. The pain had been too raw, the rejection too embarrassing. Instead, she had channeled her emotions into her art, creating paintings filled with remorse and sorrow.

Those too she had hidden from view, fearing they would reveal too much of her bruised soul.

"I have no wish to enter the marriage mart at my advanced age," Emma said honestly.

"You are hardly in your dotage," Dorothea protested. "Forgive me for mentioning it again, but your art does not appear to hold your interest as keenly as it once did. I am merely suggesting that 'tis time to look for a new passion."

"Perhaps." Emma tapped her chin thoughtfully with the tip of her finger. "A lover?"

Dorothea gave a faint shudder, then shifted her head into her shoulder, covering what was obviously a grin. "Cease trying to shock me, Emma. Talk such as this could easily curdle my milk."

Emma felt her lips twitch. The notion of taking a lover was completely absurd, but it was fun to tease her sister. "All right then, no lover. But no husband, either," she quickly added.

"Oh, dearest, I respect that you aren't a woman who can easily accept others determining the course of your life, but tell me that you will at least consider marriage," Dorothea pleaded.

Emma blanched. This was hardly the first time Dorothea—or Gwen—had broached the subject. Yet Emma's reply remained the same.

"If it means so much to you, then yes, I shall consider it," Emma replied in a noncommittal tone.

"Marriage is far from perfect," Dorothea said. "Truthfully, it can be a real challenge sometimes, but there is nothing on earth that can compare to being loved and cherished by a man whom you love in return."

Emma felt a surge of emotion seize her throat. If only Dorothea knew the truth. That was exactly what she had wanted with Sebastian. He had been the man she had dreamt of sharing her life with for so long.

Even now, though she knew and accepted that Sebastian was forever lost to her, it was impossible to imagine sharing her life so lovingly and intimately with another.

She had tried to change her thinking, ignore her feelings. Admittedly, not as intently as she should, but she discovered, as so many before her, that love is impossible to control. No matter how hard one wished it, you could not turn it on and off like an oil lamp.

"Please, do not fret over me, Dorothea," Emma exclaimed, smiling brightly to emphasize the point. "I am fine on my own."

Dorothea's fervor seemed to fade into acceptance, but Emma was not fooled. This battle might have been a victory for her, but the war was far from over. Dorothea was bound to bring up the Season in London—and marriage—again.

The mantel clock in the nursery struck the hour.

"Goodness, is that the time?" Dorothea shifted the now sleeping babe from her shoulder and cradled him in her arms. "I promised Philip and Nicole that I would watch them ride their ponies this afternoon."

"I'll care for Harold until Nurse arrives," Emma offered.

Dorothea nodded gratefully. She crossed the chamber and gently placed her son in the ornately carved wooden cradle—the same one that had housed her husband and his father before him.

Harold's nurse entered a few minutes later. As Emma quit the room, she noticed the older woman gently adjusting the babe's blanket before settling herself in a chair next to the cradle.

Emma wandered downstairs, trying to decide how

best to spend the afternoon. She should write to her sister Gwen and politely decline her invitation to visit London, but that task held little appeal. The sun was shining, the sky was blue and cloudless, beckoning her out of doors.

She took a shawl and went outside. She started walking toward the lake, then continued beyond the water to the Grecian folly. Though it had no practical purpose, Emma appreciated the classic lines and unusual architectural elements of the building. Carter was always threatening to tear it down, but it had sheltered many a wayward walker during an unexpected rainstorm—including Emma and Dorothea—and for that reason alone it remained standing.

Emma's usual route often included a stop at the folly to catch her breath before turning east and making her way to the formal gardens closest to the house. Today, however, she decided on a different course. Invigorated by the fresh air and pleasant temperatures, she went west, following a previously unexplored path through the estate's forest.

Emma felt her heartbeat accelerate as she walked farther and farther into the woods, navigating the various twists and turns. The path became narrow and overgrown, attesting to its lack of use. Logic told her she should turn around and head back, but a sense of daring emboldened Emma to continue moving forward.

She pushed her way through the thickest of the underbrush and burst forth into a clearing, pulling up in surprise. Looming directly in front of her was a structure unlike any she had ever seen. Completely square, devoid of windows on the front and sides and made of dark wood, it rose in the clearing like a vision from a fairy tale. All that was missing were trailing vines and a look of abandon.

A barn? Nay, it was too wide and tall and the location was too far from any of the working or grazing fields. Its purpose must be to store items for the estate. But what?

Curious, Emma approached.

The large, heavy door was unlatched and open just enough for her to poke her head inside. She saw a sharp, stark burst of light in the distance of the cavernous chamber, given off by a long string of lit lanterns hanging from the rafters in the center of the room.

Emma blinked repeatedly, gasping when her vision cleared as she beheld a most astonishing . . . contraption? It looked to be a machine of some kind, massive in size, overwhelming in majesty. There were drums, gears, cogs, wheels, shafts, and pulleys jutting out at odd angles, and metal chains hanging from the top that dragged on the ground.

A man, with his back toward her, stood on a ladder, attempting to fit the gears of two large wheels together while a second man was positioned below him, tugging on a lever attached to a large drum. Each was so engrossed in their individual tasks, they took no notice of her.

"Good afternoon, gentlemen."

The two men froze. The one working on the lever straightened and swiveled his head to stare at her, his expression hard.

"Viscount Kendall?"

It took Emma a few moments to recognize him. Gone was the elegant nobleman she remembered;

replaced by a man with a rough, raw edge, who viewed her now with an unmistakable glint of displeasure in his eyes.

"Miss Ellingham?"

"Yes. Hello." Emma curled her toes, pressing them against the inside leather of her boots. She should leave, of course, for it was clear that he was annoyed, but the allure of the behemoth *thing* in front of her was too strong.

She had thought about him now and again this past year, wondering how he was faring. Before Dorothea entered her confinement, they had visited Lady Sybil often. The older woman had confided that her son was improving, yet still struggling to come to terms with his aborted wedding.

Lady Sybil had mentioned how solitary the viscount had become and Emma was aware that there had been talk about Lord Kendall in the village. He had all but withdrawn from society, becoming something of a recluse, even appearing only sporadically at church services on Sundays, which raised brows and set tongues wagging.

Was *this* what had been occupying his time? How fascinating!

"You have caught me at a most inopportune moment, Miss Ellingham."

The viscount slowly released the lever and took a step toward her. The last time she had seen him he had been decked out in his wedding finery. Today he was far more casually dressed—or rather undressed. He wore no coat, and his gaping white linen shirt showcased a wide view of his naked chest, which glistened with sweat.

His shirtsleeves had been rolled to the elbow and Emma's eyes caught sight of his hands. They were sturdy, strong, and marked by the calluses of physical labor.

His hair was longer than fashionable, caressing the nape of his neck, and his face sported several days' growth of whiskers, emphasizing the cut of his jaw. He smelled faintly of leather mingling with a spicy, male scent that sent her nose twitching with interest.

"I apologize for trespassing, my lord. And for disturbing your . . . your . . . business?"

"Business? Ah, yes."

He gazed at her suspiciously before taking her gloved hand and making a short bow over it. At least it was an attempt at manners, no matter how insincere.

"I took a different path through the woods," she explained. "I was unaware that your lands so closely bordered the marquess's property."

The viscount briefly looked away. "This is my acreage. There is no disputing that my workshop is built on my land."

"I never implied that there was any impropriety." Emma turned her head and slowly perused her surroundings. "So this is your workshop? Most impressive."

"Yes, this is where I spend the majority of my waking hours, often starting my work before dawn." He stiffened. "Surely you have heard the rumors about me? How I've become a recluse, a man so heartbroken he cannot bear to face the world? How my very sanity is in peril?"

"I believe I once told you that I do not listen to gossip," she replied, tilting up her chin. "And, I shall add, nor do I believe it."

He tugged down his sleeves and covered his bare arms, then reached for his coat and shrugged into it.

"It must be disappointing to find me here, alert and engaged, instead of raving like a madman in an asylum, bitter and drowning in self-pity."

"I would never believe such a dreadful tale," Emma declared defensively. "Though anyone with compassion in their heart would not deny that you had a right to grieve the loss of your marriage."

"It's been nearly a year." His expression changed, seeming to focus inward. "Self-indulgent, prolonged pity is remarkably boring. For oneself as well as those around them who are forced to witness the suffering."

His words struck a chord. Emma too had hidden her grief over Sebastian for much the same reasons. Being sunk in a cloud of melancholy was hardly something to share with the sisters who loved her.

"This magnificent machine is proof that you have moved far beyond pity," Emma said. "Did you design it?"

"There is no need for you to feign an interest in my work for the sake of being polite," he said bluntly.

"Lord Kendall, did you just say work?" Emma favored him with an exaggerated eye roll. "The *ton* will be scandalized if they discover a gentleman working. With his hands, no less. Oh, the horror."

The hostility in his eyes slowly drained away. "I trust that you will keep my secret?"

"I might." She pursed her lips in thought. "But only if you show me your creation. What is it?"

"A threshing reaper."

"Ah. A most auspicious name." Emma tried going around him to get a closer look, but he blocked her path. "What does it do?"

He smiled grimly. "Nothing of substance just yet. My hope is that it can be used by farmers to harvest wheat instead of performing this arduous task by hand with a sickle. The thresher will then separate the grain and seed from their chaff and straw. I've read of other apparatus performing similar work, but my design is different, unique as it will do both.

"If Norris and I can get it to function properly, the current harvesting and threshing methods will be obsolete."

Her brow rose. "And the workers who now perform these tasks. What of them?"

His eyes widened at her question. "The reaper will do all the physical work, but the men will need to walk beside it and rake the wheat stalks into piles. They will then pitch the bundles into the feeder of the thresher.

"Again, the machine will do the work much faster and more efficiently than the current threshing method of beating the stalks by hand with a flail or trampling them with animal hooves. This will allow us to plant and produce more wheat, hopefully making the possibilities of food shortages less likely. A benefit for all, I believe."

Emma shook her head in puzzlement. 'Twas an odd occupation for a noble gentleman—inventor. Yet it appeared the viscount was committed to it. Her eyes swept about the workroom and she noticed a large rectangular table set off to the side with huge sheets of parchment spread over it.

Plans for the reaper thresher? Emma angled herself, attempting to see those, but found her way obstructed by a solid wall of male flesh. Frustrated, she blew out a breath and confronted him.

"Are you trying to get rid of me, my lord?"

The viscount tilted his head, his dark eyes sparkling in the lantern's glowing light. "Yes."

* * *

Jon waited for a show of temper. A flash of anger in her eyes, the stomp of her foot, a haughty toss of her head. Or instead, would there be a blush of embarrassment, downcast eyes and a stammering apology?

No, the anger seemed more in character with what he knew of Miss Ellingham, and he had a most peculiar anticipation of it.

But she fooled him utterly and instead laughed with genuine glee. The sound drew Jon's attention to Emma's mouth and he was surprised to realize how dainty it was, how sweet, soft, and inviting her lips looked. Clearing his throat, he shifted his gaze from her lips to the graceful curve of her neck, then lower to the bare gleam of her creamy white skin, peeking over the shawl that hung low on her shoulders.

His breath hitched and he felt a sudden, unwanted heat. Why? He had seen far more delectable skin on other females who favored the current fashion of low-cut bodices with breasts nearly spilling forth. Emma was dressed in a modest day gown, with a neckline that hardly plunged. It scooped, stopping a good three inches before reaching her breasts.

However, it did allow a tantalizing glimpse of the smooth, white flesh of Emma's upper chest. A most enticing sight.

Jon drew in a deep breath and pulled away, red-faced to realize he had been leaning forward and leering at her. Her brows knit together in puzzlement.

"I mean no offense, Miss Ellingham, but my assistant and I have a considerable amount of work to do," he said bluntly.

"Ah, and I am in the way." She nodded, then tilted her head as if a thought had just occurred. "If I promise to sit quietly in the corner and ask no questions, may I stay? I confess to being fascinated by your creation."

"I . . . uhm . . ." He struck at the ground with the toe of his boot. He had been working on this design for months, in hopes of obtaining a patent once the machine was perfected.

Given the current propensity among inventors for stealing parts of each other's designs, Jon and Norris had agreed to keep their work a secret until it was perfected. 'Twas ridiculous to think that Miss Ellingham would abscond with any proprietary information—then again, one never knew.

Besides, her sparkling eyes and lovely appearance would provide a distracting presence that he did not need.

"Perhaps another time," he compromised.

"I assure you, my lord, that I can take a not-so-subtle hint." She laughed lightly and held out her elegant hand. He took her gloved fingers in his and brushed his lips over the knuckles. "I shall leave you and your assistant, Mr. . . . ?

"Norris."

"Yes, Mr. Norris, to your work."

Jon escorted her out of the workshop. She turned and started toward the path in the woods. It was a long walk back to Atwood's estate. Perhaps he should offer to send for his carriage and drive her there himself?

Bloody hell, why was he acting so rashly? He had just told her that he needed to work—with Norris. Wasting time getting her home would hardly help accomplish that task.

With effort, Jon kept silent as Miss Ellingham left, knowing it was the wisest course of action. Yet he stayed in that spot until all sign of her had completely vanished.

* * *

As she walked along the now familiar path through the woods, Emma realized that her fingers were moving restlessly, gathering and releasing the fabric on her skirt with an almost frantic urgency. She grasped the edges of her shawl and pulled the garment tightly across her chest in an effort to stop the movement— yet her hands merely transferred the movements from her skirt to the shawl.

What in the world?

It happened again and Emma paused. She knew what it was, yet could hardly credit it. 'Twas a distinct, familiar, unforgettable feeling that she had firmly believed was forever lost to her.

A slow, steady smile came to her lips as she recognized and acknowledged what was happening.

Pencil, charcoal. Sketch. My hands are telling me what my brain is slow to acknowledge. I need to draw. I need to create. I need to sketch Lord Kendall's machine.

Chapter Four

Jon watched Miss Ellingham retreat through the woods, fully expecting her to turn back and offer another reason that she should be allowed to stay. Her lovely face had been set with determination, letting him know that she was not going to be easily dissuaded. Yet the leaves barely moved and the area remained quiet, with only natural sounds of the woods filling the air.

Jon almost felt an odd twinge of disappointment when sufficient time had passed without seeing her anymore, confirming that she had indeed gone.

"I dinnae think the lady meant any harm, my lord." Norris's voice broke through Jon's musings. "She was merely curious."

Jon turned and faced his assistant. Norris's Scottish accent was always more pronounced when the man was flustered and caught off guard. In a strange way it was almost a relief for Jon to find that he was not the only man to be affected by Miss Ellingham's presence.

What was it about her, precisely, that sent his mind to places it had no business going? She wasn't coy, she didn't flirt, she didn't try to blatantly manipulate him. Her interest in his work was not peppered with insincere or inflated flattery. Nay, she appeared genuinely curious about the machine and wanted to know more.

This was precisely why he had to insist that she leave. He had refined the design for the reaper thresher countless times over the last few months, achieving the same dismal results—it failed to work as he imagined.

And the very last thing he wanted to do was to announce this failure to anyone—including himself.

"This workshop is my private domain," Jon insisted. "Distractions by ladies are neither encouraged nor welcomed."

He took several deep breaths, attempting to clear his head. The pungent scent of warm metal and fresh leather was familiar and comforting. This machine, this work, had been his salvation after Dianna left him.

Surrounded by the logic of science, he had been able to exhaust his mind, quiet his maudlin thoughts and forget his heartbreak. His work had allowed him to accept what had happened, to put it firmly in the past. Here in his workshop, Jon had found a purpose that gradually morphed into a passion.

Even as a boy he had been fascinated by any sort of machinery, drawn to the structural elements, the various mechanisms and control components that made it work. It was not considered a proper course of study for a titled gentleman and heir, but the lessons in mathematics and history had provided a solid foundation of understanding when he first began this project.

Finding himself at loose ends last spring, Jon began reading scientific journals, which in turn sparked his imagination. He had a workshop built, hired Norris after corresponding with him for several months, and gotten serious about perfecting the design for a useful piece of farming machinery.

"Do you think the lady will return?" Norris asked.

"Not unless she is invited." Jon resumed his position at the base of the machine and grasped the lever. "And I can assure you that an invitation from me will not be forthcoming."

Norris scratched his head. "She seemed very keen to learn more about our work."

"Aye, but her curiosity will have to remain unsated." With a sharp nod, Jon turned his full attention to the lever, determined not to give Emma Ellingham another thought.

Emma's thoughts were swirling as she walked back through the dense copse of trees. Visions of gears and wheels and cogs flitted through her mind so intently she was tempted to stop, find a sturdy twig, and begin sketching in the dirt.

Her lips twitched, then formed a smile. 'Twas nothing short of amazing, but Emma never questioned the driving force behind her need to sketch, to draw, to create. It had been gone for so long from her life, and now that it had so abruptly returned, she was forced to acknowledge how much she had truly missed it.

As she wound her way through the formal gardens, Emma glanced at the elegant sundial placed in the center of the rose bushes. Startled, she lifted her head, noting the position of the sun, which confirmed that the afternoon was nearly gone. She had stayed out far longer than she anticipated.

Sincerely hoping that her long absence had not been noticed by her sister—and caused any worry—Emma hurried toward the front of the manor.

"Miss Ellingham! Miss Ellingham! Oh, I say, what good luck."

She turned to find Mr. Hector Winthrope standing at the manor's front door. Emma stopped dead, wondering if he were coming or going and fervently hoping it was the latter. She was far too anxious to retreat to the privacy of her room with her sketchbook and pencils to stop and attempt to make polite conversation with the man.

Or even worse, pretend to be interested in anything he had to say. No doubt her sister Gwen would say that Emma was being uncharitable, but quite frankly Emma found Hector Winthrope to be one of the most overbearing, boring gentlemen that she had ever met.

He was always eager to share his observations and opinions with anyone and everyone. The problem was, Emma was never as eager to hear them.

His lack of interesting conversation was something that she might have been able to overlook, had he not also been such a small-minded, priggish man, who possessed the most inflated sense of self-importance. Even on the best of days, 'twas a trial to avoid being outwardly rude to him.

"Good day, Mr. Winthrope."

"I was just paying a call on Lady Atwood and was horribly disappointed to find that you were not at home." His face flushed a rather unbecoming shade of red. "I'm so pleased to have caught you."

"Oh?" He approached and Emma felt herself stepping backwards, easing away slowly so as not to appear too obviously impolite.

"I came today to take you for a drive in my new curricle. It arrived from London this very morning."

Emma followed the rather dramatic sweep of Mr. Winthrope's arm as he proudly pointed to the carriage in the drive, immediately wondering how in the world she had overlooked the vehicle.

It was, quite simply, a sight to behold. The carriage possessed an exceedingly large set of wheels painted the most garish shade of yellow Emma had ever seen. The narrow upholstered seat was set at least six feet off the ground, causing her to crane her neck to view it fully.

The vehicle was hitched to a pair of sleek-looking, perfectly matched mares who were stomping their hooves impatiently, while a nervous-looking stable lad tried to keep them under control.

"I, uhm . . . Oh, Carter, come and see Mr. Winthrope's new carriage."

Emma waved energetically at her brother-in-law, who had turned tail and tried to escape the moment he spied her and Mr. Winthrope. She saw Carter's shoulders heave in a sigh, and with a pained expression on his handsome face, the marquess joined them. He met Emma's gaze with a look of trapped annoyance that matched her own, but was far too well-bred to display his feelings.

"Preparing for a bit of racing, Winthrope?" Carter asked, running his hand over the top of the wheel. "You had best be careful when driving these winding country roads. I've seen far too many overturned curricles in my day, along with the bruises and broken bones of their drivers."

Mr. Winthrope blanched. "I would never be so reckless, my lord, with such a valuable piece of equipment."

"That's a relief," Carter exclaimed. "Now if you'll excuse me—"

"I know the hour is late, but I was hoping to take

Miss Ellingham for a carriage ride, Lord Atwood. Unless you object?" Mr. Winthrope's brow rose in worried speculation.

Emma's initial sense of panic was replaced by a surge of relief. Ever since their daughter, Dianna, had run off on her wedding day, leaving Viscount Kendall at the altar, the Winthrope family had struggled to maintain a respectable place in local society.

As the highest-ranking noble in the county, Carter's approval was paramount to maintaining their tenuous hold. A polite refusal from him would easily extract her from any obligation to accept Mr. Winthrope's invitation.

"Of course I have no objection to Emma riding with you," Carter replied graciously.

What? Emma barely suppressed a groan and shook her head vehemently. "How could you," she mouthed to Carter behind Mr. Winthrope's back.

Her brother-in-law grinned wickedly, then cleared his throat. "Normally, I would not hesitate to encourage Emma to accept, Winthrope, for I know how much she enjoys being out in the country air. However, I fear she will clutch your arm much too tightly while perched atop your curricle, endangering you both."

"I can assure you that I am a most careful driver," Mr. Winthrope boasted. "An excellent driver, in fact. Miss Ellingham will come to no harm."

"'Tis the height of the carriage that will cause the most trouble," Carter confided, reaching for her hand and soothingly stroking it. "Poor Emma is most fearful."

The eager expression on Mr. Winthrope's face fell.

"Ah, I should have realized a woman of her delicate nature would have that sort of reaction to such a masculine, sporty carriage," he replied knowingly.

"Good of you to be so understanding, Winthrope," Carter said cheerfully.

Afraid of heights? Emma pulled her hand out of Carter's and covered her mouth to hide her smile at the exaggerated falsehood. When Dorothea and Carter were courting, he had taken them both on an outing to the medieval castle ruins on the edge of the estate. For nearly two hours Emma had dutifully played chaperone, yet when he had offered to show them the view from the tallest tower, Emma declined, claiming a fear of heights.

In truth, she had seized upon the chance to offer the couple a private moment, and Dorothea's mussed hair, flushed cheeks, and slightly swollen lips when they returned let Emma know they had made the most of the opportunity.

Two weeks later, Carter had proposed.

"I suppose next time I could bring Mother's barouche," Mr. Winthrope said dubiously, casting a look of longing at the curricle.

"Or I could loan you Philip's pony cart for a sedate ride to and from the village," Carter offered.

"A pony cart?" Mr. Winthrope's throat bobbed and he let out a nervous titter. "Perhaps we should take a stroll instead of a drive, Miss Ellingham?"

Oh, dear. Emma hastily choked back a squeak of frustration. His dogged determination to spend time with her might have been considered flattering if it weren't so unwelcome. Her general lack of romantic interest in men notwithstanding, it would take a much different type of man than Hector Winthrope to capture her attention.

What precisely do I have to say to make him go away? Forever.

"I sincerely thank you for your invitation, Mr. Winthrope, however I'm afraid I must decline," Emma said. "'Tis nearly time to start my weekly art lessons with my niece and nephew and I must not be late."

Mr. Winthrope stared at her in confusion. "I thought you were a guest of your sister's. I did not realize that you *work* for the marquess."

Emma clenched her teeth at his condescending, affronted tone. Honestly, he made it sound as though she were emptying chamber pots and mucking out horse stalls.

"I consider it a great privilege to share my knowledge and love of art by instructing the children," Emma replied frostily. "I would never consider it *work*."

"Nor would I," Carter added.

"I did not mean to imply . . . that is to say, I intended no insult," Mr. Winthrope stammered. He glanced nervously at Carter, removed a large white linen handkerchief from the breast pocket of his coat, and dabbed at the sweat on his forehead. "I do hope that you have not taken any offense."

"Of course not," Carter replied cheerfully.

"Good day, Mr. Winthrope," Emma said firmly, and then because he looked so utterly miserable, she charitably softened her dismissal with a slight smile.

A visibly flustered Mr. Winthrope climbed into the carriage. He teetered for an instant as he reached the high, narrow bench, eventually regaining his balance. His mouth opened and closed rapidly, then apparently thinking it best to say no more, Mr. Winthrope lifted the reins, tipped his hat, and took off down the gravel drive.

"That was an awkward exchange. I hope that he won't be returning anytime soon," Emma said with a sigh.

"Oh, I believe that he will." Carter's mouth tightened into a grin. "I had suspected, but this latest encounter confirms it. You have an admirer, Emma."

"Hector Winthrope? Bite your tongue, Carter."

"Nay, my eyes did not deceive me. He was practically ogling you when I arrived."

Emma swatted her brother-in-law's shoulder goodnaturedly. "Stop teasing me. I am far too old for Mr. Winthrope—or any other man—to be ogling."

"I disagree. You are a very charming lady, made even more so by your lack of artifice. That could be the very thing that stirs his interest."

"You are my brother by marriage and thus compelled to make such foolish statements." An unwilling smile came across Emma's lips. "Me and Winthrope? I cannot fathom anything more ridiculous. Besides, I've gotten the distinct impression that he prefers his women docile, adoring, and obedient."

"Rather like a dog?" Carter offered.

"Exactly like a canine," Emma replied, wincing inwardly.

"True, you are quite different in temperament than the staid, pompous Mr. Winthrope. Perhaps that is what intrigues him. He sees you as a puzzle he wishes to solve."

Emma snorted. "Judging by his conversation, I'm doubtful he has the patience or the intellect for solving puzzles."

They walked through the front door, held open by a silent footman standing at attention. Carter nodded his thanks and the young man broke into a pleased grin at the acknowledgment.

"My opinion of Mr. Winthrope mirrors yours,

Emma. You deserve much better," Carter admitted. "There are many fine men who would be honored to court you, and I confess it would please me greatly if you found someone that you would like to marry."

Emma groaned. "Heaven help me, not you too, Carter. I already told Dorothea that she is wasting her breath trying to convince me to spend the Season with Gwen, making *new acquaintances*. I would be miserable mingling with the debutantes, their matchmaking mamas and the young bucks trying to evade them. Please believe me when I tell you that marriage is the last thing on my mind."

"The right man could easily change it," Carter predicted.

Sebastian's handsome face invaded Emma's mind. Flustered, she shook the image away, surprised to realize she succeeded in doing so without the usual stab of deep-seated pain in her heart.

Strange.

They reached the staircase and Emma parted from Carter. He turned to go to his study while she hurried up the stairs, thoughts of Mr. Winthrope, his curricle, and marriage firmly pushed aside, replaced by the ever-growing need to start sketching Lord Kendall's remarkable machine.

For two days, Emma sketched. After so long an absence from serious work, it felt strange at first, holding her pencils and charcoal, yet it soon grew enticingly familiar, like the renewal of an old and dear friendship. The connection between her hand, mind, and emotions put the feeling of once again being *herself* back into her heart. It was an uplifting realization, brought low only by the frustration of the results of her work.

Ah, but that too is a part of the process!

On the third morning, Emma awoke very early, feeling tired from a restless night. Barefoot, she padded across her bedchamber and opened the heavy drapes. Dawn was just beginning, bringing a faint red light through the windows. She could hear the chirping birds singing to the approaching morning, a light-hearted, welcoming sound.

Emma took several deep, determined breaths and grabbed her sketch pad. Slowly, methodically, she flipped through the pages, examining each sketch before removing it and placing it on the floor in front of the window.

When the pad was empty, she knelt and started sifting through the dozens of drawings scattered on the carpet, critically sorting them. On an ever-growing pile in the corner she put the rejects. The rest she carefully lined in two rows, dismayed to admit these measly few were the best of the lot.

She needed to choose one—or two—as a guide for her painting. One by one she held them up to the light, turning them to and fro, yet none seemed right. Oh, they were well drawn and filled with interesting details.

However, none of the sketches effectively captured the spirit of Viscount Kendall's glorious machine. None brought it to *life.*

Emma sat back on her heels and sighed. It seemed almost bizarre that an object made of wood and steel would awaken her artistic muse and move her to such emotion. Yet once stirred, the drive she felt would not be denied—nor compromised.

Emma slowly examined each sketch a second and then third time before acknowledging the truth. She needed to see her subject, to touch it, to watch it wind and bend and move in order to try and adequately capture the feeling of raw power it stirred within her.

Would the viscount allow it? He had been far from enthusiastic during her visit the other day, ushering her away from his workshop as quickly as possible. She doubted he would be very enthusiastic at the idea of her returning.

Well, there was only one way to know. She must ask him.

Pleased to have a plan, Emma surged to her feet. She sat at her writing desk and removed a sheet of parchment. The opening salutation and first line were simple to compose. The rest, well, that proved far more difficult.

Four sheets of crumpled parchment later, Emma decided this was not the best way to make her request. No, she needed to do so in person. And there was no time like the present.

Deciding not to wake one of the maids, Emma proceeded to wash her hands and face, then pulled a simple walking dress from her wardrobe. She intentionally selected the lavender gown made of soft wool, for its comfort and practicality. With contrasting fabric buttons that fastened down the front of the tightly fitted bodice, Emma was able to dress without assistance.

She brushed the tangles from her hair and fashioned a single braid that hung down the center of her back, tying the end with a matching satin ribbon. Hardly a sophisticated look, but this was not a social call. This was business. Donning her cloak, she stuffed two pencils in the left pocket, picked up a fresh sketch pad and tucked it under her arm.

The household was just beginning to stir as she made her way quietly down the center staircase. She slipped into the breakfast parlor, startling a chambermaid who was laying a fire.

"Oh, miss!" the young woman exclaimed, jumping to attention. "You gave me such a fright."

"I'm sorry, Katie," Emma said sincerely. "I would have made some warning noise if I knew you were in here."

"No need to apologize, Miss Emma." Katie was blushing with guilt at the mere notion. "I wasn't complaining."

Emma smiled. "Of course."

"Are you going out?" Katie asked, glancing at Emma's cloak.

"Just for a walk," Emma replied, shifting her feet. She preferred to keep this visit to herself, as it was not entirely proper for her to meet with the viscount alone.

Besides, Dorothea and Carter had been oddly obsessed with the notion of her finding a husband. In their enthusiasm, they could very well misinterpret her need to see Lord Kendall and reach the wrong conclusion.

"Shall I ask Cook to prepare breakfast for you?" Katie asked.

"No, thank you. I shall eat with my sister when I return." Emma shifted the sketchbook under her arm. "Most likely I'll be back before Lady Dorothea comes down to the breakfast parlor, but if she does ask about me, please let her know I've gone for a morning stroll."

"Yes, miss."

Katie curtsied as Emma left the room.

The morning mist had cleared and Emma was

pleased to find the terrace empty. The sweet smell of wildflowers wafted through the air, the whisper of wind fluttering the budding leaves. She briefly considered stopping at the stables and asking one of the stable lads to saddle a horse, but feared the path through the woods was too narrow for a horse and rider to negotiate together.

There was also the possibility that one of the grooms would insist upon accompanying her, knowing Carter would balk at her riding out alone. That would be completely unacceptable. In this, as with most things she did, Emma preferred privacy.

The air was cool, the ground wet with morning dew. By the time Emma had crossed the perfectly manicured lawn and entered the path through the woods, the hem of her gown was soaked.

Having traveled upon it there and back the other day, Emma discovered her trampling feet made the route more defined and easier to follow. When she reached the end, she was even able to catch a glimpse of the building through the leaves before she fully emerged from the woods.

Heart thumping with excitement, Emma approached the entrance, disappointed to find that the door was tightly shut. Undaunted, she raised her closed fist and knocked, knowing she needed to make a substantial bit of noise to be heard. Then she smoothed her skirt, straightened her shoulders, and waited.

And waited.

The emerging sunshine pleasantly warmed her shoulders. A second, louder set of knocks seemed to echo through the vast and cavernous interior, yielding the same results. No answer. Had she come all this way for nothing?

Disappointed, Emma pushed against the sturdy lock, surprised when it easily twisted. For a moment she stood there frozen, and then she felt a swell of triumph. She rarely gave in to impulsive behavior, but the temptation was impossible to resist.

Smiling, she swung the door wide and stepped inside.

"Hello. Viscount Kendall? Mr. Norris?"

Her voice shot to the rafters and back before silence descended. Eyes darting in all directions, Emma quickly confirmed the room was empty.

Well, except for one glorious object.

Several lanterns were lit, casting an almost heavenly glow over the viscount's machine. Slowly, reverently, Emma approached. She pulled off her glove and with an unsteady hand ran her fingers over a pair of gears. The coolness of the metal was unexpected, startling in a way, as the machine appeared so alive to her.

Anxiously reaching into her pocket, she pulled out a pencil. She shifted her sketchbook and opened the tablet to a fresh page. For a long moment she stood and stared, then with breathless excitement racing through her veins, Emma began to sketch.

Chapter Five

The sound of her pencil scraping over the paper added to Emma's joy. It all felt so *right*! Her head bobbed continuously as she tilted it upward to look at the machine, then down at her parchment. Her fingers flew, trying to keep pace with her mind and imagination.

Gleefully, Emma turned the page and started a second sketch. She was so focused on her work that she barely registered the presence of someone at her back until a pair of strong arms closed around her. She screeched in surprise and dropped her sketchbook.

"Release me!" Emma demanded in a shaky voice.

The hold on her loosened and she whirled around. Viscount Kendall stood before her, his eyes gleaming.

"How did you get in here?" he questioned, regarding her suspiciously.

She stifled a scoff at the ridiculous question. How else would she have entered but through the only door?

"The door was unlocked," Emma exclaimed, struggling to catch her breath. "I knocked, rather loudly, but I assumed you and Mr. Norris were too deep into your work to hear it."

Emma saw Lord Kendall's back stiffen. "In my haste to gather additional supplies, I must have forgotten to lock the door." He muttered a low oath beneath his breath. "However, that hardly constitutes an invitation for anyone to simply barge in to my workshop uninvited."

She hesitated. "I was very much hoping that an invitation from you would be forthcoming."

"Why?" he asked, his voice wary.

Emma favored him with a bright smile. She needed his permission in order to sketch the machine. Antagonizing the viscount was hardly the way to gain it.

"I confess that I have been constantly thinking about your machine since I first saw it. I was hoping that you would allow me to watch you work. I promise that I shall stay silently in the shadows to avoid disturbing you and Mr. Norris."

A muscle twitched in his cheek. "Our work is not ready for anyone to view."

"But I've already seen it," she protested.

"Purely by accident. Initially." He crossed his arms over his chest and heaved a sigh of exasperation. "Frankly, Miss Ellingham, I cannot help but be suspicious of your behavior this morning."

Emma willed herself not to take offense at the thinly veiled accusation. "I understand that if your machine eventually works as you and Mr. Norris intend, it will be very lucrative for both of you. Therefore, discretion and secrecy are paramount in order to prevent a rival from stealing your designs. I respect that and give you my word that I will say nothing about what I have seen in your workshop."

A dubious expression crossed the viscount's face, but Emma remained hopeful. He placed his hands on his hips and glanced at the ceiling. 'Twas clear he was considering her request, and though she felt an anxious need to present him with more and more reasons why he should, Emma held her tongue.

There were few things more distracting and annoying than having someone yammering in your ear. Never more so when you were trying to think and make an important decision.

"It seems an innocent enough request, if I may say, my lord," Mr. Norris interrupted.

"You may not." The viscount bristled.

Emma smiled gratefully at the assistant and he gave her a sheepish shrug. Even though it was unsuccessful, she certainly appreciated his effort and support.

The viscount appeared to have come to a decision. Emma tried reading his expression. 'Twas impossible. But then he heaved a sigh and the scowl between his brows eased.

He's going to say yes!

The butterflies fluttering in her stomach soared. Unable to contain her grin, Emma stepped forward. So did the viscount, but he stopped abruptly when his foot hit the sketch pad she had dropped earlier.

They reached for it at the same time, but Lord Kendall's arms were longer, his movement faster. He snatched the pad and positioned it under the light. He studied the first drawing, then lifted the page and viewed the second. He turned to her and Emma found herself blushing over his long, penetrating look.

"Will you kindly explain *these*, Miss Ellingham?"

* * *

Jon stared at her in bafflement. If he didn't know better, he would have to conclude that she was stealing his designs.

Actually, did he know better? His acquaintance with her was brief and there was no denying that he was holding the proof of her duplicity in his hand.

"I sketch," she said softly, taking the pad from his hand. "And paint. 'Tis such an integral part of me, part of who I am, well, at least it was as far back as I can remember. But something changed this past year— I don't how or why, but I lost it. Eventually, I was forced to accept that it could be gone forever, that I might never regain that part of myself.

"And then I stumbled upon your workshop and saw your machine." Her eyes lit with an inner glow of wonder. "The spark came rushing back, the excitement returned. I'm at a loss to explain it, I just know that it is there and for that I am grateful."

"Ah, miss, that's beautiful." Norris released a sentimental sigh.

Good God! Norris was in his late forties, with a wife and five children, and here he was, swooning like a schoolgirl. Apparently, Miss Ellingham had a strange power over men of many ages. Jon blew out a frustrated breath, refusing to be drawn in by his assistant's enchantment with the girl. Her explanation seemed— far-fetched?

"Artists paint portraits and landscapes," the viscount challenged. "Sometimes a still life."

"We paint what inspires us, moves us, speaks to us," she countered.

Shaking his head in disbelief, Jon couldn't hold back his consternation. "There is no life in a machine, no beauty."

"There is power and strength." Her eyes grew wide with wonder. "Even majesty. I long to capture it on canvas."

She spoke with such reverence that he had no choice but to believe her sincerity. The conclusion momentarily threw him into a quandary. It seemed like such an innocent request—on the surface. There had to be more to it. Jon sorted through the various possibilities in his mind, finding no answers.

He cast a critical eye over the reaper thresher, unable to understand her fascination. Or more importantly, condone it. Sadly, inherent trust in others was a quality that no longer existed in him. Not after Dianna had made him look like such a fool.

"Your interest in our work is flattering. Nevertheless, I must ask you to leave," Jon said.

"Oh, dear. Won't you reconsider? Please?"

He hardened his resolve against the hopeful expression on her face. She was a lovely woman, but he had learned the folly of allowing a pretty female to so strongly influence his decisions.

"My decision stands," he said firmly.

"Oh, I am disappointed to hear it," she said in a small voice.

A bolt of emotion seared through Jon and it took a moment for him to identify it as guilt. Why? He owed her nothing. Quite the contrary. He owed himself—and Norris—the necessary privacy to complete their work.

Yet witnessing Miss Ellingham's dejection was difficult. Her shoulders slumped, her eyes lost their fiery excitement. He felt like a cad, a villain.

"It's not ready," he admitted, needing to somehow soften the blow. "And until it is, I cannot share it with the world."

She looked taken aback. "I can assure you, that I have no plans to exhibit my paintings."

Her sincere declaration should have reassured him. It did not. The risk of having the design stolen was the least of his worries. Enduring a public failure and possibly humiliation was the main reason he needed to keep his invention unseen. By anyone.

For the past year he had kept himself totally away from London society and mostly away from local society, yet the gossip, whispering, and speculation over being stood up by his bride still lingered. Jon had reluctantly accepted that it would forever be a part of his public persona.

Yet the very thought of being once again mired in a situation that exhibited him as a failure and a figure to be pitied, brought him a sense of gripping fear. That humiliation he could, and would, avoid at any cost, even if it meant disappointing the very delightful Miss Ellingham.

He rubbed his fingers against his temples, trying to recall her exact words. "What if you succeed in capturing the power and strength and what did you call it— ah, yes, the majesty of my machine? Would you not want to share that with others?"

"If I give my word, then I keep it." She bristled noticeably. "I do see a beauty that perhaps others do not, yet there is no need to mock me for it, my lord."

There was a glimmer in the depths of her blue eyes that made Jon draw in his breath. She was lovely in an uncommon way, not soft and delicate, but strong and intelligent. Seductive qualities made even more appealing by her unawareness of their power.

"It was not my intention to ridicule you or your art." He dipped his chin, ashamed to have lashed out because of his own insecurities. "Truthfully, the reaper thresher is not functioning the way we had hoped. There's a flaw in the design that Norris and I are trying to correct. Consequently, the final product might look vastly different from this model."

"I can appreciate the strong desire for perfection," she said. Turning her chin, she looked him directly in the eye. "And the fear of failure."

Jon felt a rush of heat on his neck. Silently, he watched her remove the two sketches from the pad. With a sigh of regret, she held them out to him. As Jon reached for them, he heard Norris sniff with disapproval.

Though the viscount was able to ignore his assistant's censorious look, he admitted Norris had a point. The sketches were merely parts of the machine. He doubted anyone besides himself and Norris—and Miss Ellingham—could understand what they meant.

"Keep the sketches," he said, pulling his hand back.

She stared at him in confusion. "Are you certain you don't wish to destroy them?"

"Though you must believe otherwise, I can assure you, Miss Ellingham, I'm not that big an arse."

"Emma." She managed a brief smile. "Allowing me to keep the sketches shows great trust. Dropping the formality of our address seems the next logical step. Don't you agree, Jon?"

Her words warmed the knot of tension in his chest. He liked how she boldly used his name without waiting for permission.

"I'm honored." He bowed.

"You should be." Her sassy reply made him smile.

"As should you," he countered.

She brushed her hand over the smile on her lips. The action drew his attention to their plump sweetness and he quashed a ridiculous urge to taste them.

"I wish you and Mr. Norris the best of luck. And I promise that I shall not return to your workshop without an express invitation."

She nodded, looked at Norris and then at him before leaving.

Jon swallowed and made himself relax. There. He tried convincing himself that would be the end of it. She would wait for an invitation that would never be forthcoming. The sharp disappointment would fade in a few weeks and she would forget all about his invention and find something else that inspired her to paint.

Could it be that easy? Probably not. Jon had caught that glimmer of a challenge in Emma's stunning blue eyes as she left.

He smirked grimly. *The end of it?* Not bloody likely.

As she walked back to the manor, Emma found herself pleating the fabric of her skirt between her fingertips. Her disappointment was sharp, the sense of failure slightly depressing. For a brief, glorious time she had felt a pure sense of joy as she sketched, a connection to the woman she had been.

Alas, that fleeting moment was gone in the blink of an eye and she doubted there would be an opportunity to recapture it. She was surprised—and pleased—when the viscount had allowed her to keep the two sketches she had drawn. But that unexpected gesture had not fooled her.

There was no denying the swift, calculating look on the viscount's—*Jon's*—face when she mentioned how she hoped to be invited to see the reaper thresher when it was completed.

True, he had smoothed away the scowl nearly as quickly as it appeared, but Emma had seen it.

Seen it and understood it.

There would be no invitation. That much was clear. Her initial burst of disappointment was difficult to hide from him, but she had managed. She had been gracious and accepting, while having absolutely no intention of being so easily put off.

There had to be a way to get into that workshop without compromising her promise. All she needed to do was find it!

Thoughtfully, Emma trudged through the woods, clutching at the lower branches as she went. She was slightly out of breath when she came to the clearing. If she hurried, she could be in the breakfast parlor before Dorothea, leaving her sister unaware that she had ventured out this morning.

Yet returning held little appeal. She needed more time alone with her thoughts.

Emma turned. Quickening her pace, she decided to head for the main road. Following the road would eventually lead to the manor's front drive. The tree-lined entrance was imposing, designed by a master landscaper, providing the perfect backdrop for the elegant manor house.

Perhaps the sight would inspire her muse. Carter and Dorothea would certainly appreciate a painting that captured the grandeur of their home. The piece might not move Emma to heights of delight, but at least she'd once again have a brush in her hand.

Narrowing her eyes and cocking her head, Emma gazed critically down the long gravel drive. Her attention was so enraptured, it took a few moments to realize the sound she was hearing was an approaching carriage.

Emma looked up. *Could it possibly be? Oh, damn, it is!*

With a distressed squeal, Emma leapt into a nearby bush. Her cloak caught on a bramble, but she tugged hard, hearing the fabric rip as she freed herself. No matter. She crept farther into the foliage, successfully concealing herself.

The carriage rumbled past, blinding shards of sunlight bouncing off the bright yellow wheels. Squinting, Emma had a clear view of the driver, but it was not Mr. Winthrope's considerable person that held her attention, but rather the woman who sat beside him.

She was dressed in a fashionable red cloak that cascaded over her shoulders and down her back like a blanket of delicate wool. Her wide-brimmed bonnet concealed a good portion of her face; however, Emma caught a fleeting glimpse of a delicate nose, high cheekbones, and golden-blond tendrils of hair.

The woman sat very close to Mr. Winthrope, their knees touching, yet Emma allowed that could have been a result of the deep curve in the road forcing the contact as they slid against each other. From what she could tell, the pair were silent, though Emma supposed Mr. Winthrope needed to concentrate on keeping his horses under control at that fast speed rather than engaging in conversation.

Emma waited a full minute after they had passed before emerging from her hiding place. Brushing the leaves off her arms, she clutched her sketchbook tightly, pleased with her success at avoiding Mr. Winthrope.

If only persuading Jon were as simple! Alas, that would require more than luck and a bit of quick thinking. Yet surely there was a way to get him to change his mind about allowing her to paint his machine.

And whatever it was, Emma was more determined than ever to find it.

Jon was in a hurry. He had just spent the better part of an hour with the blacksmith going over the specifications for three new parts he needed for the reaper thresher. The man had been respectful, even while his honest puzzlement over the order shone through, and had promised delivery by the next day.

The blacksmith was an honest man and a skilled craftsman and Jon was confident he would produce quality pieces. Yet it remained to be seen if they would work as Jon hoped.

Frankly, his patience was growing thin. There had been so many setbacks trying to get a successful, working design for his machine that Jon was starting to feel discouraged.

Head down, moving at a blistering pace, Jon rounded the corner, barely missing a collision with a finely dressed female. At the last moment he caught a glimpse of the lacy flounce at the hem of her walking gown and her bold red cloak, and stepped to the side.

She let out a surprised gasp and took several small steps backwards. Jon lifted his head to apologize and received the shock of his life.

Dianna Winthrope.

He felt as though he'd been hit between his eyes with a brick. He blinked. Twice. But the vision before him remained solid and real.

"Dianna?"

"Jon!" She froze, a shocked, helpless expression on her face.

His heart sped up and he cleared his throat. "I was unaware that you had returned."

"We have only recently arrived."

"We?"

She blushed and lowered her chin. "Mr. Dickenson and I. We are married."

"I see." So the rogue had done the honorable thing and married her. Good? Jon was unsure how to react.

He had thought of her constantly for months after their wedding debacle, wondering how she was, where she was, what she was doing. 'Twas only recently that he no longer lay awake at night with the image of her lovely face haunting him, wondering how she felt about him, how she had so easily walked away from the future they had planned.

The questions that had swirled in his head, the words he had anticipated saying to her if they ever met again, crowded his brain. Yet he spoke none of them.

Dianna appeared fragile. Behind the sweetness of her smile was a hint of despair. Why? Did she regret leaving him? Would she do things differently if given the chance?

Did he even want to know? It no longer mattered now. She was married—to another man.

"Are you here to visit your family?" Jon finally asked.

"Heavens no. Papa has refused to speak to me. I believe that my mother might have relented and allowed me in the house, but she would not go against my father's wishes.

"I did briefly see my brother, Hector, this morning. He took me for a ride in his new curricle." Dianna's brow furrowed into a deep frown. "It was a most unpleasant visit. My brother remains as angry as my parents and vows that it shall be years before he can forgive me."

"Then why have you returned?"

Color bloomed in her cheeks. "Mr. Dickenson has come into an unexpected inheritance that he is here to claim. He is the new Baron Brayer, a noble title which includes a sizeable amount of property."

Jon racked his brain, trying to recall precisely when the older Lord Brayer had passed away. It had to have been at least four or five months ago. Why such a delay in their return? Had it truly taken that long to locate Dickenson?

"I was unaware of a lineage relationship between Dickenson and Lord Brayer," Jon mused.

"As was I. From what I understand, 'tis a rather distant connection. But a valid one all the same," she hastily added.

Jon cleared his throat. "Does this mean that you will be living here?"

"Apparently. The land is entailed, so we must remain for at least part of the year. I'm sure my husband will also enjoy staying in London, though I am uncertain if he will bring me with him when he goes to Town."

Dianna bit her lower lip and Jon felt his heart skip a beat. He had always found that nervous habit of hers impossibly endearing.

He looked away. This was madness. He had no right to find anything about Dianna the least bit appealing. Jon spared a glance across the street and noticed that they had attracted considerable attention from the local villagers. A few brave souls ventured closer, obviously hoping to overhear any conversation, while most gawked from afar.

"We seem to be causing a bit of a commotion," he remarked to Dianna beneath his breath.

"They will look and gossip from afar, fearing they will be tainted if they dare to approach or speak with me. I have quickly learned that I am universally scorned," Dianna said, her voice quivering with sorrow. "Even my husband's widowed aunt takes great pleasure in looking through her lorgnette at me as though I were a nasty bug."

"Then you should act like one and bite her," Jon suggested, his heart twisting at her pain.

Dianna's laughter rang out sweetly, the sound knotting his chest. *Oh, how deeply I loved this woman.*

"You always could make me laugh," she said wistfully.

"Sadly, that wasn't enough, was it?" he asked, not bothering to conceal his expression of irony.

"Attempting to make amends with your former love in a public square, my dear? How vulgar."

They both turned in surprise. Gerald Dickenson's indignant tone was matched by an expression of disgust as he stepped beside his wife. He possessively grabbed her arm and Jon noticed Dianna momentarily flinched before regaining her composure.

"Goodness, you do love to tease, Gerald." Dianna smiled nervously and patted her husband's shoulder. He shrugged her off in annoyance.

"Dickenson." Jon nodded his head, attempting a politeness he was far from feeling.

"It's Lord Brayer now, or haven't you heard?"

"Oh, I heard," Jon replied lightly.

Dickenson faced him with a belligerent stance, his lips curving down in disdain. A scruff of whisker shadowing his face gave him a swarthy, almost menacing appearance. He was a few inches shorter than Jon and a year or two older. Women often labeled Dickenson handsome, with a brooding quality they called romantic. Witnessing it firsthand, Jon thought it appeared more childish than anything else.

"I suggest that you leave at once, Kendall," Dickenson said coldly. "The last thing that any of us need is a fresh scandal, as it would surely put Dianna firmly beyond the pale of respectability with no chance of ever recovering. 'Tis bad enough that she is vilified by one and all."

"And whose fault is that?" Jon challenged.

"Hers," Dickenson promptly replied, a flash of anger springing to his eyes. "Dianna lacked the moral fortitude to resist my charms and fulfill her promise to marry you. She is, however, merely a weak woman, so I suppose one is forced to make allowances."

What a brute to attack his wife so viciously and assume none of the responsibility for her predicament! Jon glanced covertly at Dianna, trying not to feel any sympathy for her, but that was impossible. She was staring beyond her husband at a fixed point in the distance, her expression blank.

Jon wasn't given to impulsive gestures, but the need to reach out and comfort Dianna was so strong he almost acted upon it. The only thing that prevented him from extending his arm and pulling her close was the worry that Dickenson would somehow make her suffer for it.

"Should we return home or do you wish to stroll through the village?" Dianna asked her husband.

Dickenson preened, momentarily appeased. "A walk is a splendid idea. Being seen is the first step toward forcing them to accept you. I cannot have my wife be on the receiving end of so much outright animosity. It reflects badly upon me and my position among the local society."

"I am sorry, Gerald," Dianna said quietly.

"We must present a united front or else your scandalous behavior will never be forgiven or forgotten and my good name will be forever tarnished," Dickenson stated brusquely.

He then bestowed a barely civil nod of farewell at Jon and pulled Dianna away. It took Jon a few moments to believe that the meek, subservient creature who walked beside her husband with her shoulders hunched and her eyes downcast was the vibrant, teasing, vivacious woman he had once loved.

What the hell had happened to Dianna?

Chapter Six

Emma was lost.

The burning feeling in the pit of her stomach that she had so staunchly tried to ignore for the past hour was persistent and telling. Her mood had alternated between hope and dread and there was little doubt dread was becoming far more dominant as the reality of her situation took hold.

She was lost.

She thought she had taken careful note of her surroundings as she walked, assured she would be easily able to return home if she failed to *accidentally* encounter Lord Kendall. However, recognizing the cluster of trees with the low bush that leaned noticeably to the right, Emma conceded that she had already circled past it.

Three times.

Things were not going at all according to plan. She had spent the day in her room, sketching the tree-lined drive and manor house, desperately hoping for a burst of artistic inspiration that never came. The project had kept her hands busy, but failed to fully engage her mind.

Time and again she had turned to the image of the gears on the viscount's machine, yet she held to her promise and refused to put her ideas to paper. Knowing that she would be unfit company, Emma had taken an early dinner in her room. Dorothea had stopped to see her, quickly retreating when she saw that Emma was working. Yet the smile of delight on her sister's face had made Emma feel like a fraud.

The manor sketch was no resumption of her art. It was an activity merely marking time until she could get to what she really wanted to sketch and eventually paint: the viscount's glorious machine.

Frustrated, Emma had restlessly paced her chamber, sifting and discarding numerous plans, convinced she had to do *something*. Perhaps a chance meeting in the woods *near* Lord Kendall's workshop would remind him of her request and prompt him to change his mind and graciously extend an invitation for her to view his work?

Emma now admitted it was far-fetched and a tad desperate. Trouble was, she had a tendency to do foolish things when she was so intent upon achieving a goal, and this evening was a prime example of how that could get her into situations like this one.

And thus she stood, stranded and lost in the viscount's woods, with darkness approaching and no one aware of her predicament. Dorothea had no idea Emma had left the house, nor did any of the servants. No one would be looking for her, at least not until the morning.

The distant rumble of thunder added yet another layer to her anguish. Emma shivered, unable to control the chills that raced through her.

Could it get any worse?

A fat raindrop splattered on the tip of Emma's nose and she silently cursed herself for once again tempting fate.

A rustle in the bushes drew her attention away from her misery. "Hello! Is anyone there?"

The noise repeated, louder this time, indicating it was closer. Yet why no response to her calls? Was it an animal of some sort? A vicious animal?

Steeling herself, Emma faced the source of the sounds, trying not to let her imagination run wild. She had walked through other sections of forest many times, seeing deer, birds, rabbits, and squirrels. Surely any other woodland creatures who lived in this area posed no great threat, being far more afraid of her than she need be of them.

The rain began falling at a steady pace, quickly soaking her bonnet and the shoulders of her cloak. Emma stood dripping, holding her breath, waiting. And then he was there, riding down the path, through the rain, his horse kicking up clumps of mud with each step.

Viscount Kendall.

Emma stepped out of his way. His hat was pulled low over his brow, his shoulders hunched forward in an attempt to evade the raindrops. For an instant Emma worried that he would not see her standing off the path, but then he lifted his chin and their eyes met. She saw the surprise there—and the irritation.

Thankfully he was too much of a gentleman to simply ride past her. She took a deep breath and spoke, letting her voice carry through the pelting wind and rain.

"I fear that I've gotten myself lost. Would you be so kind as to lend me some assistance, Jon?"

One brow rose, but he didn't speak as he pulled his horse beside her. Instead, he steadied his mount, leaned forward and extended his arm. Emma gulped. Surely he didn't expect her to vault onto his horse?

"Give me your hand," he commanded.

Emma raised her head, judging the high distance and swallowed again. "I'm not an acrobat," she croaked.

"Neither am I. Give me your hand."

Heart pounding in her chest, Emma did as he requested. Their hands met and she felt the strength of his fingers tighten around hers. Her feet left the ground and she noticed the muscles in his arm rippling through his coat as he lifted her.

Gracious, he was strong!

Emma scrambled onto the back of the slippery horse, miraculously managing to keep her seat. The moment she was settled, Jon commanded his mount to move forward.

Emma wrapped her arms around the viscount's waist and kept her head burrowed against his shoulder. He felt warm and solid, an anchor of strength and safety against the perilous weather. With her head down, she could make out little of their route, but she trusted that Jon knew the way.

The rain continued pelting them with a steady stream of cold water. Emma sniffled, preparing herself for a miserable ride home, but they suddenly drew to a stop. Were they already home? Had she been so ridiculously close to the manor house and not realized it?

Jon dismounted, then reached up and pulled her down. Emma felt her half boots sink into the mud when she landed, but she thankfully kept her balance.

Blinking, she looked up at the plain façade of the viscount's workshop looming before her and thought she should feel a jolt of pleasure.

Instead, she felt guilty.

"Why have you stopped here?" she asked, shouting to be heard above the howling wind.

A muscle in the viscount's jaw flexed. "'Tis the closest shelter. We'll wait until the storm passes and then I'll take you home."

He unlocked the door and ushered Emma inside, pulling his horse in behind them, as it would have been cruel to leave the animal exposed to the harsh weather. The workshop was dark, but it took only a moment for Jon to light the lanterns. Soon a golden glow spread over the space. Sparing her a quick glance, the viscount secured his mount in a corner and then began rummaging through the items laid out on a workbench in the far corner.

"What are you doing?" Emma asked through chattering teeth.

"Looking for Norris's bottle."

"Oh." That explained nothing, of course, but he was so intent upon his task, Emma felt it was unwise to pester him.

"Ah-ha! Found it. Now all I need are some glasses." He cocked his head questioningly toward her. "Or we could take turns swilling from the bottle. No? Yes, well, I agree 'tis far too uncivilized. I'm sure if I keep looking I'll find something more appropriate."

While Jon continued his hunt for glassware, Emma removed her sodden bonnet and cloak, shaking off the excess water. The workshop offered much needed protection from the elements, but was damp and cold

inside. She looked for a hearth or some other source
of heat, disappointed to see there was none.

"Can I help?" she asked, folding her hands to stop
their trembling.

"No need. I've found them." He handed her a
none-too-clean-looking glass filled with amber liquid.

Emma accepted the offering, her nose wrinkling
when she caught a whiff of the contents. "What is it?"

"Scotch," Jon replied. "I knew that Norris would
have a bottle stashed in here somewhere. He is, after
all, a Highlander."

Emma stared suspiciously into her glass. It smelled
vile, yet she knew several men who enjoyed the liquor.
It must be an acquired taste. Shivering, she brought
the glass to her lips, willing to try anything to chase
away the chills.

Wisely, she took a small, cautious sip. It burned the
back of her throat when she swallowed, but as promised, created a warmth that spread languidly inside
her. Encouraged, she continued sipping, surprised to
suddenly notice her glass was empty.

"May I have some more?" she asked, holding out
the goblet.

"If you are having another, then so must I." Jon's expression barely flickered as he refilled her glass and
then his own. "Are you trying to get me drunk, Miss
Ellingham?"

"Emma," she said softly, not liking his regression to
formality.

His brow lifted and she could see amusement spark
in his eyes. "I suppose it would be a waste of breath
asking what you were doing in my woods in the middle
of a rainstorm? *Emma.*"

Emma lifted her glass and stared at him over the

rim. She liked hearing her name fall from his lips. It sparked a feeling of warmth in her chest that she knew had nothing to do with the liquor she had just consumed.

"I was hoping that a chance encounter in the woods would afford me the opportunity to engage you in friendly conversation, so you would view me as I am, not a threat but an admirer of your invention," she admitted.

"I applaud your resourcefulness." The amusement in his eyes deepened. "And if that failed? What next?"

She blew out a breath. "Well, another, albeit brief consideration, was widening my eyes and fluttering my lashes at you when we next met."

He barked with laughter. "Reducing yourself to insincere flirting to get your own way, Emma? You wound me with such trickery."

"I said that I gave that rather featherbrained plan only a very brief consideration. I didn't employ it," she replied, flashing him a defensive smile. "Will you at least afford me some credit for my restrained behavior?"

"I might." Jon finished his whiskey and firmly tapped the stopper into the bottle. "If you tell me why you abandoned your flattery plan."

She shrugged, seeing no good reason not to reveal the truth. "I'm not exactly certain how it is done."

"Flirting? Surely a woman with your good looks has had her share of suitors."

Now it was Emma's turn to laugh. "I'm hardly the sort of woman who is sought after the minute they leave the schoolroom. There have been a few men who demonstrated some mild interest, but 'tis hardly a long list of besotted gentlemen clamoring for my hand in marriage."

"Just your hand? I would hope they were as interested in the rest of you."

His eyes met hers and Emma clearly saw the teasing humor in their depths. Then his gaze dipped to her breast, his eyes smoldering with heat. But only for an instant. So quickly she wondered if she had imagined it.

Or wished for it?

Hastily, Emma sipped on her drink, cradling the glass between her hands. Gracious, she was acting like a goose!

"I saw Dianna in the village today," he remarked in a hushed voice.

Caught in mid-swallow, Emma coughed, nearly choking on her drink. "Miss Winthrope?"

"The very same. Granted, I felt as shocked as you look right now, Emma." He let out a laugh, but Emma heard the difference this time. There was no mirth or enjoyment in his tone—it sounded more like pain than pleasure.

"What was she doing in the village?"

Jon reached for the whiskey bottle and began twisting the stopper. "She has returned, apparently to stay. Oh, and she is no longer Miss Winthrope, but rather Mrs. Dickenson." He refilled his glass, then downed the contents in one long gulp. "Actually, I should refer to her as Lady Brayer. Dickenson has inherited a title. He is the new Baron Brayer."

"That's awful."

"Yes. I confess that I'm not pleased."

The lines of misery on Jon's face touched Emma's heart. It seemed grossly unfair that he should be subjected to such pain after all that he had endured.

Wanting to lend some sort of comfort, she stepped forward. But the toe of her wet boot caught on the uneven ground and she tripped.

She reached out a hand blindly for support and Jon expertly caught her by the waist. With a startled cry, Emma instinctively threw her arms around his neck to keep herself from tumbling to the ground.

They turned their heads at precisely the same moment, bumping noses. Emma squeaked in surprise, but there was an even greater shock to come when the viscount angled his head and kissed her lips.

Supple tendrils of pleasure shimmered inside her at the unexpected contact. His mouth was softer than she would have imagined, his lips lush and warm. She might not have had many opportunities to flirt with handsome gentlemen, but she had experienced enough kisses in her life to know that this one was shockingly powerful.

And utterly delightful.

Jon's hand moved through her hair, holding her in place, but truthfully Emma had no wish to escape his spellbinding embrace. His tongue swept into her mouth, teasing and tantalizing and the warmth spread through her entire body.

Emma's breath quickened at the intriguing taste of him and she boldly pushed herself closer so they could drink more deeply of each other. Her eyes closed as she reveled in the delicious feelings he evoked and she found herself trembling with unexpected pleasure.

Jon broke away and Emma heard herself sigh and whimper with regret at the loss of his lips. Yet to her awe and delight, Jon began feathering kisses along her brow, down her cheek and finally brushing his lips against the nape of her neck. Emma felt as though she was melting, her entire body shimmering with pleasure.

His kisses made her dizzy. Or was it all that whiskey? He kissed her again—almost as though he knew her quandary—and Emma had her answer. 'Twas his kisses. They were truly intoxicating, making her breathless and light-headed.

Emma leaned into him and they shared one final, soul-shattering kiss before Jon lifted his head. The expression in his eyes made her stomach flip and flop with restless excitement. But then he let her go and stepped away from her.

The sharpness of her pleasure was slowly fading, yet the warmth remained. Dazed, Emma gazed at him in wonder, raising her hand to touch her swollen lips.

"That was most improper," she whispered in a breathless voice she did not recognize as her own.

"Yes. Yes, it was, yet I do not regret it." A faint line of worry furrowed his brow. "Do you?"

"No regrets," she said softly. "They are, in my opinion, a pure waste of time. Life, as they say, is far too short. Why spend it in misery?"

"Why indeed."

The deep rumble of his voice sifted through her. Emma's hand reached out, but she pulled it back before smoothing the hair away from his brow.

What had gotten into her? They might have shared the most wondrous kisses; however, that did not mean she had the right to enact such an intimate gesture.

A sudden crack of thunder reverberated through the workshop, breaking the sensual mood. Thank goodness. Emma had enjoyed their kisses—far too much than was sensible. She needed to push them from her thoughts. Immediately.

These kisses were an anomaly, due to too much

whiskey for her and too much emotional turmoil for Jon. Seeing Dianna so unexpectedly today had rattled him.

'Twas perfectly understandable. More than likely he had seized the sudden opportunity to kiss her to help him escape the pain he was feeling. The kisses meant nothing to him. And while they were most delightful, Emma knew they had to mean nothing to her, too.

"It sounds as though the storm is getting worse," she commented, striving to return the appropriate boundaries to their interactions. Almost as if to emphasize her point, a loud pattering of raindrops pelted the roof.

"I hope it ends before complete darkness." Jon frowned, glancing up at the ceiling. "What of your sister and Atwood? No doubt they will be worried if you don't return soon."

"Actually, they are unaware that I left the manor," Emma admitted, fervently hoping her absence would not be detected. It would cause a minor uproar if she and the viscount were discovered here, alone.

"That was most unwise," Jon commented.

Emma nodded in agreement, bracing herself to hear much more about her obviously foolish actions. "I fear I can be quite reckless when it comes to pursuing my art."

"Then we must ensure that you are back where you belong before you are missed," he said.

"Yes." Emma inwardly breathed a sigh of relief, appreciating how he refrained from lecturing her. She scanned the workshop. "Would you like to work while we wait for the rain to stop? I'll sit in the corner to give you privacy."

"With your back turned and your nose pressed against the wall?" he asked jokingly.

"Like a naughty child?" The image made Emma smile. "'Tis a fair punishment, considering that I have not fully kept my promise to stay away."

"Norris and I are at an impasse, I'm afraid. We can't do anything until the new parts I've designed are made." He grimaced as another clap of thunder shook the pane of glass in the single window positioned high on the back wall. "It sounds as though we shall be here for a while. We might as well get comfortable."

The viscount inclined his head and Emma noticed a settee covered in dark green fabric and a matching wing chair nestled in a corner. At his invitation, Emma sat on the settee while Jon settled himself in the chair.

"I was—"

"Have you—"

Jon smiled ruefully. "Ladies first."

"I was wondering if you always had an interest in creating and building mechanical things?" she asked. "I can easily imagine you as boy, tinkering with gears and pulleys."

Jon looked over at the reaper thresher, sighed, then gazed back at her. "I suppose I was an oddity, even as a child," he mused.

"Gracious, that's not at all what I am implying." Emma anxiously bit her lower lip. She was trying to be cordial and friendly and instead had succeeded in insulting him.

"I was different from other boys. My restless nature has always been inclined to embrace the creative possibilities of solving a problem." He cocked his head thoughtfully. "I never truly pursued it, and after I met Dianna I completely abandoned that curiosity."

"Are you pleased to have recaptured it?" Emma asked.

"Yes." He sat back in his chair. "Though I had hoped to one day have both in my life."

Emma stared at her hands. She could understand his need. Having someone to love—and love you—could only enhance the creative side of oneself.

"I'm still searching and trying to recapture my artistic muse," she admitted. "Well, I was. And then I saw your magnificent machine."

He gave her a sidelong glance. "Are you trying to play on my sympathies to give you permission to paint the reaper thresher?"

Emma inched forward. "Would it work?"

"No."

She laughed, uncertain why the rejection didn't wound. Perhaps because she knew she would eventually wear him down? Or maybe the glow of his kisses had softened the blow.

More likely those kisses have addled my brain.

"Tell me about your childhood, Emma. I know you have two sisters. Are there any other siblings?"

"No. Just the girls." Emma paused. She rarely spoke of her past, realizing it was not deliberate. The truth was, no one of her recent acquaintance had been interested enough to ask her about herself. Even Hector Winthrope, the man Carter claimed was enamored with her, had never broached the subject.

Then again, Hector never referred to anything other than that which was of interest to him.

"My parents died young; within a year of each other," Emma began. "Father went first, then Mother passed, many said of a broken heart. I was five, so my memories are fuzzy, but I recall feeling frightened and uncertain and there were awful nightmares that woke me each night.

"Uncle Fletcher and Aunt Mildred became our guardians. They were kind in their own way, but it wasn't the same as Mother and Father. Thankfully, I had Gwen and Dorothea to ease my fears. I understand now that without my sisters' love and comfort, things would have been even more difficult. I'm grateful too that I have some memories of the devotion my parents had for each other and for their daughters."

Jon met Emma's eyes with sympathy. "As a boy, I longed for siblings. Brothers, sisters, it didn't matter which or how many of each. To my parents' sorrow they were unable to have any other children but me."

"How sad."

"They never overtly expressed any regrets, only gratitude they had me."

"They were indeed fortunate on that account."

Jon shrugged his shoulders, looking uncomfortable at her observation. "At what age did you begin to paint?" he asked, leaning back in his chair and crossing his arms over his chest.

"A few months after Mother died," Emma replied.

His brow rose. "Coincidence?"

"I don't know," she answered, for the first time wondering if there was a connection. "I have always liked to draw. Gwen persuaded Uncle Fletcher to buy me a set of watercolors, hoping it would ease my nightmares. It did help."

Perhaps that could explain the root of her intense—almost obsessive, at times—need to express herself. Was that part of her grieving? A part that so profoundly shaped the woman she became?

Shifting the subject, Emma asked what other machines Jon wanted to design. 'Twas a subject he quickly warmed to and they fell into easy conversation.

Even the silences between them were unrestrained and comfortable.

They grew quiet again and Emma stared for a moment at the flickering shadows the lanterns cast against the walls. She glanced over at him. His eyes were closed, his breathing even, and she realized that he had fallen asleep.

No wonder. From what she could tell, he had been working like a demon these past few days. Apparently the physical exhaustion, coupled with the emotional shock of seeing Dianna this afternoon, had finally caught up with him.

Emma took advantage of the unique opportunity to study Jon while he slept. She had never seen him so relaxed, unguarded. He was slumped in the chair, his long legs sprawled in front of him, his head angled back. A lock of thick dark hair fell across his brow, giving him a gentle, almost vulnerable countenance.

There were streaks of mud on the doeskin breeches clinging to his muscular thighs and an even thicker coating of mud on his black Hessians. His cravat was simply tied, his waistcoat discreetly patterned, his deep blue coat fitted perfectly across a pair of broad shoulders.

His looks were more rugged than classically handsome, yet no matter what label was given, they were exceedingly appealing. Even more so because of what she knew of his character.

He was an honorable man, though his kisses earlier had shown he possessed the capacity to be every bit of a rogue.

She smiled at that thought.

Emma swung her legs onto the cushions of the settee and reclined against the padded arm. She was relaxed, but cold. Crossing back to where she had left her cloak, she retrieved the now dry garment. Noticing Jon's greatcoat near her own, she grabbed that also.

Slowly, carefully, so as not to wake him, Emma draped the coat over Jon. She then resumed a comfortable position on the settee and buried herself beneath her own outerwear. The warmth of the whiskey had faded, but being dry and covered kept her from shivering.

Emma yawned. She had eaten very little dinner and consumed two glasses of potent liquor on an empty stomach. Naturally, her eyelids felt heavy. After several valiant attempts, she gave up the struggle and allowed them to close.

It took but a few moments for her join the viscount in slumber.

Emma awoke with a start, jerking upright. Glancing upward, she saw a thin, gray streak of light filtering through the single small window placed high on the back wall of the workshop.

Was that the dawn? Good Lord, had she truly spent the entire night here?

The lanterns had gone out. Her eyes scanned the semidarkness, coming to rest on the body sprawled in the chair across from her. Tentatively, she leaned forward, stretched out a hand and gently touched Jon's shoulder with the tips of her fingers.

He stirred and mumbled and Emma snatched her hand back. What was she doing? Waking him was a terrible idea. It was better, far better, if she simply slipped away on her own.

Emma tensed, waiting anxiously to see if she had disturbed him enough to rouse him, but thankfully his breathing remained soft and steady. Heart racing, she listened for the sounds outside the workshop, hearing no rain on the roof.

A good sign. She could move faster if she didn't have to navigate her way through a storm. It might be possible to return to her bedchamber undetected and no one need ever know she did not sleep in her bed last night.

Holding her breath, Emma moved quietly, intent upon not making a sound. She slipped out the door, then flung her cloak over her shoulders and tied on her bonnet.

Dawn was just breaking, but the light was faint enough to see where she needed to go. The ground was wet and slick. Knowing the last thing she needed was to fall and possibly injure herself, Emma tread carefully.

Yet the moment her feet hit a dryer surface, she began running.

Chapter Seven

Jon awoke alone, to a quiet, semidark workshop. "Emma?"

The settee was empty. He turned his head, quickly scanning the room. Damn, the workshop was empty too. Well, except for his horse standing quietly in the corner. Jon swore again. Clearly she had left on her own. But when? The moment the rain stopped? The moment he had so rudely fallen asleep?

He ran his hand over the cushions of the settee, but the cold fabric gave him no clues. Following his next instinct, Jon bolted to his feet and headed for the door. He would ride immediately for the manor to make certain Emma had reached home safely.

If anything dire had happened to her . . .

He reached for the door, then paused. He could hardly present himself at the Atwoods' residence in his current disheveled state. 'Twas obvious he had slept in these clothes. His sudden appearance at such an inappropriate time would raise questions that he was unable to answer.

Not to mention how odd it would look if he called at the house with the singular purpose to inquire if Emma was there. No, he would follow the path she always used through the woods, to make certain she was not on it and confirm what he sincerely hoped— that Emma's sensible nature had prevailed and she had waited until there was enough light before traipsing through the woods.

Bloody hell, she certainly knew the way, he thought with a grin. She had traveled the damn path between the two properties enough times in the past few days.

Feeling slightly less anxious, he led his horse from the workshop, vaulted onto its back and searched for the path. Finding it empty, he turned his horse and rode for home. He looked forward to having a hot bath, a shave, and changing into clean garments before calling at the manor.

The household was just beginning to stir as he slipped in through a side door. He deliberately avoided the servants, yet somehow his valet materialized the moment Jon stepped into his bedchamber. Naturally, the stoic Gilmore said nothing about the state of his employer's clothing and asked no questions about where he had been all night.

Instead, the valet arranged for a bath, brought out fresh clothing, sharpened Jon's razor, and inquired if the viscount would require breakfast to be served earlier than usual. Jon's stomach growled at the mention of food. 'Twas all the answer Gilmore needed.

When Jon entered the dining room an hour later, the sideboard was filled with silver covered servers. He filled his plate with a heaping pile of eggs, bacon, blood sausage, fried potatoes, buttered kidneys, toasted bread, and blackberry preserves. He downed a cup of hot coffee, refilled his cup, then dug into the appetizing fare.

As his stomach filled, his mood improved. He spread a generous portion of blackberry preserves on a slice of toasted bread and reflected on the events of last night.

Was it fate or merely bad luck that kept throwing Emma Ellingham in his path? He smiled. Nay, 'twas neither. 'Twas Emma herself. He had never met such a forthright, determined woman.

Why had he kissed her? Impulse? He rarely gave in to it. Circumstance? Well, she had literally fallen into his arms and when their lips came so close, it seemed the most natural thing in the world to lean in and capture them. They had tasted far sweeter than he had hoped and her eager response had stirred his senses.

As they kissed, he had been seized with a desire to not just feel her mouth beneath his, but capture it and make her his own. It surprised him. This possessive, conquering emotion was something he had never felt. It had taken considerable effort to control and restrain it.

Even his most passionate moments with Dianna, the woman he had loved so deeply, had been more reticent. Why then was he so undisciplined when he kissed Emma?

'Twas the question that Jon was still pondering when his butler entered the room, his normally impassive face grave.

"The Marquess of Atwood is here, my lord," the butler announced. "He regrets calling at such an early hour, but insists he must speak with you immediately on a matter of utmost urgency. He is awaiting you in the drawing room."

Bloody hell.

Jon took a vicious bite of his toast, and cast a quick glance at the ornate clock his mother had especially selected for the dining room. Not yet eight. Damn, it was certainly serious if Atwood was here at this hour of the morning.

Emma!

It had to be about her, Jon reasoned. She must have been discovered returning home in the early morning hours. Or else she hadn't returned at all? The delicious breakfast he had just consumed congealed into a hard ball in the pit of his stomach.

"Inform the marquess that I will be with him shortly," Jon commanded.

"Very good, my lord." The butler bowed and left the room.

Jon took a deep breath and placed the remainder of his uneaten toast on his plate. Brushing the crumbs from his fingers with surprisingly steady hands, he wiped the corners of his mouth with a linen napkin and rose from the table as though he had not a care in the world.

However, his sense of foreboding intensified the moment he entered the drawing room. The marquess did not greet him with the usual smile and handshake. Indeed, Atwood's face sported a most ominous expression.

"I apologize for disturbing you at such an uncivilized hour, but this couldn't wait," Atwood said.

"So my butler has informed me. What's wrong?" Jon asked, a surge of fear flooding his veins. If anything dire had befallen Emma, he'd never forgive himself.

"Gerald Dickenson, the new Lord Brayer, is dead," Atwood said flatly. "He was found early this morning in his study by one of his servants, lying in a pool of blood with a knife protruding from his chest."

"Christ!"

Jon swallowed, remembering Dickenson's boorish

behavior when they had met in the village the other afternoon. In truth he could not say that he was saddened by the news. Still, it was a rather brutal way to die.

Atwood's eyes narrowed. "Two of the footmen who were on duty told me that their employer had a late night visitor. They saw this man and Brayer entering the study, then next heard the baron shouting in anger and an equally loud raised voice replying."

"The assailant?"

"Most likely."

"Nasty business." Jon shuddered.

It was a quiet, placid community, with no crime to speak of beyond a petty theft now and again or a drunken brawl at the local pub. This was truly shocking.

"I'm afraid there is more." Atwood's lips thinned into a hard line and Jon felt the hair on the nape of his neck begin to rise. "The footmen were both able to identify the man with Brayer."

"That should prove helpful."

Atwood frowned. "They say it was you."

Jon's head whipped around. "Me? That's ludicrous. What business would I have with him at any hour of the day or night?"

Atwood lifted his brow. "He ran off with your bride on the morning of your wedding. Some would find that reason enough to confront him."

"As much as it pains me to admit it, we both know that was as much Dianna's doing as his," Jon said, heaving a sigh.

"Did you call upon the baron last evening?" Atwood asked.

"Absolutely not!" Jon insisted vehemently. "If those footmen claim to have seen me, they are very much mistaken. Surely the servant who admitted this man to the house caught a better look at his features and can verify it wasn't me."

Atwood shook his head. "The hour was late. Apparently he did not call at the front door."

"Well, he gained admittance somehow." Jon scratched his head.

Atwood shrugged. "I can only assume that Brayer let the killer into the house. And further assume it was someone known to him."

Jon could feel his face beginning to heat. Atwood's tone held a note of accusation and his eyes were narrowed with suspicion. 'Twas disheartening to discover a man he thought was his friend would believe him capable of such an act.

"I give you my word, as a gentleman, that it wasn't me," Jon insisted, squaring his shoulders and looking Atwood directly and steadily in the eyes.

"Your word?"

"I swear that I was not in any way involved."

Atwood watched him carefully, a muscle ticking in his jaw. "I believe you, Kendall. However, as magistrate of the county, I require more than just your word. There were, after all, two witnesses who swear it was you."

"The footmen are mistaken," Jon repeated.

"Well, 'tis a simple matter to prove them wrong. You need only to have someone verify your whereabouts last night. If you can prove that you were somewhere else, anywhere else, it would be impossible for you to have been involved in Lord Brayer's death."

I've somehow gotten away with it!
Emma stared at the reflection in her dressing table

mirror and breathed a great sigh of relief. She had snuck into the manor just after dawn broke, creeping up the servants' stairs, flattening herself against the wall in the corridor to hide her shadow from the maids who were beginning their daily chores.

Once safely in her bedchamber, Emma had quickly removed her clothing, pulled on a nightgown, and climbed into bed. She dozed fitfully until a maid timidly knocked on her door, asking if she needed anything.

It was the usual morning routine, but today instead of turning the girl away—as she often did—Emma requested a breakfast tray to be brought to her room. As expected, Dorothea soon appeared in her chamber, worried that something might be amiss.

After assuring her sister that all was well—though Emma wasn't entirely certain that she had convinced Dorothea—she ate every bite of her breakfast. Then she picked up her sketchbook.

Visions of the wheels and cogs of the reaper ran through her mind, but she tamped them down. Instead, she found herself sketching a strong jaw, a straight nose, and a pair of intense, deep-set eyes.

Jon.

Tossing the sketchbook aside, Emma came to her dressing table and began brushing her hair. The steady stroke of the brush through the long strands always managed to relax her. When her nerves had settled, she pinned the shining strands into a simple chignon, softening the look by leaving a few curling wisps around her temple.

Emma stepped outside onto the south patio and Dorothea greeted her with a pleasant smile. The day was lovely; filled with sunshine and clear blue skies.

"Where are Philip and Nicole?" Emma asked as she

took the seat beside the cradle where baby Harold dozed.

"At the stables, waiting for their father. As you know, Carter often takes them riding at this time of the morning and they are anxious to get started." Dorothea sighed. "I do hope he returns home soon. I would hate for the children to be disappointed."

Emma leaned into the cradle and drew in a deep breath, reveling in the sweet scent of her baby nephew. "It's not like Carter to miss a standing appointment, especially with his children. Where has he gone?"

"To see Viscount Kendall."

Emma lunged forward, catching herself before she landed on top of the baby. "He's gone to see Viscount Kendall? Really? About what?"

Dorothea raised her shoulders in a delicate shrug. "I have no idea. I was still asleep when he left this morning. He scribbled a brief note that tells me nothing." Dorothea smiled. "'Tis so typical of a man, is it not, to leave out all the interesting details."

Mind racing, Emma muttered an incoherent reply. Had Carter somehow discovered where she had spent the night? Had he gone to see the viscount to confront him on the matter? The events of last night—and her early morning return home—echoed over and over in Emma's mind, yet she saw no way her secret could have been revealed.

"Is everything all right, Emma?" Dorothea asked. "Your face has suddenly gotten rather pale."

Emma cringed. Thankfully, Harold chose that moment to stir and waken. She gathered the baby in her arms and lifted him from the cradle, then gently handed him to his mother.

"Do you think he's hungry?" Emma asked, grateful for the chance to change to subject.

"He's always hungry," Dorothea replied with a laugh. She discreetly adjusted her clothing, somehow managing to modestly cover herself, while putting the babe to her breast.

Emma's mind continued to race as Dorothea's attention became completely focused on her child. This could be bad—very bad. If it became common knowledge that she and the viscount had spent the night together . . . oh, God, there would be hell to pay!

Unease settled in the pit of Emma's stomach, but then she scolded herself for so quickly assuming the worst. There could have been any number of reasons why Carter needed to see Jon at such an early hour. Granted, she currently could not think of a single one, but that did not preclude the existence of a good reason.

A reason that had nothing at all to do with her.

Thankfully, Emma managed to get her wayward thoughts under control just as her brother-in-law appeared on the patio. He kissed his wife, gently stroked Harold's bald head, and settled in a chair.

"Have you eaten?" Dorothea asked her husband.

"Just now," Carter replied. "I was famished and Cook prepared all my favorite breakfast foods the moment I arrived home."

Emma could not hold back her smile. Cook adored the marquess and took great delight in spoiling him at every turn.

"Well, I'm glad that you have sustenance for your outing with Philip and Nicole," Dorothea said. "They are waiting for you in the stables."

Carter nodded. "I'll join them in a few moments."

"Can you tell you us what so urgently took you away

this morning?" Emma asked in what she hoped was only a curious—and not desperate—voice.

"Terrible business, I'm afraid." Carter sighed and rubbed his hand across his chin. "Gerald Dickenson was killed last night. His servants discovered him this morning on the floor of his study with a knife in his chest."

"How horrifying." Dorothea pulled the baby tightly against her chest, cradling his head protectively. "Has the person been caught? Are we in any danger?"

"We are safe, though I have instructed the servants to be vigilant and alert me immediately if they encounter any strangers on the grounds." Carter leaned into Dorothea. "I believe this attack was personal. The baron knew his killer."

"That's dreadful." Dorothea propped the babe on her shoulder and began gently patting his back. "But I thought your note said that you had gone to see Viscount Kendall."

"It did. I did." A hint of frustration crossed Carter's face. "Kendall is the prime suspect. Two of Lord Brayer's footmen swear they saw Kendall entering the baron's study with him late last night. A loud argument then followed. A few hours later, Brayer's body was discovered."

Emma's mouth fell open. She remained still for several moments as her mind tried to comprehend the implications of Carter's revelations.

Suspected of murder? Jon?

"That cannot be true," she whispered.

"Kendall denies it, most vehemently, and personally I believe him," Carter replied. "Yet as much as I would like to, I cannot so easily dismiss the accounts of two eyewitnesses. Especially when Kendall has no one other than himself to refute the footmen's claims."

"No one?" Looking perplexed, Dorothea raised her brow. "Surely one of Kendall's servants or Lady Sybil saw him at some point last night and can vouch for his whereabouts?"

"Apparently not. Kendall claims to have spent the night in his workshop. Alone."

The babe let out a loud belch and Carter's solemn expression broke into a fond smile. Reaching out, he took his youngest son into his arms.

"Goodness, this is most unfortunate for Kendall," Dorothea exclaimed as she discreetly buttoned the front of her gown.

"But there is no real proof that the viscount was involved," Emma protested. "These footmen did not see Kendall strike their employer."

"True, yet Kendall will need to mount a spirited defense to prove his innocence."

"Defense? Has he been charged with the crime?" Emma asked, her heart racing.

"I had no choice," Carter said with obvious regret.

"Dear Lord," Emma whispered.

"Gracious, this only gets worse and worse." Dorothea tucked a loose strand of hair behind her ear. "I shall call on Lady Sybil directly. She must be beside herself with worry."

"The viscount said nothing else about his activities last night?" Emma pressed. "Nothing at all?"

"There appeared little to tell," Carter replied. "Regrettably."

A wave of panic swept through Emma. She knew precisely why Jon had said nothing. It was obvious that he was protecting her reputation. Yet at what cost?

Granted, he knew that he was innocent of this

heinous crime. *The real killer will be found and Jon will be set free.*

Yet even as the words echoed in her mind, Emma knew that justice was not always fair. The guilty were not always caught and innocent people paid and suffered for crimes they did not commit.

She cast an anxious glance at Dorothea and Carter. They would be most distressed hearing what she needed to tell them, but the stakes were too high to keep silent.

"There is something that I have to tell both of you," Emma said slowly, searching her mind for the right words.

"Oh, my, you suddenly look very solemn and serious, Emma," Dorothea exclaimed.

"This concerns Lord Kendall," Emma replied, careful to keep any emotion from her voice, hoping that if she remained calm and matter-of-fact, so would her sister and brother-in-law. "I can state with absolute certainty that he is telling the truth. He was at his workshop all of last night and well into this morning."

Carter and Dorothea exchanged a puzzled look.

"Emma? How on earth can you make such a bold statement?" Carter asked.

Emma shivered. "I know this is true because he wasn't alone. I was with him in the workshop last night until very early this morning."

Disbelief appeared to rob both Carter and Dorothea of speech. They didn't speak for several long moments, and when the silence was finally broken, they both began talking at once.

"You cannot mean to say—"

"What in the hell—"

"It was all perfectly innocent," Emma said, rushing to explain. "I walked over to his property, hoping to run into him in the area by the workshop and have another look at the machine he is working on, but I got lost and it began to rain.

"Thankfully, Lord Kendall found me. We took shelter from the storm in the workshop, but the rain never stopped. As the hour grew late, we fell asleep. I awoke first and hurried home, sneaking into the manor before anyone saw me."

Carter and Dorothea once again grew silent, staring at her in amazement. Emma could feel her cheeks burning with embarrassment. "It was all perfectly innocent and respectable," she repeated, gesturing helplessly.

Carter gave her a skeptical look. "You spent the night alone with a man. I doubt that anyone will agree it was innocent or respectable if this incident is revealed."

Emma rubbed her forehead nervously. "But it must be told," she exclaimed. "'Tis the only way to prove Jon's innocence."

"Jon?" Dorothea's brow rose fractionally at the familiarity. "Emma, is there something else you wish to tell us?"

"No," Emma replied vehemently.

"Carter?" Looking uneasy, Dorothea turned to her husband. "What should we do?"

Carter's jaw firmed. "Emma's right. It could take weeks, even months to find the real killer. Or worse, he might never be found. This is the only way to quickly prove that Kendall was not involved in the baron's death. She must tell the truth."

"It will cause a scandal," Dorothea warned.

"It will save a man's life," Carter replied. "I'll have a note sent to the other magistrates and convene a meeting at the reverend's residence this afternoon. Emma will tell them what she knows about the events of last night."

"Would it not be better to have them summoned here?" Dorothea questioned.

"No. They need to support my decision to let Kendall go and I want to avoid any appearance of intimidation. Emma must be believed or else her revelations will be for naught."

Emma swallowed a deep breath of air. "Why would they think I am lying?"

"You are a woman," Carter said bluntly. "Directly contradicting the word of two men."

Dorothea's eyes widened and she turned to Emma. "Would you like me to come with you, Emma? For moral support."

Emma's stomach dipped. She had not anticipated needing to tell anyone other than Dorothea and Carter about spending the night with Jon. And the possibility that she would not be believed had never once crossed her mind.

She forced a brave smile to her face. "I think it best if only Carter accompanies me."

Dorothea leaned forward and slid her arms around Emma. "As you wish."

Emma felt a rush of tears gather in her eyes. The repercussions from the scandal she was about to create by revealing her involvement with the viscount would also taint Dorothea and Carter. Yet Dorothea remained supportive.

Emma was grateful. It helped give her some much-needed courage to do what was necessary to save Jon's life.

* * *

The queasiness in Emma's stomach increased dramatically when they arrived at the reverend's cottage. By the time the coach came to a full stop, it felt as though there were butterflies battling inside her. Carter exited first, gestured the footman aside, and offered her his hand.

Grateful for the support, Emma took a deep breath, squared her shoulders, and stepped down. She continued to cling to her brother-in-law when the reverend's wife greeted them at the door and held on even tighter when the older woman led them to a modestly decorated drawing room.

The reverend and two other gentlemen waited for them. Carter introduced Squire Hornsby and Mr. DeBore, and Emma could tell by Carter's respectful manner, these men clearly had standing and influence in the community. She swallowed hard, knowing Jon's fate rested upon these men believing her.

Refusing any refreshments, Emma awkwardly took a seat. She would have preferred to remain standing, as it would afford her a fast way to exit, but if she didn't sit, the men would have to also stay on their feet.

"Emma has something important to tell us about Lord Brayer's murder," Carter said directly.

All eyes turned toward her. Emma felt her heart lurch, yet she was grateful Carter had gotten so quickly to the matter at hand. He nodded at her encouragingly, putting her very slightly at ease.

Emma took a deep breath. "Lord Kendall has explained that he was at his workshop last night at the time Lord Brayer was attacked and killed. However, he has omitted one very important fact. Lord Kendall was not alone. I was with him."

She paused a moment to let that revelation register. The men exchanged glances before casting a nervous eye in Carter's direction. He nodded, silently giving his permission for them to question her further. Emma braced herself.

"For how long?" the reverend asked.

"Until dawn," Emma replied.

Squire Hornsby sucked in a whistling breath, while the reverend appeared properly shocked. Emma tried to maintain her composure, but it faltered a bit when she noticed that Mr. DeBore was unable to completely contain his smirk.

"So, you would have us believe that Kendall is not a murderer, merely a debaucher of innocent young women?" Mr. DeBore asked.

"He is neither," Emma said firmly, her face heating. "He was a perfect gentleman. We were caught in the rainstorm and fell asleep. Nothing inappropriate occurred between us."

"Based on this new evidence, I am releasing Kendall," Carter announced, moving forward to stand at Emma's side.

"Not so fast," Squire Hornsby interjected, raising his hand. "There are two men who say otherwise. They swear that it was Kendall with Lord Brayer."

"They are mistaken," Carter said firmly, shooting a look at the squire that would have most men quaking in their boots.

The squire opened his mouth again, and Emma held her breath, waiting for the next objection. However, Hornsby must have thought better of it, as his mouth quickly closed.

Though Carter claimed he wanted to avoid intimidating his fellow magistrates, he had apparently changed his mind. The three men exchanged nervous glances.

The reverend cleared his throat. "I think Lord Atwood makes a valid point."

Squire Hornsby snorted, yet voiced no other objections. Nervously, Emma looked to Mr. DeBore. He nodded his head slowly in agreement.

The trembling in Emma's belly quieted. Jon would be freed.

But at what price to her?

Chapter Eight

Emma sat primly in the brocade chair, her hands clasped demurely in her lap while Dorothea paced in front of her, muttering beneath her breath.

"I will say it again, Emma, as Viscount Kendall will be here shortly," Dorothea sputtered. "He is an honorable man. He knows the sacrifice that you made by coming forward and clearing his name. Carter and I are both certain that he will propose. And when he does, you must accept."

"You are overreacting," Emma replied, striving for a soothing tone.

"I wish that I was," Dorothea announced, her face clouding with concern. "I can see no other way, nor can Carter. We were up half the night, racking our brains for an alternative, yet I fear that this is the only possible solution."

Emma stilled. It was foolish of her to have been lulled into a sense of false security, to have believed that she might emerge from the incident unscathed. Yet it had all been surprisingly calm and normal when she and Carter had returned from the reverend's house yesterday afternoon.

Dorothea had not pressed her for details, though

Emma was certain Carter had told his wife everything the moment they were alone. The unpleasantness of the meeting with the magistrates had gradually begun to fade and Emma had deliberately pushed away any lingering anxiety over the experience.

Then, at supper, Carter received a note from Lord Kendall, expressing his gratitude and confirming the nobleman had been released from prison and the charges against him dropped.

There had also been a note for Emma.

> *Miss Ellingham,*
>   *It is my sincere hope that you will receive me when I call at Ravenswood Manor tomorrow morning.*
>   *Your servant,*
>   *Kendall*

Brief, formal, and to the point. Emma had crumbled the fine velum into a tight ball and shoved it into the pocket of her gown. She clutched it now as she gazed at her sister.

"I was fully aware that there would be gossip to endure once the truth about that night was revealed," Emma said slowly, determined to make her sister understand—and support—her position. "However, you must believe me when I tell you that I am unafraid of any scandal that may result from it, for I have done nothing disgraceful or reprehensible. All I did was tell the truth to ensure that an innocent man was set free."

"Unfortunately, the truth involved a scandalous revelation and the price for retaining even a modicum of your good name is your freedom."

Dorothea sent her a compassionate look that dispatched a cold shiver down Emma's spine.

"No," she whispered.

"You are ruined, Emma," Dorothea said gently. "You spent the night, alone, with a man who is not your husband. That, by most people's standards, is unacceptable."

"Nothing happened between us," Emma insisted.

"Then why do you blush such a charming shade of red each time you say that to me?"

Emma blanched, damning her sister's observant eye. Jon's kisses had awakened something fiery within her, a passion that even in her naïveté she realized could consume her. It intrigued her, even tantalized her, yet she knew she had the strength to resist it.

Marriage! Nay, 'twas an impossibility. Having seen the joy her sisters experienced sharing their lives with men whom they loved—and loved them—Emma knew it would be a daily struggle for her to settle for far less.

"The appearance of impropriety is hardly a good enough reason to take such a bold step as marriage," Emma said. "We barely know each other."

A kind sympathy lit Dorothea's eyes. "Be that as it may, 'tis your only choice."

Emma felt a grip of panic seize her chest. She knew all too well that stubborn set of Dorothea's jaw meant her sister had made up her mind—and it would be nigh on impossible to change it.

"Since when have you been so beholden to the dictates of the *ton*?" Emma questioned desperately. "You have no hesitation in flaunting society's conventions when it comes to raising your children."

"Nursing my babes within the privacy of my own home is hardly comparable, Emma."

Emma let out a long, deep sigh. "I'm not certain I can do it."

"Oh, Emma." Dorothea clasped Emma's hands. "Kendall is a fine man, with a deep sense of honor. He could have revealed the truth himself, yet he chose to protect you. I know that he will treat you with courtesy and respect. 'Tis not a bad foundation upon which to build a good marriage."

Emma felt her heart slowly sink as the vise of reality closed around her. Dorothea was right. It was going to be impossible to weather this scandal. There was no other choice. Despite all her misgivings, when the viscount asked, she was going to have to say yes.

God help them both.

The longer Emma sat, alone, in the drawing room, the more intense the enormity of her impending meeting with the viscount, and its consequences, rattled her. He had arrived nearly an hour ago. Coward that she was, Emma had hid abovestairs, catching only a brief glimpse of him as he was whisked into Carter's study. The two had been in there all that time, no doubt discussing the terms of the marriage contract.

Marriage contract! Have I utterly lost my mind?

Too uneasy to sit any longer, Emma sprang from her chair and began pacing in front of the long windows. The sun was struggling to move out from behind an enormous cloud. A sign of things to come? Yet what would mark a victory for Emma—the emergence of light or the darkness of rain?

She wanted to approach the situation with logic instead of emotion, but it was impossible. Marriage was an emotional and physical commitment. Or at least it should be.

He had deeply loved another woman, she reminded herself. *A woman who is now a widow and free to marry again—after a respectable period of mourning. Yet propriety and honor will instead force him to take me as his wife.* The reality of that bothered Emma far more than she cared to acknowledge.

And I loved another man. Does that not make us the perfect society couple?

The ironic humor should have brought a smile to her lips; instead Emma was unable to completely suppress the sob that rose in her chest. With a shudder, she covered her mouth with her hands.

Maybe Lord Kendall will refuse to make the match, she thought frantically, yet even as the idea was forming in her mind, she rejected it. Dorothea had spoken truthfully when she remarked that the viscount was an honorable man. He would do the *right* thing, damn the consequences.

Emma hung her head and felt the first tear slide down her cheek. She brushed it away, but a second fell fast and then a third, and soon she was sobbing until her face felt flushed and hot, her nose was running and her eyes felt gritty.

When the tears finally subsided, Emma collapsed into a chair, her head lolling against the soft cushion. She fished a handkerchief from the pocket of her gown and blew her nose.

I feel as though something has died.

Marrying Lord Kendall would change everything. *If I am another man's wife, Sebastian will be truly and irrevocably lost to me. Forever.*

Sebastian was never mine to lose, the logic in her brain shouted. *He always thought of me as a younger sister, never as a potential romantic partner. Sebastian married another woman, a woman he loves and admires, a woman who has given birth to his children.*

"I know that," Emma muttered to herself. Yet apparently knowing and truly believing it were entirely different things.

She was so deep in thought—and misery—she failed to hear the knock on the drawing room door or the sound of footsteps approaching until they had stopped in front of her. Startled, Emma raised her chin.

Viscount Kendall gazed down at her. His jaw was freshly shaved, his hair neatly trimmed, his clothing crisp and newly pressed. Apparently, he had taken extra time with his appearance before coming to see her.

She stood and hastily ran a nervous finger over the tip of her twitching nose, then touched her hand to her brow. "I didn't hear you come in," she said lamely.

"I imagine you have a great deal on your mind," he said gently. His piercing eyes seemed to penetrate deep into her soul and the look of compassion on his face made her turn away.

"Oh, yes."

Emma felt his hands close over her shoulders and he slowly turned her around. "You've been crying," he stated.

Emma sniffed. She must look ghastly. Swollen, puffy eyes, red nose, disheveled hair. Would that be enough to scare him off?

Determined to have her say, Emma met his eyes. His face was exhausted and she realized how selfish she had been, thinking only of herself. He had been through a difficult and traumatic ordeal.

"Are you well?" she asked. "Did you suffer any ill effects from your incarceration?"

He gave her an ironic smile. "I was in the gaol less than twelve hours."

Emma released a strained laugh. "Of course. How foolish of me! So much has happened in such a short span of time, I fear my wits have been scattered to the four winds."

"Yes, a great deal has happened," he agreed.

"Thankfully it has all been put to rights."

"Almost. There is one additional, most important matter that needs to be settled."

Pulse pounding, Emma shot him a sideways glance. The knot choking her throat was growing and the tightness in her chest made it difficult to breathe.

"Miss Ellingham. Emma. Would you do me the great honor of becoming my wife?"

They stood facing each other in charged silence. *Bloody hell!* Jon fidgeted with the gold button on his waistcoat. He hadn't thought much beyond making the proposal. He had assumed she would gratefully accept and they would next work out the details.

Indecision bloomed clearly across Emma's face and she tightly fisted her hands at her sides.

Arrogant, presumptuous fool! Jon mentally berated himself for not preparing for her refusal. Had he learned nothing from his prior attempt at getting himself a wife?

"I should have realized that, like your two sisters, you would wish to marry for love," he said, regretting that he had been so damned anxious to get this over with he hadn't considered Emma's feelings.

She had a mind of her own and a strong, independent streak that enabled her to follow it. Atwood had given his blessing to the union and settled a generous dowry upon her. Yet he had insisted that Jon would have to secure Emma's consent to the union or it would not take place.

Apparently, the marquess had had an inkling about his sister-in-law's reaction. Damn, the least Atwood could have done was warn him!

Emma's cheeks flushed. "I am unlike my sisters in many ways. In all honesty, marriage is not something that I have ever seriously considered."

He wasn't sure if he should be heartened or discouraged by that remark. Jon had always believed that the main focus of any woman's life was to marry—and have children. Once again, Emma had proven herself to be unlike most females of her class.

"Are you disinclined toward marriage in general or specifically with me?" he asked.

She hesitated. He braced himself.

"Except for a few, brief conversations, we are strangers," she protested, her luminous eyes reflecting her inner turmoil and uncertainty. "Marriage is such a permanent, drastic step."

"You know as well as I do that the only way for us to avoid an irrevocable scandal is to marry," he said, trying to implore her with a practical argument.

She shut her eyes and shook her head rapidly. "You are exaggerating. Yes, there will be talk and unkind words spoken against both of us. However, I believe that while your reputation will suffer initially, in time it will recover."

"And what of your reputation, Emma?"

"True, a female is not afforded the same consideration by society. My reputation will never be fully restored." She grimaced. "However, that hardly matters to me. I am included in society events because of my two sisters and the positions of their husbands. 'Tis no great loss if I am no longer welcome at certain parties or balls."

"Well, I shall always feel a deep sense of guilt if you are shunned," he replied. "Especially knowing that I could have shielded you from such a fate." He cleared his throat. "I can give you a comfortable life, Emma, with all the prestige and benefits of my rank and fortune. I vow to treat you with kindness and respect, to honor my vows of fidelity, as I expect you to honor yours. You shall want for nothing, including the freedom to pursue your art or anything else that strikes your fancy."

A disquieting irony lit her eyes. "Ah, pity and bribery. The hallmarks of a truly desperate man."

"Marry me," he said firmly.

Jon could feel his hands clench and unclench as he waited for her response. After the heartbreak of Dianna, he had consigned the idea of marriage to the very back of his mind, determined not to think about it for as long as possible—if ever.

His title was old and dignified, but not especially important. His estates were not entailed, he could leave his land and fortune to whomever he pleased. Perhaps a worthy charity or an institute of higher learning and innovation.

If he failed to produce a legitimate heir it would be of no major consequence to anyone, except perhaps his mother, who hinted now and again how much she would like to have grandchildren. His title would pass to some distant relative, most likely a cousin who resided in the Americas and would have little interest in it without the money.

After failing to make Dianna his wife, Jon had been

comfortable and accepting of all those possibilities. Then everything changed yesterday when Emma had sacrificed her reputation to save him.

"What are you thinking, Emma?" he asked, when he could no longer bear the suspense of her silence.

She inhaled unsteadily. "I am wondering how I have managed to create such a shambles of my life in less than twenty-four hours."

"You could have kept silent," he countered. "Perhaps you should have. We both know that I am innocent of the crime."

Her eyes widened with dismay. "And risked the possibility of you being found guilty? And executed? Carter said it could take months to find the real killer. Or worse still, the culprit may never be found."

The wave of feelings invading him took Jon by surprise. Initially he had been offended at the idea of a woman rushing to his defense. As a man, 'twas his role to protect the weaker sex. Yet he now felt humbled at having a champion for his cause. Emma had put herself at risk to save him—without hesitation.

He could not help but admire her courage and conviction, her selfless sacrifice. All the more reason he could not let her suffer for her actions.

"I'm grateful for your help and honesty. Thank you," he said simply.

"I could do no less," she replied softly.

They stared at each other for another long moment.

"Would it be so terrible to be my wife?" he asked, taking a step closer and reaching for her hand.

"I don't know you," she replied quietly. "Nor you me."

"That's not so unusual," he insisted. "Many couples marry under similar circumstances."

"Yes, and live to rue the day." Emma shuddered as she gently extricated her hand from his.

"Your two older sisters married men they loved. Is that why you hesitate?" he asked.

"I can assure you that I harbor no girlish daydreams of love and romance." Her gaze grew thoughtful. "However, if I must marry, then I have some conditions."

Jon felt himself stiffen with caution. "Conditions?"

"I should like to spend the majority of the year living at your estate here, in the country." She peeked at him from beneath her lashes. "I will of course accompany you to London anytime you deem it necessary, but I find as I grow older, I have little interest in the social events of the Season."

"That is easily agreed upon. I, too, prefer the country life." He took another step forward, close enough this time so that he could see the blue of her eyes. "Anything else?"

"Yes." She cleared her throat. Loudly. When she finally spoke, her voice dropped a full octave lower. "I do not want a marriage of convenience. I want a true union, with children. At least two, if we are so blessed."

Damn! She was full of surprises. Never in a million years would he have expected her to lay such a request at his feet. Emma was quite correct in her earlier statement. They barely knew each other.

Jon stared at her thoughtfully. "And you thought I might object to such a request?"

Her brows knit together as the color rose to her cheeks. "Frankly, I had no idea what you would think. I only know that you are not making this marriage proposal of your own free will."

Ah, so that is the crux of the matter. He looked at her earnestly, trying to convey his sincerity with his entire body. "But I am, Emma. No one is forcing me."

"We are being manipulated by this situation," she

insisted. "A union between us was the furthest thing from both our minds. There is no point in denying it."

"'Tis true that ever since things went so badly for me last spring, I have not been of a mind to marry," he admitted. "However, I can assure you that this is what I want. And not only because honor demands it.

"I am pleased that you want to have children. Frankly, until you mentioned it, I hadn't realized that is something that I, too, would like to experience."

Emma's expression barely altered. Silently, he prayed that the sincerity and honesty of his words would strike a chord within her and persuade her to make the right choice.

Finally, she exhaled. A long, deep breath that gave Jon no clue to her decision. Then she bowed her head.

"All right. I accept. I will marry you, Lord Kendall."

"Jon," he corrected, taking her hand again.

His first inclination was to lean down and seal the bargain with a kiss, yet oddly that felt too intimate. Instead, he lifted her delicate hand to his mouth and kissed her knuckles softly.

His senses rose to alertness. A vision of her enfolded in his arms, their lips pressed together, danced before his eyes and wolfish, sensual thoughts invaded his mind. She was a luscious creature, unaware of her feminine powers.

And she was going to be his. It would be pure pleasure, and a bit of a challenge, to discover her hidden depths.

Thank God he had always relished a challenge.

Reluctantly, Jon released Emma's hand, but the sweetness of her delicate flesh lingered on his lips. She managed a shy smile and for the first time since entering the drawing room, he felt optimistic.

* * *

Later the next afternoon, while staring anxiously into her dressing table mirror, Emma tried not to think too much about Jon's final words before she had agreed to become his wife.

I can assure you that this is what I want. And not only because honor demands it.

Had he been telling the truth? She had believed him at the time, yet a day later she was beginning to wonder if she had exaggerated the moment in her mind in order to accept the inevitable.

Stop being so maudlin! Emma shook her head, mentally berating herself. She was making a difficult situation much worse with these gloomy, dire thoughts. She needed to focus on the positive aspects of marrying the viscount.

Jon had promised her independence, and she took him to be a man of his word. Hopefully, there would be children one day, another joy to anticipate. He had promised they would spend the majority of their time in the country, which meant she would be living on an estate that bordered Dorothea's home, still another reason to be thankful.

Lord Kendall was a fine man. He believed that respect, loyalty, and fidelity were traits to be valued in a marriage. Jon's words had given her hope in possibly achieving those in this marriage.

And what of love? Emma frowned. *Alas, that must be forgotten.* She was trying to be realistic and honest with herself. They had each already endured the deep pain of losing a love they had cherished. It would therefore be exceptionally foolish to expect they would come to passionately love each other.

Actually, the bigger fear was that only *one* of them would fall to the emotion and the other would reject it. And the way that her luck always seemed to run, that person would be her.

The pain of her past whispered in Emma's head. With a rogue's smile that could easily melt the heart of any maiden, Sebastian had told her that he loved her. And then ruined it all by adding, as a sister. A companion, a trusted friend and confidant. Not as a woman.

Emma pushed back on the pain and the memory— as she always did—regretting that she had never been able to truly banish it. But she was older now and hopefully wiser. Never again would she gift her heart to a man who was unable to cherish and protect it.

The steady patter of rain drew Emma's attention to the window. An omen? Nay! She refused to indulge in any ridiculous superstitions. Determined, she lifted the crown of fresh flowers resting on her dressing table and carefully pinned it to her hair.

Emma narrowed her eyes at the mirror. There. Now she looked like a bride, even though she didn't precisely feel like one. 'Twas still difficult to comprehend that in less than a day a marriage license had been obtained, the ceremony arranged, and the reverend convinced to perform it.

The combined power of Carter and Jon's wealth and privilege was never to be underestimated. She would do well to always remember it.

"You look beautiful, Emma," Dorothea said as she entered the bedchamber.

"Do I?" Emma's stomach leapt with nerves. "I thought I looked rather pale. Should I use some rouge?"

"There's no need." Dorothea gave her a warm hug,

pressing her cheek to Emma's. "Though it hardly shows, I'm sure you are nervous."

"Terrified," Emma admitted.

"And what about tonight? Is there anything you wish to ask me about what will happen on your wedding night?"

"I'm not a ninny. I know how babies are made," Emma protested.

"Sharing your bed with a man is not only a physical experience," Dorothea responded primly. "Though it does help lessen the shock, knowing what to expect."

Questions swirled, too delicate to ask, yet Emma was tempted. That is, until she caught a look at her sister. "Are you turning red, Dorothea?"

Dorothea shrieked and buried her face in her hands. "I believe that I am."

"Oh, dear, if just speaking of marital relations causes such embarrassment, how am I to ask you about them?"

Dorothea lowered her hands and straightened her spine. "I assure you that I can speak coherently on the subject."

"Well, I'm not certain I'm ready to hear it." Emma bristled. "I have enough misgivings about this wedding as it stands. No need to add more."

"'Tis natural for a bride to be nervous, even a tad apprehensive," Dorothea said, adjusting the crown of flowers on Emma's head.

"Far more than a tad," Emma remarked in an ironic voice.

She glanced back at the mirror. Dorothea's fumbling had knocked the flowers slightly askew. Not enough to make her look disheveled, but enough to ruin the appearance of perfection. Oddly enough, that made Emma feel slightly better.

"Everyone is waiting," Dorothea said gently. "Are you ready?"

Emma took one final glance at herself in the mirror and sighed. But then she straightened her back, steadied her nerves, and rose from the chair. "Yes."

Chapter Nine

Jon felt his chest tighten the moment Emma entered the drawing room. She was a vision in blue. The silk gown clung to her curves in all the right places, showcasing the essence of her womanhood. The color of the gown offset the creamy whiteness of her complexion and brought out the blue in her eyes.

Her hair was swept off her neck, piled simply upon her head and circled with a simple coronet of fresh flowers that matched the small nosegay she carried. Her throat was bare and he suddenly thought how elegant and lovely she would look wearing the Kendall sapphire-and-diamond necklace.

Lady Atwood stood at her side and they walked together toward him. Solemnly, Jon held out his hand and when Emma clasped it, he immediately covered it with his other hand.

"I'm sorry to have kept you waiting," she murmured.

"I feared you might have changed your mind," he admitted.

"I did." She pulled in a long breath. "At least a half dozen times last night and twice more this morning."

She almost sounded cheerful. Or was that a maidenly show of hysteria?

"Then may I assume your presence here means you have decided to marry me?"

"You may." She nodded her head, then thrust out her chin with determination. "I've set the course and am now committed to follow it."

Emma's no-nonsense attitude should have provided him with some relief. It did not.

Casting them an annoyed look, the reverend cleared his throat and pressed his lips together in a flat line of irritation. Miffed, Jon returned the reverend's stare measure for measure. He still wasn't certain exactly how Atwood had persuaded the clergyman to perform the ceremony, as it was obvious he disapproved.

A panicked yet determined bride, an ornery officiant, and buckets of rain falling from the sky. Bloody hell, this wedding was fraught with even more drama than his previous fiasco with Dianna.

Perhaps he was a man not meant to ever marry?

However, time for reflection was long past. As Emma said, the course was set. The ceremony was brief and subdued. Calling forth his own annoyance, Jon ignored the censorious looks the reverend threw their way. He spoke his vows, listened intently as Emma repeated hers, then placed the ring on Emma's finger.

The reverend concluded the ceremony with a less than enthusiastic blessing. Emma released a long sigh, turned and embraced her sister. The move startled Jon, as he was hoping they might share a gentle kiss. However, he was soon receiving congratulations of his own—a handshake from Atwood, a tight, emotional hug from his mother, and finally a warm hug from Lady Atwood.

With a merry smile, Lady Atwood next invited them

all to adjourn to the dining room for the wedding feast. The reverend immediately declined the invitation. His wife's lips pursed into a sour look of disappointment, yet she offered no objection to her husband's dictates.

The family gathered around the dining room table. Lord and Lady Atwood's two older children joined them. 'Twas clear the pair were close to Emma and that she, in turn, had a great affection for them.

Their excited chatter lent a festive air to the meal and Jon was glad that the convention of keeping children separated from adult celebrations had been ignored.

As they all took their seats, Jon glanced at Emma. She looked as dazed as he felt. He took a long sip of the French wine in his crystal goblet to chase the dryness from his throat. Striving for normalcy, he placed the crisp linen napkin in his lap.

"I'm sorry that your other sister, Mrs. Barrington, was unable to attend the ceremony today," he said.

"As am I." Remorse filled Emma's eyes. "Gwen and Jason are in France for a few weeks. A message would never have reached them in time to be here this afternoon. I pleaded, but Carter and Dorothea insisted that we mustn't wait, that it was essential we marry as soon as possible."

A frisson of guilt stabbed at Jon at the necessity of such haste. He should have considered Emma's feelings. As it stood, marrying so swiftly did not ensure they would mitigate the worst of the scandal that was sure to follow. Waiting a few days for Emma's sister should have been given more serious consideration.

"We can go and visit them, if you'd like," Jon offered. "Or invite them to come to us for an extended stay."

A spark of lightness entered her eyes. "That's most

kind. Thank you. They will attend the Season when they return from the Continent, but I shall write to Gwen and extend an invitation."

Ah, their first exchange as husband and wife. And it had gone smoothly. Jon took another sip of his wine and started to relax.

The first course was served—a fresh pea soup. It was soon followed by courses of fish, fowl, beef, vegetables, and salad. Jon had not felt especially hungry when he sat down, yet he found himself consuming generous portions of most of the dishes.

Emma, he noted with a slight frown, was moving the food around on her plate and stacking it into neat, colorful piles. Her wine also remained untouched.

"The food is delicious. I fear I am being rude eating so much," he commented. "Though I suppose I must make up for what you are not consuming."

Emma's mouth curved slightly and she took a dainty bite of asparagus. "My nerves are still fluttering, which causes my stomach to be unbalanced."

"Filling it might help," he suggested.

"Perhaps." She took another small bite and then a sip of wine. "Or it might cause anything I've placed inside to suddenly, violently appear."

Jon blanched. Good Lord, had she just implied she might cast up her accounts if she ate? "I had not realized you felt so ill. Do you need to lie down?"

"Actually, I do feel better after eating," she said, accepting a second serving of roasted duck. "You need not look so worried. It will stay down. I won't embarrass myself. Or you."

A hint of color graced Emma's cheeks and she appeared a bit more relaxed. Breathing easier, Jon took her at her word.

"Lady Atwood has done a remarkable job on such short notice," he remarked, as a trio of footmen entered the dining room with yet another course.

Emma nodded. "Dorothea was up most of the night going over the details and rose far earlier than usual this morning, ensuring that all would be ready. She spent considerable time with Cook devising the menu and even longer with the gardeners. I think half the blooms in Carter's gardens and most in the hothouse were cut to make all the flower arrangements."

"Her efforts are noted and appreciated," Jon said.

"She did perform miracles in a mere day. It was important to her on many levels. Dorothea told me that she wanted this to be a memorable occasion and as *normal* a wedding as possible."

Jon nodded absently, uncertain what to make of that remark. True, the wedding had been planned and executed in haste. And it was fair to say they had but a brief acquaintance with each other. Yet that was hardly an uncommon start for a marriage among the nobility.

In fact, the marriage of many couples of their class was viewed as a business transaction, the establishment of familiar connections, the exchange of wealth and position. And of course, the continuation of their noble bloodlines.

It suddenly occurred to him that despite the delightful kisses they had exchanged two nights ago, Emma might be feeling particularly nervous and anxious about the physical intimacy they would share later that night. She was far from a prude, but he believed her to be a virgin.

Could that account for her queasy stomach?

That thought lingered, troubling him. Jon sipped

his wine. Perhaps he ought to ease her nerves and suggest putting off the consummation for a few days, until they were more comfortable around each other. She might appreciate the considerate gesture.

Damn. Just the thought brought on a sharp stab of disappointment. He wanted her in his bed. She was his wife. The woman he had just vowed to honor, cherish, and protect. That reminder brought on a powerful possessiveness inside him that was as surprising as it was strong.

He intended this to be a simple, straightforward relationship. One of mutual respect, admiration, and when appropriate, affection. One that was devoid of intense emotions—like this possessiveness—which clouded sensible judgment and actions.

Would they be able to achieve it?

Jon's reflective mood was broken by the marquess. Atwood stood, raised his glass, and offered a toast to their union and added wishes for their future happiness. The others echoed the sentiments, with smiles and laughter. Beside him, Jon felt Emma still.

He leaned close and asked, "What are you thinking?"

She stiffened further. "Everyone has been very kind."

"Yes. What else?"

She turned toward him, holding his eyes as she sipped from her goblet. "The truth?"

"Always."

A flush rose in her cheeks. "As I look around the table and observe my sister, Carter, and your mother, I cannot help but realize they seemed far more pleased over our nuptials than either of us."

He cast a glance at those she mentioned and realized that Emma was right. "Damn depressing, isn't it?"

She appeared startled, but then her demeanor transformed and she smiled broadly. "I agree."

"What do you propose we do about it?" he asked.

"Lower their expectations?"

Jon's lips quirked into a slight grin. He always appreciated a quick wit. "Shall we start a row?"

"Quietly at first, and then escalate to shouting?" she asked, her eyes gleaming with humor.

"Ah, now that would be a scene to remember."

"And cherish," she added.

Jon reached for her hand and gave it a gentle squeeze. She responded in kind. The feelings of warmth pouring through his chest surprised him.

Sharing this silly, conspiratorial moment together lightened his heart, making him consider that there could be more, much more, between them than a congenial, pleasant relationship.

The idea piqued his interest more than was sensible. Practical. Yet much to Jon's chagrin, it refused to disappear.

The clock struck three chimes, indicating it was past time to depart. The remains of the meal had long been cleared from the dining room and the conversation had slowed to a trickle.

Realizing it could be delayed no longer, Emma caught her sister's eye, nodded and stood.

Everyone followed her lead. Jon placed his hand in the small of her back and she could feel the warmth of his palm through the fabric of her dress. It was a protective gesture, part of his duty as her husband.

Husband. A shock went through her, along with a sense of disbelief. Emma tamped it down. 'Twas done. Falling to pieces after the fact was a useless waste of emotion and energy.

Everyone followed them out of the house, standing

beneath the porticos to say goodbye. The rain that had persisted earlier in the day had thinned to a mist, shrouding the horizon in a foreboding landscape.

It looks like something out of those gothic novels Gwen loved to read when we were younger. All that is missing is the howling of a wild beast in the distance.

Shaking off those bizarre thoughts, Emma turned toward Lady Sybil to bid her farewell.

The older woman's eyes were suspiciously moist. "I wish you every happiness, my dear."

"Thank you." Emma clasped her mother-in-law's hand tightly. "Are you certain you won't return home with us?" she asked.

"Oh, my no," Lady Sybil replied. "A newly married couple is entitled to their privacy. For ages I have been promising my dearest friend, Eileen, that I would come and stay with her for an extended visit, and this is the perfect time. My bags are packed and loaded on the coach. I will be departing for Lincolnshire the moment the fog lifts."

"We shall miss you," Emma said truthfully. "Don't stay away too long."

"Only a month," Lady Sybil replied, hugging her fiercely. "Or two."

Dorothea embraced Emma next. "Please give your marriage a fair chance," her sister whispered in her ear. "I truly believe that you can find happiness."

Emma merely raised her brows. This was hardly the moment to verbalize the many doubts and uncertainties she was feeling.

The carriage arrived. Emma accepted Jon's outstretched hand and he assisted her inside. The door shut and the panic and apprehension that had begun rattling around in Emma's chest when they left the dining room settled firmly in her stomach.

The drive to Jon's home was short, silent, and un-eventful, yet unfortunately did little to ease Emma's nerves.

A footman hurried to pull down the carriage steps and gallantly offered his hand to help her descend. Emma was relieved to see his livery was simple and less formal than the servants in her sister's household. She was far from prepared to take on the running of a grand, formal house.

She waited for Jon to join her and they entered the manor arm in arm. The servants were lined up in the foyer, eyes front, waiting politely to greet them. The butler and housekeeper approached and were introduced. Mr. Hopson and Mrs. Fields offered what Emma determined were sincere congratulations on their marriage and wishes for a long, happy life together.

Emma then moved slowly down the daunting line of underlings, silently repeating their names and positions as they were presented to her, in the hope it would aid her in remembering them. As for their duties, well, judging by the spotless condition of the foyer it was clear they all worked hard.

Jon followed closely behind her and she noticed he was pressing a guinea into each one of their hands. She was pleased to discover that he was honoring this long-held tradition. Since they had not been married at the church, he had been unable to toss coins to the village children, another tradition she enjoyed witnessing.

"What time would you like supper served, Lady Kendall?" Mrs. Fields asked.

Emma smiled vaguely, then jolted, realizing the housekeeper was addressing *her*. "Uhm, well, we have just eaten a rather substantial meal," she hedged.

"Of course." The housekeeper nodded, but Emma saw the older woman's brows draw together. "I'll inform Cook there will be no supper service this evening."

Emma blinked. In all likelihood some sort of celebratory dishes had been prepared for the viscount and his bride. Though Emma knew it would be difficult to eat again, it would be rude not to at least sample the food.

"Do you think the dishes will be spoiled if we eat later than usual, Mrs. Fields?" Emma asked.

"Oh, no. Cook will naturally accommodate whatever schedule you prefer."

"Well, then, just for tonight we shall dine at eight thirty," Emma replied, knowing that was more the city fashion than the country.

"Very good." Mrs. Fields broke into a conspiratorial smile. "Cook will put the extra time to good use, decorating the special cake she's prepared in honor of your nuptials."

"How thoughtful. I'm sure it will be delicious." Emma glanced down the row of servants who were still standing at attention. "Once Lord Kendall and I have enjoyed it, I would like you to make certain that each member of the staff is given a slice."

Mrs. Fields nodded approvingly. Emma felt a rush of relief. Starting off on the right foot with the housekeeper would help make her transition to mistress of the household run much smoother.

If only there was an easy way to do the same with her husband.

"If you will excuse me, Emma, I have some papers in my study that require my immediate attention."

What? He is abandoning me already?

Jon gazed at her expectantly and for the briefest of instant Emma wondered what he would do if she objected.

"I am quite comfortable being left in Mrs. Fields's capable hands," Emma replied, pleased to hear her voice gathering strength.

"Until dinner."

He bowed and Emma watched him disappear from view.

"Shall I show you to your suite, my lady?" Mrs. Fields asked.

"That would be lovely." Emma paused as a sudden, troubling thought occurred. "I have not displaced Lady Sybil, have I?"

"Oh, no. The viscountess—the dowager viscountess," Mrs. Fields corrected herself with a smile, "moved out of those rooms ages ago."

"Good."

"I supervised the unpacking of your garments this morning," the housekeeper informed Emma as they climbed the long staircase. "I hope it all meets with your satisfaction."

"I'm sure it will," Emma replied.

"Lord Kendall told me to arrange for any changes that you wish to make to your chamber," Mrs. Fields added.

Emma nodded vaguely, as she was too busy focusing her attention on the marble sculptures that graced the second-floor hallway. They were magnificent, as were the gilt-framed paintings. Emma had been inside the manor on several occasions, however she had never ascended to the higher floors.

They made several twists and turns before reaching her rooms. The moment she entered, Emma knew there would be little to change. Decorated in pale shades of green, the chamber was serene and soothing. Swags of silk drapes were drawn back from the windowpanes with matching ties, and the pattern on the carpet was a pleasing combination of white, gold, and green.

The furniture was a rich, dark hue, yet delicate, with clean lines and pleasing shapes. There were large windows on two walls that even on this overcast afternoon flooded the room with natural light. Emma was pleased to note that there was not an abundance of decorative vases or figurines to clutter the space.

The bed was an elegant four-poster piece, set high off the floor. Emma noticed the silk-covered stool discreetly placed to the side and realized she would need to make use of it to get into bed every night.

Unless my husband decides to carry me.

Shocked and uncertain where that errant thought had emerged from, Emma turned her complete attention back to Mrs. Fields. The housekeeper showed her the sitting room, which led to her private dressing room. At the back of it, Emma immediately noticed the door that no doubt connected her rooms to the master's chamber. She swallowed hard at the sight.

A timid knock provided a welcome distraction.

"Ah, here's Dory. 'Tis my understanding that you did not bring a lady's maid. If you approve, Dory can serve in that capacity. She's young, but has a fine talent with a needle and arranging hair."

"I'm sure she and I will get along splendidly," Emma replied, liking the choice of a maid closer to her own age. "Hello, Dory."

The maid smiled and bobbed a curtsy. "Lady Kendall."

Emma sighed inwardly, telling herself she had to

cease being startled every time she was addressed by her new name.

"We'll leave you now to rest," Mrs. Fields announced. "Just ring if you require anything."

Jittery at being left alone, Emma spent a few minutes exploring her rooms, then flopped down in one of the gilt chairs set in front of the fireplace. She glanced at the ornate porcelain clock on the desk, dismayed to read the time. Not yet five o'clock!

She now regretted asking supper to be served so late. What was she going to do with herself until then?

An exploration of the house might be enjoyable, especially if she discovered more art treasures. But the house was vast and the potential for getting lost high. Best to wait for another day.

Emma glanced out the window. The rain had ceased; the fog dissipated. Ah, yes, fresh air was precisely what she needed. Invigorated now that she had a plan, Emma exchanged her elegant leather slippers for a pair of sturdy walking boots.

She smiled and nodded at the servants she passed on her way outside. The grounds of the estate were not as elegant or extensive as Carter's, but there was a charm to the less formal, almost unrestrained wildness that appealed to Emma.

Standing at the edge of the woodlands, she clasped her hands together and immediately felt the ring that now resided on her left hand. The bottom of the band was smooth, while the top had textured edges that encased the gems. Four evenly matched emeralds set in a straight line.

She tipped her hand to view them. They sparkled up at her, winking as though they knew she was not the woman meant to be wearing this ring. Idly, Emma wondered if it was a family piece, as there would not have been time enough to have one made. Yet it fit her finger perfectly.

She watched the sun begin to set. She entered the house and asked a footman for directions to her chamber. Her new maid, Dory, awaited her, eager to show her skills. Distracted, Emma allowed the servant to select a fresh gown from the wardrobe, help her dress, and fuss over her appearance.

Jon seemed momentarily startled when she entered the dining room, his eyes widening when they traveled over her hair. Grinning shyly, Emma self-consciously patted the side of her head.

"Yes, 'tis a rather elaborate hairstyle for an at-home meal with no guests. But Dory—she's my new maid— was anxious to make a good impression and demonstrate her skill with a curling iron. I didn't have the heart to object."

"It's very . . ." His voice trailed off.

"Fussy and overdone," Emma answered with a slight laugh. "I know. I promise to restrain Dory's enthusiasm in the future. For both our sakes."

"Good. I'd hate to have to insist you remain indoors and out of sight."

Emma bit her lip as a bubble of laughter rose to her lips. "Do you honestly believe that you could keep me hidden?"

"Probably not." He paused and his expression turned mischievous. "But I would feel it was my duty to try. For the sake of the community."

"You are a most considerate man, Jon," Emma remarked, fighting back another wave of laughter.

"I try." He strolled to the sideboard. "Would you care for a drink?" he asked.

"Yes. I'll have whatever you are having."

His brow rose, but Emma met his penetrating gaze with one of her own. She assumed that he was drinking something far stronger than the ratafia or sherry that was always offered to ladies.

Well, if he needed fortification, then so did she.

There was a merry clink as he removed the crystal stopper from the decanter, lifted it, and poured a hefty amount into two glasses. Emma admired his graceful movements and his broad shoulders.

Emma accepted the glass that was pressed into her hand with a slight nod of thanks. They sipped their drinks in silence. Emma took very small swallows, in hopes of relaxing, but she was cautious not to drink too much.

Jon had not said if he intended to come to her bed tonight, but just in case he did, she intended to be in full control of her senses. Dinner was announced, and arm in arm they proceeded to the dining room.

Jon dismissed the staff, indicating they would prefer to serve themselves. Emma gazed down at the multitude of dishes and sighed.

"By any chance, do you have a dog or two you allow inside the house?" she asked.

"Why?"

"We need some help consuming this food."

"I can assure you that Cook would be far more insulted to discover you have fed the meal to the dogs rather than leaving most of it uneaten."

"Well, then we must soldier on," she said with false cheer, filling her plate with a spoonful of nearly every item.

An hour later, they admitted defeat.

Wiping her mouth with her napkin, Emma pushed herself away from the table and rose to her feet. "It has been a long, eventful day. If you will excuse me, I shall retire for the evening."

Jon's expression remained unchanged. He swirled the brandy in his goblet slowly before taking a sip. "Very well. I shall be up to join you in an hour."

Emma's mouth went dry and her heart began to beat wildly in her chest. The question of whether or not her husband planned on consummating their marriage tonight had just been answered.

Chapter Ten

Jon tied the sash on his dressing gown and padded across his bedchamber in bare feet. He walked through his sitting room, and for a moment stood and stared at the door connecting his chambers to Emma's. Taking a deep breath, he reached for the handle, then drew back his hand.

Uncertainty rippled through him. It was slightly beyond the hour that he said that he would come to her. She was expecting him. Yet should he knock and give her warning? Did he wish to start this part of their marriage so formally?

It seemed ridiculous, however it was also a considerate gesture. He tapped his knuckles on the center of the solid wooden door, then opened it, drawing the line at waiting to be granted permission to enter.

The chamber was bathed in soft candlelight, the fire in the grate banked to a red glow. A quick glance revealed that Emma was already in bed.

Anxious or terrified? He was about to find out.

Raising his own candle higher, Jon approached the bed. For a long moment he simply looked at his bride. Her breathing was slow and steady and he wondered if she feigned sleep. Was she dreading the consummation of their vows?

A depressing thought.

He stepped closer. The flickering light gleamed across Emma's womanly form beneath the sheets. He imagined himself spreading a slow path of tender, erotic kisses down the length of those luscious curves, heating her body to the edge of passion and then bringing them both to a screaming release.

She mumbled suddenly and turned onto her back. Her unbound hair spread across her pillow like a silken cloth, strands of amber mixed within the brown. He wondered how many brush strokes it had taken to untangle that monstrosity of a hairdo she had sported at dinner.

"Emma," he whispered.

She stirred again, murmuring. The covers slipped, revealing bare shoulders. He drew in a sharp breath. She wasn't wearing a nightgown. She wasn't wearing anything.

The chamber suddenly felt very hot.

Jon went still as seductive fantasies took hold. There was something deeply erotic about a woman prepared and waiting to be awakened with physical pleasure. Taking a deep breath, he sought to temper his hunger and rein in his burgeoning desire.

Establishing a physical bond between them would bring a sense of normalcy to their marriage. But not if he fell upon her like a ravishing beast.

He cleared his throat. Loudly. Emma's eyelids fluttered and she slowly opened her eyes. The uncertainty he saw there hit him like a bucket of frigid water, effectively dousing his ardor.

He had no idea what had possessed her to leave

her nightgown off. Maybe her sister had advised it. Whatever the reason, it did not negate the fact that she was inexperienced.

He needed to move slowly or else this could turn into a disaster for both of them. This first taste of pleasure they shared as husband and wife should be more than the urge to satisfy a physical need.

Tenderness and sweet words would help make that happen. He could be tender and gentle. But the sweet words? Could he say them to a woman he didn't love? Would it sound forced? Insincere?

"Jon?" Her eyes were fully open and she was watching him with a mixture of curiosity and unease.

"Were you expecting someone else?" he joked nervously.

She seemed startled by his remark. Wincing slightly, she sat up, affording him a delicious view of her gorgeous breasts before hastily pulling the sheet to her neck. He'd never seen a woman with such fine skin, creamy white with a faint glow of a blush-colored rose.

"Whatever do you mean?" she queried.

"A joke, madam, and a poor one at that."

Silence hung between them for what felt like an eternity. Yet in truth it was but a few moments.

His gaze roamed her face and form. The bed was so high they were nearly at eye level.

"You're shivering, Emma," he finally said.

"Nerves," she replied.

He put his hands in hers. "Do you want me to leave?" he asked, calling himself ten times a fool for suggesting it. But if that was what she wanted . . .

"'Tis our wedding night."

"There will be other nights."

She worried her lower lip between her teeth. "Do you want to go?"

Hell no! He swallowed, adjusting the front of his dressing gown to hide his bulging erection. "I want this part of our marriage to be enjoyable for both of us," he admitted.

She blushed. "A sentiment that I share."

He moved closer. "You are a virgin." He said it deliberately, not as a question but as a statement to avoid insulting her.

"Are you?" She bristled.

Jon smiled, ignoring the indignant challenge in her tone. Even nervous and uncertain, Emma's strong spirit refused to be crushed.

"There is no judgment in my words, only inquiry," he clarified. "Women are usually shielded from the facts of carnal relations, which in turn can lead to all sorts of misinformation and anxiety."

Rather than appreciating his forethought, she appeared affronted by it. "I'm not naïve or ignorant. I know what's going to happen. Dorothea explained everything."

"Ah, understanding and experiencing are two very different matters."

A deep frown appeared on her face. "Yes, well, of course."

"Is there anything you would like to ask me?"

Eyeing him cautiously, she shook her head. "You are not a virgin," she said, copying his prior tone, making her words a statement, not a question.

"Does that bother you?"

Both of her eyebrows lifted. "I suppose 'tis best if one of us knows what to expect."

His lips quirked into a grin. "Now why do I get the

distinct feeling that you would prefer to be the one with the knowledge?"

She smiled and lowered her chin. "I don't care much for surprises."

"Nor do I." He reached down and touched her cheek with his knuckle, stroking it slowly. "I want this to be pleasurable for you, Emma."

She raised her chin. Her eyes opened wider, sparkling and clear as a summer sky. "I trust you," she whispered.

Damn! Such a simple, pure statement, yet it touched him deeply. "An excellent beginning."

It was time to make Emma truly his wife.

Emma rubbed the soft sheet between nervous fingers and tried to steady her breathing. She had fallen asleep waiting for him. Jon. Her husband.

She hadn't heard him enter her bedchamber. She'd been dreaming. Strange, disjointed images had swirled through her unconscious mind, leaving her feeling restless, unsettled. Then the soft, whispered sound of her name had pulled her back to reality.

And now Jon stood beside her bed, silhouetted in the romantic glow of candlelight, dressed in a long silk robe. The sight of his solid, powerful frame raised the hair on the back of her neck, bringing a tingling sensation through her body.

He said that he wanted this part of their marriage to be pleasurable. She believed him. She remembered the kisses they had shared in his workshop. They had been enticing, exciting, sparking her curiosity. She felt an attraction for him that she concluded was desire.

Yet she was still nervous. This was the most intimate,

vulnerable act between a man and a woman. Was she ready to experience it with him?

Jon leaned forward and gathered her in his arms. The palms of her hands rested against his chest. Even through the layer of his robe, Emma could feel the solid strength of his muscles as he eased himself against her.

"Forgive me for waking you," he said huskily, his fingertips skimming over her hair. "You must have been very tired."

"I haven't slept much these last few nights," she admitted.

His eyes gleamed. "Then I shall apologize in advance for keeping you from your slumber again tonight."

Jon's face was so close that Emma could feel the clean warmth of his breath, and her senses went weak with anticipation of the kiss that she knew would be forthcoming.

She lifted her arm to hold him close and felt the sheet slip as her breasts popped from the covers. She had not intended to come to bed naked, but the delicate nightgown Dorothea had suggested she wear had been ill-fitting, pushing so tightly against her breasts it had been difficult to breathe.

Emma had removed it, trying to decide if she should search through the wardrobe for one of her plain, simple nightgowns. Instead she had slid naked between the covers and the comfort of the bed and the soft feel of the sheets had brought on a relaxed languor to her tired limbs.

But now she was very much awake. She watched her husband from under lowered lids, breathlessly waiting for him to capture her lips, but instead he strung a sweet line of kisses along her throat. A shiver went through her as his clever lips found the most sensitive spots.

With a moan catching in her throat, Emma angled her head so their lips would meet. He kissed her teasingly, sliding his tongue along her lips before parting them and slipping inside. She quivered at the contact of his hot tongue thrusting fervently between her lips, excitedly exploring her mouth.

Jon drew back. He flung off the robe and lay beside her, propping his head up on his elbow. The mattress gave beneath his weight. Chest still heaving with excitement from his kisses, Emma spent a moment admiring his naked physique. Not dispassionately with her usual artist's eye, but as a woman.

She was fascinated by the strength and beauty of his body. He was firmly muscled with a narrow waist, slim hips, and long legs. Her glance started at his broad shoulders, drew across his chest, then followed the lean contours of his stomach to his waist. The candlelight glinted off the nest of hair covering his groin, his aroused penis standing tall.

A slow smile curved her mouth. He was magnificent. She liked what she saw. Liked too that he was so comfortable in his own nudity. Unable to resist, she ran her hand across his chest, along his ribs and down to the narrow trail of hair over his belly, marveling at the rigid muscles.

She looked up into his face and saw his eyes darken with passion. His chest rose and fell sharply, his flesh trembling beneath her touch.

"Don't stop now," he whispered throatily.

Emboldened, Emma went lower and closed her fingers around his stiff penis, feeling the weight of him in her palm. Beneath the rock hard length, his flesh was hot, the skin soft. It was a moment of raw, sensual discovery that gave her a heady sense of power and delight.

"Do you like it when I touch you?" she asked throatily.

Teasingly, she ran her fingertips along his length, rubbing the moisture that seeped from the head in a slow circle, coating it in sticky warmth. His hips arched and he grabbed her chin, lifting it.

His eyes were dark with passion. He groaned, low and deep, bucking against her hand, pulsing and growing larger. "Hold me tighter," he grimaced, his face contorting in both pleasure and pain.

She did as he asked, stroking and squeezing. He moaned and reached for her, his warm hands cupping her full and aching breasts. He thumbed the nipples and they stiffened, arching into his palm.

Heat swelled inside her. She pressed closer, nuzzling her face beneath the strong cords of his neck, burrowing deeper. Jon's hand glided downward, moving over her rib cage, brushing the tops of her thighs.

The fingers clutching his penis grew slack and he pulled himself away. Deprived of her sexy new toy, Emma cried out in protest.

"No! Come back," she exclaimed breathlessly.

"In a few minutes," he murmured, his voice low and husky. "When you are ready to take me inside you."

His warm, wet lips pressed against the curve of her breast. Emma twisted, allowing him greater access and he greedily accepted her invitation.

Pulling the nipple into his mouth, he sucked. Emma held back a moan of excitement. Her mind was spinning out of control and all she could do was bask in the arousal.

Jon's mouth left her breast and traveled lower. Down her side, across her stomach. He kissed her inner thigh, then spread her legs wider with his strong hands. She could feel the warmth of his breath on her damp curls as he bent his head closer. Though her body throbbed and ached, she tensed, unsure if she was ready for such intimacy.

"Jon, I . . ."

"Relax," he cooed.

Was he joking? Wantonly spread and exposed before him and he expected her to relax?

Emma's hands flailed at her sides as she concentrated on trying to conquer her embarrassment. His fingers joined his mouth and tongue, kneading and stroking and she cried out. She could feel her inner muscles tighten and she became lost in a web of passion.

The languid strokes of his tongue over her delicate flesh drove her wild. Restlessly, Emma spread her legs wider, her body straining toward him. The embers of desire caught inside her, spreading heat throughout her trembling body.

"Let it happen," Jon coaxed.

She groaned and felt her inhibitions slipping away at the excitement of his wicked caresses. His tongue darted out, licking and laving her sensitive core. Shivering, Emma buried her fingers in his hair, moving her legs and lower body urgently as the sensations built and climbed within her.

The rush of blood pounding in her ears reminded Emma of the sea. The world around her slipped away as she concentrated only on the wild pleasure that Jon was stirring within her. Biting her lips to keep her screams at bay, she struggled to reach fulfillment.

Then suddenly, unexpectedly, it broke over her. Brightness lit behind her eyes and Emma threw back her head and gasped as the heat spread from her core and crested through her entire body in a shower of hot ecstasy.

Emma shuddered, willing her heavy breathing to steady and fighting the urge to pull the sheet and cover her face. Abandon. Total and utter abandon. The feeling was indescribable—raw and exposed, yet amazingly joyful.

Her thoughts and body floated and drifted as she basked in the afterglow of pure pleasure. Gradually she became aware of a tender caress starting on her thighs and ending at her ankles. She looked down the length of her body.

Jon raised his head and gazed into her eyes. He was still positioned between her splayed legs. Emma blushed, hoping the candlelight hid her reaction, then laughed at herself for being so foolish.

Now I feel flustered and inhibited! After letting him . . .

Emma's thoughts scattered when Jon loomed suddenly above her, bracing himself on his forearms.

"You enjoyed it," he said, a note of smug pride in his voice.

"What gave me away?" she quipped, hiding her shyness with humor.

His mouth opened over hers and he kissed her deeply. She smoothed her hands down his broad back, down the valley of his spine then up to the ridge of his tight buttocks. He adjusted his position and laced his fingers with hers, raising her arms above her head.

Then he sank down, covering her body with his.

Heart to heart. Following her instincts, Emma lifted her hips and twined her legs around his, opening herself. He responded by pressing against her entrance, slowly, firmly, steadily.

She felt her body stretch to accommodate his length as he claimed her, going deeper and deeper and then a sudden, sharp, stinging pain made her catch her breath.

"You are a virgin no longer." He stilled. "Do you need more time to adjust?" he asked, his gaze wide and searching.

Emma wiggled her hips, trying to escape the burning fullness. Somehow, he remained still. She could feel the trembling in his shoulders, the rock-hard strength of his body.

"Could you wait?" she inquired, marveling at his control.

He let out a sharp, hollow bark that quickly turned into a groan. She felt his fingers sliding over her breasts, down her stomach and twisting between their bodies. He pressed firmly on her womanhood, sending a tingling, restless feeling racing through her.

"Better?" he whispered.

She licked her lips and felt the now familiar ache tugging low in her belly. "Yes. Oh, yes."

Jon growled and started rocking back and forth, slowly, gently, each thrust stretching her as he pushed deeper inside. Emma closed her eyes and arched her back, straining toward him. They moved together in a slow, sensual rhythm, her hips rising to meet his thrusts. There was a slight soreness, but the sensations were too wondrous for her to care.

His eyes fluttered closed and she noticed the rhythm become faster and deeper. Her excitement mounted along with his and she felt the beginnings of a second climax, the restless waves seeking completion. They gathered and pulled at her until they suddenly tore apart.

She cried out in fulfillment. Jon crushed her to his chest and thrust harder, his body jerking into hers. He, too, cried out and his seed flooded her womb, pulsing, warm and alive. She braced herself, expecting him to collapse on top of her when the shuddering ended.

But instead he bestowed a sweet, tender kiss on her lips, then rested his forehead against hers. His breathing was ragged, his body covered in a fine sheen of sweat. Staring into her eyes, he asked calmly, "Are you all right?"

Her throat closed with a sudden burst of emotion. Fearing her voice would crack, Emma nodded.

He shifted off her. She felt his flesh withdraw from her body and experienced a piercing sense of loss. He lay on his back beside her, his arm bent at the elbow covering his eyes.

Emma turned on her side, squirming closer to lie against him. She wrapped her hand around the thick muscle of his upper arm and pressed her face against his shoulder.

"That was—" She sighed, unable to express her emotions in words.

He pulled himself closer and kissed the tip of her nose. "Try to sleep, Emma. 'Tis late," he commanded.

Sleep? 'Twas impossible. Not after what she had just experienced, what they had just shared.

She opened her mouth to protest just as Jon turned onto his stomach. He curved his arm around the pillow beneath his head and Emma's lips fell silent as she admired the broad lines of his shoulders and back.

They were perfectly formed, as if carved from marble and polished to a shine. With his eyes closed and his features relaxed he looked young and carefree. There was a faint, self-satisfied smirk upon his face and she felt a stab of pride knowing that she had managed to put it there.

Her husband. The man she was bound to for the rest of her life. And possibly beyond, if scripture was to be taken literally.

Gracious!

Trying not to dwell on the thought that she was a married woman, Emma followed her husband's dictates and closed her eyes.

Within minutes she was asleep.

Chapter Eleven

When Emma woke the next morning, she was alone, the bed empty. She brushed her hand over the pillow that lay beside her and felt the slight indent where Jon's head had rested. His scent—so bold, masculine, and enticing—lingered faintly, but he was long gone.

Had he slipped from the chamber the moment she had succumbed to sleep? Or had he slept by her side?

Did he want to maintain their closeness or was he indifferent to it? Was it purely a physical act for him? For her? Her heart was not fully engaged, but she had certainly felt some very intense emotions that went beyond pure satisfaction last night.

The chamber door opened. Emma rolled over and raised her head.

"Good morning, my lady," Dory said as she drew back the curtains.

A dull light flooded the chamber. Sitting up, Emma ran her fingers through her tousled hair, telling herself she was not disappointed to see her maid, instead of her husband.

"What time is it?" Emma asked.

"Half past eight."

Emma smiled at the irony of waking up at her usual time, despite all that had happened in the last twenty-four hours. The body truly was most resilient, even as the mind and emotions were in turmoil. Accepting with thanks the robe Dory held out to her, Emma shrugged into it. She walked across her bedchamber and went behind the screen, relieved to find a pitcher of hot water waiting there, along with clean clothes and towels.

Grateful for the privacy, Emma washed away the soreness between her legs. She noticed streaks of blood on the cloth and was thankful that Dorothea had warned her of that possibility.

She heard the sheets being pulled from the bed and hoped her young maid would not be alarmed when she saw the bloodstains.

With Dory's help, she dressed, tactfully declining the maid's offer to arrange her hair. Pleased that she was able to find her way to the dining room without assistance, Emma hesitated before entering, bracing herself to see Jon.

She strolled through the doorway with her head held high, but her fluttering nerves were for naught—the room was empty. A single place was set on the polished wood table, the chair in front of it facing the window.

"Has Lord Kendall come down yet?" she asked the stoic footman who stood at the sideboard waiting to serve her.

"Yes, my lady," the servant replied as he pulled out a chair for her. "'Tis his lordship's usual custom to have his morning meal very early."

"Oh, I see." Emma sat in the offered chair, wishing she had stayed in her chambers. She rarely ate in the morning and had only come down with the expectation of seeing her husband.

"May I bring you some coffee? Tea? Chocolate?" The footman looked at her expectantly.

"Chocolate, please," Emma said, deciding she needed something hot and bitter this morning.

A second footman appeared. He was younger than the first, with an eager expression proclaiming his desire to please. Hastings, she thought. Or was his name Howard?

"Shall I prepare a plate for you, my lady?" he asked. "Or would you prefer that Cook make something else?"

Emma glanced at the sideboard that fairly groaned under the weight of so many silver covered chafing dishes. It seemed inconceivable that Cook had somehow left out any possible item one could consume in the morning.

"A small serving of eggs and a slice of bacon would be lovely, along with toast and jam," she replied, taking a sip of the hot chocolate.

"Coddled or scrambled?" the footman inquired.

Gracious, so many damn decisions! "Which do you recommend?" she asked.

"Everything Cook makes is delicious," the footman stammered, his cheeks reddening.

"Then I shall have a small portion of both," Emma declared.

She nodded her thanks when the footman placed a plate of hot food in front of her. Then he bowed and tactfully withdrew.

Thank goodness. It was going to be difficult enough choking down half the food on her plate without having an audience. Honestly, she really needed to see about getting a dog. A large one, with an even larger appetite.

Emma looked out the window as she buttered her toast, but saw little through the swirling mist. Her mind was occupied with her wayward husband. It had not occurred to her that Jon would desert her this morning.

After the night of passion they had shared it was going to be challenging enough facing her husband with calmness and serenity. The longer she waited, the more frayed her nerves would become.

Knowing there was little she could do about it, Emma turned her attention to her meal. After stuffing herself with as much of Cook's very tasty eggs as possible, Emma conceded defeat. Dismayed to see a quarter of the plate was still full, she piled the rest of the eggs and bits of bacon on a slice of toasted bread and topped it with a second slice. She then wrapped the food in her linen napkin, shoved it in her pocket and left the dining room.

A stroll was certainly in order—if she kept eating like this, the seams of her gowns would be strained to the point of bursting.

As Emma walked down to the terraced gardens, the breeze fluttered her skirts. It was turning into a fair day, as the morning sun was quickly burning off the fog and mist. Setting off at a brisk pace, she wandered down the sloping lawn, squinting against the sunshine.

There was no one about. She assumed the gardeners and groundskeeper were busy working on another part of the estate. Maintaining a property of this size surely took a large staff and endless hours of hard work.

A movement far in the distance caught her eye. She squinted. A horse and rider cantering across the open fields? Jon? Emma's heart skipped a beat. She raised her arm to block the sunlight and strained her eyes for a better look.

Nay, there was no one atop the beast.

And it wasn't a horse.

It was a dog. Black as midnight, with a sleek, muscular body, long legs, and a large head. It moved much like a horse, gaining ground swiftly as it raced across the field. For an instant she envied the freedom and delight it exuded.

Suddenly, three men appeared from a copse of trees and the animal quickly changed direction. Shouting and waving their arms, the trio chased the beast, who was now running directly toward Emma.

She felt a moment of sheer panic as it approached, having nowhere to take shelter. Hoping the large beast was friendly—or at least disinterested in her—Emma took a deep breath and stood her ground.

The dog sailed past her with barely a glance, keen on escaping the men who were chasing it. Emma turned to see where it would go, but it abruptly skidded to a halt, raising its massive head. She could see its black nose twitching.

Emma looked back down the hill. The three men were getting closer.

"Run!" she commanded to the animal. "Or they will catch you."

At the sound of her voice, the dog's ears lifted. Cocking its head, the animal trotted toward her, nostrils flaring. Emma stepped back in fear, but the beast's dark brown eyes moved upward to meet her own.

They were gentle and sweet and she soon realized that she had nothing to fear.

"Aren't you a handsome fellow," Emma exclaimed. "Whatever have you done to get those men so angry with you?"

Coming closer, the dog sniffed, nudging its head against Emma's side. Startled, she stepped back. The dog followed. Then he sat, looking up at her expectantly.

Clearly, he was begging. For what? She had nothing to give him. *Oh, gracious!* With a smile, Emma pulled the napkin from the pocket of her gown. The dog's tail began wagging so swiftly Emma swore she felt a breeze.

"Would you like some breakfast?" she asked, breaking off a piece of toast, bacon, and egg.

The dog's eyes grew wide with excitement at the sight of the food. He moved closer, yet remained politely sitting. Cautiously, Emma fed him, watching the large bite disappear in a single gulp.

"You really should chew your food," she admonished, giving him another piece.

"You've caught him, Lady Kendall! Well done!"

Gasping for breath, the three men finally reached her. She recognized them from the line of servants she had met yesterday. The man who had spoken was the head groundskeeper, the other two were his assistants. Unfortunately, she could not recall any of their names.

Emma stared at the trio. "Do you know this animal?"

"He's been pestering us for months, digging up all the new plantings," the groundskeeper explained.

"And that's not all he's been doing," another man grumbled.

The groundskeeper poked him in the side and the man lowered his gaze.

Emma was intrigued. "Oh? Please, tell me of his other crimes."

The groundskeeper, a short, stout fellow with graying hair at his temples, rubbed his red cheeks. "That mongrel has gotten himself into our kennels. One of his lordship's prized hunters whelped a litter of pups last week. Her coat is pure white, but her pups are all black, with paws as big as my fist. There's no doubt who sired that bunch."

They all gazed down at the dog. As if sensing he was the subject of their conversation, he began wagging his tail again.

"Well, aren't you the little Romeo," Emma said with a laugh.

She petted the dog's large, square head, stroking its long, silky ears. The animal's eyes closed in delighted bliss and the speed of his wagging tail increased so much that it now turned in a circle.

"Who is his master?" Emma asked.

"He has none, as far as we can tell," the grounds-keeper replied. "Cook's been feeding him scraps and if he's around, he gets a meal when we feed the other dogs."

"We know he wasn't likely to leave if he was being fed, but . . ." The groundskeeper shrugged.

Emma nodded approvingly. She was glad to hear that even though he had been a pest, the staff had shown the stray animal kindness.

"You did the right thing, Mr. . . ."

"Collins, my lady." The groundskeeper touched the brim of his cap respectfully.

"I should like to keep him, Mr. Collins," Emma decided. "Just this morning I was telling myself that I truly need a dog, a large dog in fact, and now he has appeared. I believe he will make a perfectly splen-did pet."

The groundskeeper scratched his head. "His lord-ship had a pup when he was a lad, but he wasn't nearly this large."

"I doubt there are many dogs that can compete in size with this noble beast," Emma concluded. "Fortunately, the manor house is vast in size. He shall fit in quite nicely."

As if knowing he had found a champion, the dog licked the top of Emma's hand. She scratched behind his ears and he nuzzled closer.

The groundskeeper hardly seemed convinced. "He's not a proper pet for a lady, if you don't mind me saying."

"But that's part of his charm," Emma said. "He's large and awkward and most loving, precisely the type of dog that I require." Seeing that the groundskeeper was hardly convinced, Emma added, "You will come to find, Mr. Collins, that I am unlike other ladies."

She thought of the fat, spoiled lapdogs that were the fashion among noblewomen. Pugs and toy poodles carried around on pillows, sporting jeweled collars. No, that was not the kind of canine companion that she desired.

"He'll need a bath if you intend to bring him inside the house," Mr. Collins observed.

"An excellent point. Do you have time to take care of that for me? Or would you prefer that I ask one of the footmen?"

One of the younger men snickered and Emma assumed he was imagining a neatly dressed footman containing and washing the dog in a tub of soapy water.

"We'll clean him up for you, my lady," Mr. Collins said. Then casting a stern eye at the dog, he added, "He won't give us any trouble."

"I'm sure you shall do an excellent job," Emma said. "Once he is presentable, please bring him to me."

Mr. Collins whistled for the dog to come. The beast

sat back on his haunches and leaned into Emma. "Go along now, like a good boy," she commanded.

The dog lay down by her feet, crossed his paws and rested his big head upon them.

"He must know we intend to wash him," one of the younger men whispered.

Emma stifled a smile at his earnest manner, doubting the dog had any idea they planned on giving him a thorough washing. Then again, who knew exactly what the animal understood.

"I agree that he certainly is a clever fellow," she said in an idle tone. "I shall call him Sir Galahad, as he was the noblest of King Arthur's knights. My sister Dorothea has a dog named Sir Lancelot, but Galahad was renowned for his gallantry and purity."

Sir Galahad opened his mouth wide and yawned, appearing unimpressed with his lofty name. All eyes turned to the massive beast, who looked even larger in repose. Mr. Collins frowned, while his two assistants looked perplexed. With a smile, Emma unwrapped the remainder of her breakfast scraps and handed them to one of the younger groundskeepers.

He nodded in understanding, extending his palm. Smelling the food, the dog bounded to his feet and approached.

"He'll follow me now," the young man said, slowly leading the dog away.

"He does seem especially fond of bacon," Emma agreed.

"I think that you are far more clever than your dog, my lady," Mr. Collins declared as he and the other assistant hurried away.

Emma smiled, then waited until they had faded from view before returning to the manor. Finding the dog—Sir Galahad—had proved to be an entertaining distraction and had succeeded, for a time, in taking her mind off the fact that Jon had disappeared without a word to her this morning.

Why had he not waited to have breakfast with her? Or left a note, explaining where he had gone?

The answer remained elusive and thinking upon it was giving her a headache. It was going to take time to establish a comfortable relationship with Jon—she needed to be patient and practical.

In the meantime, she would occupy herself by becoming acclimated to her new role as Lady Kendall and getting her new pet settled in the household. The dog's large size and exuberant manner were sure to cause some distractions among the staff.

With a slight smile, Emma wondered what her husband's reaction would be when he met Sir Galahad, and she freely admitted that a wicked part of her hoped he would be thoroughly annoyed.

Late morning dragged into early afternoon. Emma met with Cook to consult over the week's menus, received a tour of the manor house from attic to cellar from Mrs. Fields, and attended to her correspondence, which consisted of a single long letter to her sister Gwen.

She spent a pleasant hour wandering among the lush foliage in the solarium, remembering that her first conversation with Jon had taken place there—the afternoon of his aborted wedding. Disheartened by that memory and having no desire to return to her lonely bedchamber, Emma settled herself in the drawing room.

Though formally decorated, she liked the vast

openness of the chamber and the floor-to-ceiling windows that allowed the sunlight to stream into the room.

The furnishings were tasteful and expensive, yet still comfortable. The drapes were gold, as was the upholstery on the furniture, the rugs scattered on the polished wooden floors done in patterns of gold, green, and blue.

A flurry of noise outside the drawing room saved her from complete boredom. She rose from the writing desk and opened the door. Mr. Collins stood on the other side, his arms straining to hold the length of leather cord that was looped around Sir Galahad's neck.

"It took three of us to get it done, but the dog's had a proper bath. He likes to run, so I thought it best to keep him on a lead when I brought him into the house," Mr. Collins explained.

"A wise idea," Emma agreed, as the dog strained forward to reach her. "Though he doesn't appear to like it."

"He's got a strong will," Mr. Collins said with a grunt, digging in his heels as he struggled to hold the dog.

"I admire it," Emma replied. "However, I am confident Sir Galahad will soon be tamed."

Mr. Collins raised his brow skeptically. Ignoring it, Emma took the leather leash, expressed her thanks, and closed the door. Miraculously, Sir Galahad didn't pull her across the room. Instead, he sat on her foot and leaned into her body.

Emma rewarded him with a friendly pat on the head. She removed the lead from his neck and the dog immediately began exploring the room, sniffing the floor and furniture, even going behind the long silk drapes. Enjoying his antics, Emma sat on the silk brocade settee and watched.

After taking in every inch of the chamber, the dog approached her. He scrambled onto the settee beside her, sat upright and rested his back against the arm of the sofa, his head higher than her own.

Gracious, you are a large beast.

Emma scratched his snoot and rubbed his long, silky ears. Sir Galahad inched closer, then stood, turning several times in a circle before plopping down and settling himself. With a contented sigh, the dog closed his eyes and laid his head in Emma's lap.

Absently, she stroked his head, finding an odd sense of comfort and serenity. She was relaxing, book in hand, when the door opened and Jon entered.

He was dressed casually in tan breeches that hugged his muscular thighs, knee-high black boots, a navy-blue jacket that accented the width of his broad shoulders, and a silver waistcoat. Emma felt her breath hitch.

Damn, he is handsome.

Seeing him evoked the memories of being in his arms last night, how the feel of his kisses and caresses had so completely stoked the fires of desire deep inside her. With great determination, Emma somehow managed to quash the blush that threatened to redden her cheeks.

Though she didn't want to admit it, Emma knew she was changed by the physical bond that had been forged between them. She was not so naïve as to think Jon had experienced the same, but she hoped he might feel some kind of connection to her, beyond what duty dictated.

She caught the hint of a frown on his face when he spied her. *Good heavens. I guess he intended to avoid me as much as possible.* Miffed at the notion, Emma lifted her chin.

"Good afternoon, Jon."

"Emma."

He approached, and the room was filled with the sound of a deep, low-throated growl. Jon and Sir Galahad stared warily at each other.

"Oh, by the way, I've gotten a dog," she said, pulling her chin a bit higher.

Jon's gaze shifted to her. "So I see. Where did you find him?"

"He found me."

Jon's brow lifted in curiosity. "Are you certain that's a canine? He looks more like a small pony."

"His name is Sir Galahad," she replied, ignoring the jibe, refusing to admit that she had thought the very same thing when she had observed the animal from a great distance. "He's smart and loyal and friendly. Well, mostly friendly. 'Twould probably be wise to approach him cautiously, just to be sure he likes you."

Jon halted. "Why do you sound mildly pleased at the idea of him taking a bite out of my hide?"

"Do I? How ridiculous." Emma felt her cheeks color as a symphony of emotions rioted through her. It would serve him right to get a nip from the dog for neglecting her so thoroughly this morning.

"Our dogs are kept in the kennels," Jon mentioned casually. "'Tis a far more preferable arrangement than having them lounging on the antique furniture."

"Is it?" Emma reached over and petted Sir Galahad's chest. "I find this far more appealing. He is my companion and therefore needs to be near me."

"He'll terrify the servants," Jon observed as he inched closer.

"They'll get used to him," Emma countered.

"He'll require as much food as three dogs," Jon grumbled.

"We can afford it." Emma twirled her fingers through the animal's soft fur. "I concede that you have some plausible objections, but I have my heart set on keeping him. He can be my bridal gift from you."

A look of doubt crossed Jon's face. "Most husbands gift their brides with jewelry."

"Goodness, Jon, I should think that by this time you would agree that I am not a usual bride and ours is far from a usual marriage."

Ah, well, that shut him up. She glanced at her husband beneath her lowered brows, wondering if her bluntness had offended him. And then became annoyed with herself for caring.

"Perhaps we are an untraditional couple on occasion. But hopefully not a cynical one." Jon reached into his coat pocket. "I had business in the village early this morning and then I needed to consult with Norris at the workshop. You were sleeping so soundly, I didn't have the heart to wake you. I was going to leave this on the pillow for you, but decided I'd rather present it to you myself. Your *second* bridal gift, madam."

Emma put down her book and accepted the long velvet box he handed her. Sir Galahad lifted his head, sniffing hopefully, quickly losing interest when he deduced the mysterious box contained no food.

"Thank you, Jon," she said.

His lips twisted upward in an ironic smile. "You haven't opened it."

Emma lifted the box lid, gasping when she beheld the stunning diamond necklace inside. There were seven large diamonds, joined together by a slender diamond-lined chain. They glistened and sparkled, looking luminous in the afternoon light.

"I . . . uhm . . ." Emma stammered.

"Do you like it?" he asked softly.

"It quite takes my breath away," she answered truthfully.

"Yes, but do you like it?"

Emma felt a rush of heat climb up from her chest. She rarely wore jewelry and never anything this magnificent. "Has it been in your family for many generations?"

"No. It was purchased especially for you."

Emma pressed her hand against the churning sensation in her stomach, not wanting to admit how much the gesture stirred her. Not the exorbitant cost of the gift—though it was magnificent. She would have been equally content with a simple string of pearls.

Or eating breakfast this morning with her husband. 'Twas yet another example of how little Jon really knew her. Still, he was, in his own way, trying.

"Thank you," she said again.

His expression turned serious and she knew this was not the reaction he was expecting. Jon gestured to the dog, snapping his fingers, and Sir Galahad jumped off the settee.

Jon immediately took the animal's place. His pleasant, masculine scent filled her nostrils. "If you wish, you can exchange the necklace."

Emma blinked, but then pulled herself together. She was being ungracious. And rude.

"Honestly, I'm uncertain where—or when—I would wear such an extraordinary piece of jewelry," she admitted, expelling a long breath. "But it will always hold a special meaning for me because you chose it."

He stared at her for a moment, the intensity of his gaze spreading through her like a warm breeze, making her squirm. Hoping for a distraction, Emma glanced over at Sir Galahad, but the dog had settled himself comfortably in the corner and was snoring contentedly.

Drat! Where was a piece of crisp bacon when one needed it?

Emma knew this was Jon's way of apologizing for his neglect this morning. She was, of course, willing to accept the apology. The necklace, however, was completely unnecessary; indeed, in a small way she almost felt insulted that he thought it was necessary to bribe her.

She would far prefer that they were simply honest with each other and spoke their mind. Hurt and anger left unspoken over time could easily turn into animosity.

And no amount of diamonds could overcome those feelings.

Chapter Twelve

Emma leaned closer, her face within a hairsbreadth of his own. Her expression hinted at her inner turmoil and Jon surmised his neglect of her today was the cause.

The necklace had distracted her—momentarily—but the darkness in her eyes told Jon that she was not appeased. No, Emma had not reacted how he had anticipated, with excitement and delight. Dianna would have been positively giddy with such a gift, trying it on immediately, preening before a mirror to see how it looked.

He needed to remember that Emma was nothing like Dianna. Hell, she was nothing like any woman he had ever known. And therein lay much of her charm.

He shouldn't have left her bed while she slept and then abandoned her for the better part of today. Guilt crept upon him. By rights she should be angry and upset with him. He had been inconsiderate.

He hadn't meant to be. Their night together had been an unexpected joy, wholly satisfying on a physical level, and unexpectedly deep on an emotional level.

Most surprising. He had believed such feelings were lost to him after Dianna's betrayal.

It had jarred Jon learning that they were not, putting him off-balance. To combat the feeling, he had left her bed as dawn was breaking, dressed and gone to his workshop. By burying himself in his work and putting a physical distance between them, Jon had hoped the time apart would help clarify his feelings.

It hadn't.

Transfixed now by the glittering eyes that held his with such intensity, Jon did the one thing that seemed right and natural. He dipped his head lower until his lips brushed Emma's.

She gasped, but did not deny him. Slowly, her eyes fluttered closed and she leaned closer, responding to his overture, returning his kiss. Her mouth was tender and sweet, and he took great pleasure in the taste of her lips and tongue.

He raised his hand, his fingertips tracing the smooth line of her brow. She swayed slightly and he could feel her hands curling tightly into the fabric of his jacket. He fought to control the urge to haul her fully against his body, as he deepened the kiss. Sensual pleasure ran through him, sending the blood pounding through his veins.

Behind her, Jon heard a low, distinct, canine growl. Emma broke away and turned her head to look over her shoulder. The large dog had awakened and abandoned his position in the corner. He stood beside his mistress, hackles raised. His mouth was closed—at least he hadn't bared his teeth—but the warning growl emanating from deep in his throat was quite menacing.

"Sir Galahad is most protective," Emma said with

a hitch in her breath. "He does not approve of you kissing me."

"Well, he damn well better get used to it," Jon replied gruffly. "As I intend for it to occur quite often."

That brought a hint of a crooked smile to her ripe lips and Jon found himself smiling back.

"I must assure him that he remains firmly in my affections," Emma declared.

She pulled out of Jon's embrace, turned and approached the dog. Scratching his head, she spoke to the animal in a sweet, praising tone. His tail began wagging with enthusiastic happiness and Jon felt a sudden burst of kinship with the beast—it was indeed joyful to be acknowledged and fussed over by Emma.

A commotion at the door drew Jon's attention away from his charming wife and her massive dog. His normally stoic and stuffy butler, Hopson, barged into the room, his usual mask of composure noticeably missing.

"Pray, forgive the interruption, my lord, but you have callers."

"No need to stand on ceremony and announce me, Hopson." A woman dressed in black swept dramatically into the room, her skirts billowing behind her.

"Dianna?"

"Oh, Jon. Lord Kendall. Jon." She pressed her gloved hands to her temples and shook her head. "Forgive my intrusion, but I simply had to come. I've heard the most horrid rumors and I had to assure myself that all is well with you."

He blinked. Dressed in her widow's weeds she looked especially fresh, young, and innocent. Her brow was furrowed with worry and her concern appeared genuine. For a split second Jon almost found himself lost in her deep, sorrowful eyes.

"Lady Brayer." He bowed, breaking the connection, drawing his eyes away. "My deepest condolences at the death of your husband."

"A shocking tragedy," she muttered.

"I was given to understand the incident took place in your home. You are unharmed?" Despite her treatment of him and past hurt, he never wished Dianna ill.

"I'm fine." She inhaled deeply. "I was upstairs in my bed, asleep when it happened. I have little memory of what occurred once Gerald's body was discovered and the household roused. 'Twas pandemonium."

Jon strained forward to hear her, as her voice came out in a nervous whisper.

"I'm glad that you are safe," he replied. "Though I am surprised to see you out so soon after the funeral."

"I told her this visit was scandalous and inappropriate for more reasons than I could name," a disapproving male voice intoned. "But as usual my sister refused to listen, paying no heed to logic or decorum."

Jon looked up and watched Hector Winthrope enter the room. He was short of breath, his full jowls jiggling, suggesting that he might have been running to catch his sister. Yet somehow she had escaped him.

A tide of pink flushed Dianna's pale cheeks and she looked down at the carpet. "Forgive me for being so bold, Jon."

Hector's glower darkened. Jon fully expected him to begin berating and scolding her, since Hector seemed to always relish the opportunity to act pompous and superior.

Emma stepped forward into view, adding yet another layer of awkwardness. Both Dianna's and Hector's faces flashed with surprise. Jon waited to hear the growling warning from Sir Galahad, but the dog remained silent.

Damn the beast. He was exactly the sort of distraction they needed at the moment.

"Miss Ellingham!" Hector gushed. "Please forgive my rudeness for not noticing you sooner."

Spots of bright color appeared on Hector's cheeks. His delight at seeing Emma was so obvious Jon wondered if the man would start drooling with excitement. For her part, Emma seemed oblivious to Hector's adoration.

"See there, Hector. We are not Lord Kendall's only visitors this afternoon," Dianna said triumphantly.

"I'm not exactly a visitor," Emma replied. She glanced pointedly at Jon. Apparently she was waiting for him to explain her cryptic response.

"'Tis true. She is no longer Miss Ellingham, but rather Lady Kendall." Jon inhaled a deep breath. "Emma did me the great honor of becoming my wife yesterday."

Mouths agape, Dianna and Hector stared at Emma.

Honestly, it wasn't all that shocking—was it? Emma was a respectable gentlewoman, sister-in-law to a marquess. Why shouldn't he have taken her as his wife?

The small bit of color that had remained on Dianna's face drained away. "Married?"

"I'll own I don't always pay the closest attention in church, but I most certainly would have taken note of the banns being read these past three weeks," Winthrope sputtered, a look of disbelief on his face. He pulled a fluffy white handkerchief from his breast pocket and dabbed at his damp brow.

"There were no banns," Emma said bluntly.

Hector tilted his head in puzzlement. Well, Atwood had claimed he would do all within his power to minimize the scandal—and reason—for their hasty marriage. Jon was impressed that Emma's brother-in-law had somehow managed to accomplish that feat.

At least for now. The truth would soon be learned and the scandalous whispers ensue.

"No banns? So this was a hasty, impulsive decision?" Hector questioned, his voice rising. "Why?"

"We had our reasons," Emma replied calmly.

Winthrope peered at Emma sharply, his eyes lowering to her midsection. "I see. Pray, allow me to offer you my felicitations."

The sour look of utter disappointment and censure he cast at Emma belied any sincerity in those words. He took a step forward, but Jon stopped him with a hand on his chest.

"You are gravely mistaken, Winthrope, if you believe we are expecting a child. I suggest that you think very carefully before repeating such an insulting untruth about my wife and impugning her character and reputation."

Hector's eyes narrowed nastily.

Dianna sucked in a sharp breath, her face screwed up in horror. "Goodness, Hector! And you accuse me of lacking tact. The circumstances of their marriage are none of our business."

Yet despite her words, Dianna's eyes were darting from him to Emma in an apparent attempt to comprehend the situation.

"Well, no matter the details for the hasty union, none will deny this is a most advantageous match for you, Miss Ellingham," Winthrope said, his eyebrow arching snidely. "You must be delighted."

"Lady Kendall," Jon corrected tersely, a flush of anger running through him.

There was a time when Jon had pitied Hector and his almost pathetic need to feel important and exhibit a moral superiority in all things. The man had neither great wealth nor social standing and he desperately craved both. But any lingering empathetic feelings Jon had were quickly disappearing every time Winthrope insulted Emma.

"We heard a ghastly rumor that you had been questioned and then arrested for Gerald's murder," Hector prodded. "'Tis the reason my sister insisted upon coming to see you today, Kendall, even though I strongly advised against it."

"As you are standing here right now instead of rotting in the gaol, 'tis clear the rumor was false," Dianna declared, yet her voice sounded unsteady and bewildered, as though she didn't quite believe what she was saying.

"I was falsely arrested, but it was a mistake, a misunderstanding that Emma quickly clarified," Jon said smoothly.

"And you rewarded her for her help by marrying her," Hector concluded, his eyes squinting as though he was trying to decide if he had hit upon the truth. "How interesting."

A sharp denial sprang to Jon's lips, but he held back the remarks. He owed no one an explanation. 'Twas annoying in the extreme that Winthrope's conclusions were partially accurate, yet confirming or denying the particulars of their marriage could prove embarrassing for Emma.

"If you must do so, Mr. Winthrope, I believe the

better way of interpreting our marital situation is to say that Jon rescued me," Emma said in a dignified voice.

Dianna's eyes strayed to his. "You always were so noble," she said quietly.

"Isn't he," Emma responded, moving forward and slipping her arm through his. "'Tis most infuriating."

There was no mistaking Emma's possessive gesture. It surprised Jon, even more so when he realized he was rather flattered by it.

Dianna's hand fluttered to her chest. "We must intrude upon you no longer and take our leave at once."

Hector sniffed loudly. "We should never have come in the first place, however I'm sure the viscount and his *new bride* will forgive us."

After presenting them with an exaggerated bow, Winthrope grasped his sister's hand and tugged her out the door. Dianna glanced back over her shoulder at him, her expression filled with apology, but she said nothing.

There were several moments of painful silence once the pair had left.

"Well, that was most uncomfortable," Emma declared with a long sigh. "I suppose I must take a small comfort in knowing they departed before I said something utterly rude and unforgiveable."

"I, too, bit my tongue more than once. Though Winthrope had little difficulty slinging smug remarks in our direction." Jon kept his eyes on the door, just in case their unexpected guests reappeared. "We knew that our sudden, unexpected wedding would cause curiosity and result in some gossip and speculation."

"But they had no idea we had married," Emma countered, untangling her arm from his. "Dianna came because she was concerned about you."

Jon resisted the urge to tug at his cravat, which suddenly felt too tight around his neck. Though Emma's tone had been even and steady, it felt like an accusation.

She retreated to the other side of the room, and sat again on the silk brocade settee. The dog instantly jumped up beside her. Hoping to ease some of the odd tension between them, Jon moved to join her. When he came within a few feet of his wife, Sir Galahad started barking.

"Oh, now you've decided to make your presence known," Jon said in mock disgust as he dropped into the chair across from them. "A few of those deep barks and low growls would have sent Hector Winthrope running for the door."

"And what of his sister?" Emma asked softly. "Would she have been so easily frightened away?"

"Dianna has far more courage than her brother."

Emma clenched her hands together. "Despite her defection, you still care for her."

Jon's heart squeezed a bit at the faint hurt in Emma's tone. "Caring and loving are far different. I can assure you that I would never allow myself to mourn losing Dianna for the rest of my days."

"Some things are beyond our control."

"Not this," he insisted.

Her eyes glittered, yet Emma remained silent and composed. Too composed.

"'Tis moments such as these that I seriously question my sanity in agreeing to our marriage," Emma finally said.

That stung. How exactly was he supposed to reply? Verbal assurances seemed pointless and weak.

True, their marriage had an unconventional start

and was burdened with more obstacles than most. But that hardly meant that it was doomed.

Did it?

Emma pressed her fingertips to her temples, trying to stave off the headache that was forming behind her eyes, no doubt caused by all her conflicted emotions. When Hopson had announced they had visitors, Emma fully expected to see her sister Dorothea waltz into the room, a contrite smile on her face.

The shock of seeing Dianna enter had momentarily rendered Emma speechless. She had wanted to maintain an air of nonchalance, to demonstrate that she was unaffected by the appearance of her husband's former fiancée. Former love.

It hadn't worked out precisely as Emma had hoped.

Drat! Why could she not have smiled vapidly and made inane conversation about the weather with their unexpected visitors? Why instead had she allowed the pang of resentment that settled in her stomach as she watched Jon greet Dianna affect her so strongly?

Emma hadn't understood where it had sprung from and she certainly didn't want it to linger. Yet it did.

Though it had flashed for a mere instant, Emma had clearly seen the look of betrayal cross Dianna's face when she heard of their marriage. Obviously, the other woman still carried some kind of feelings for Jon—the nature of which Emma couldn't begin to speculate about.

And though he denied it, she was certain Jon had feelings for Dianna. Were they merely the kind, considerate emotions that a well-bred gentleman had for a female who had experienced a brutal tragedy and shocking loss? Or something more?

The uncertainty did nothing to bolster Emma's confidence in her relationship with her husband, especially when he had chosen to ignore her this morning. She had entered into this marriage determined to enact no emotional scenes between herself and Jon and to avoid conflict. She was quickly learning that was going to be nearly impossible.

What a conundrum! Emma folded her arms across her chest to comfort herself. Jealousy had no place in a marriage that she was struggling to come to terms with. She wanted nothing more than to simply dismiss these unsettling feelings—but the problem remained that she had not expected to feel such strong emotions toward Jon.

They could be temporary, she told herself. A result of the physical closeness and sexual fulfillment they had shared last night. It could fade; most likely once the novelty of intimate relations wore off.

Or it could burn brighter.

With determination, Emma turned her mind away from those thoughts and bit the inside of her cheek to prevent any idiotic statement from escaping her lips. Having had years of practice, she was good at hiding what she truly felt.

"Has there been any news about Gerald's killer?" Emma asked, desperate to shift the conversation.

Coward! Not ten minutes ago she had been lamenting the need for open, honest conversation between herself and Jon and now she was running from it like a scared rabbit.

"Not that I have heard," he replied.

"I would have asked Hector if he were here on his

own, but I thought it vulgar to broach the subject directly with Dianna in the room," Emma said.

"I'm surprised Winthrope didn't mention it," Jon replied. "He relishes drama of any kind and is hardly known for his tactful or his considerate nature."

"The siblings appear to have a somewhat strained relationship," Emma observed. "Though perhaps that is normal between brothers and sisters?"

"One would hope not."

Jon offered her a gentle smile, which had an unsettling effect on her insides. A small charge of tension floated in the air between them and she wondered if he would kiss her again.

She rather liked those kisses.

After a polite knock, Hopson again entered the drawing room. Emma expected him to ask what time they wanted tea served, but once again she was wrong.

Instead, he held open the door and Dorothea sailed in, clutching her infant son tightly in her arms.

"Do forgive the intrusion, but Harold was being fussy and you know how a ride in the carriage instantly soothes him. And since we were driving so close, on an impulse I thought I'd pop in and say hello," Dorothea said with an overly bright smile.

Her face wore an innocent expression, but Emma was hardly fooled. In truth, it was miraculous it had taken her sister so long to find an excuse to check on her.

"We are delighted to see you, Lady Atwood," Jon said graciously. "And young Harold as well."

"How kind. But as I told you yesterday after the wedding, since we are now related, you must call me Dorothea," she gently reminded him.

He nodded. "As you wish, Dorothea."

Harold gurgled and cooed in his sleep. At the sound, Sir Galahad lifted his head in interest, drawing Dorothea's attention.

"My goodness, that is a very large dog," Dorothea exclaimed.

"My wife's latest addition to our family," Jon replied dryly. "Have a care for your son. This beast might decide he'd make a tasty snack."

Dorothea's eyes widened in alarm and she clutched the sleeping infant protectively. "Why ever is he allowed in the house if he is so ferocious?" she whispered.

"Lord Kendall is merely being dramatic," Emma said with a frown. "Sir Galahad is perfectly harmless. In truth, he reminds me of your dog, Lancelot."

Belying Emma's sterling defense of his character, the dog approached Dorothea and began nudging her side. She yelped, lifting Harold higher in her arms.

"You said he was harmless," Dorothea gasped.

"He is," Emma insisted, taking wicked delight in her sister's discomfort. She was confident that the dog meant no harm, though 'twas true the animal was finding her sister particularly interesting. "What's in your pocket?"

"My pocket?" Dorothea stepped away from the dog and he immediately followed. "I don't know. My handkerchief?"

"There must be something else," Emma determined. She walked around Sir Galahad and thrust her hand into the pocket of Dorothea's cloak. "Aha! A teething biscuit."

Triumphantly, Emma held the treat aloft. The dog barked in delight, then immediately sat and pressed himself against Dorothea's side.

"Oh, for heaven's sake, give the beast the biscuit before he knocks me over," Dorothea exclaimed.

Emma extended the treat, which disappeared in an instant. Then he stood, his tail wagging, his entire back end wiggling in anticipation of another treat.

"Heavens, don't you feed this poor animal?" Dorothea asked, apparently overcoming her fear of the beast.

"Numerous times a day," Emma revealed as the dog lay down at her feet.

"If you ladies will excuse me, I have urgent business that cannot wait," Jon said. "I shall have tea sent up."

He bowed formally, then turned. Once he reached the door, Jon whistled. Sir Galahad sprang up on all fours and eagerly followed the viscount out the door.

"Traitorous beast," Emma muttered beneath her breath.

"The dog or your husband?" Dorothea asked.

"Both," Emma answered.

They shared a quiet laugh. Emma motioned with her arms and Dorothea handed over the babe. Emma cuddled the warm body close, feeling an instant sense of peace. Harold was the essence of innocence and goodness; 'twas impossible to feel anything other than contentment when he was nestled so close to her heart.

Tea arrived. Dorothea poured, then persuaded Emma to relinquish the baby. They settled the dozing infant in the middle of one of the settees, pushing pillows all around to hold him in place.

Then Dorothea filled a plate with sandwiches and cakes for each of them. Emma nibbled on hers while Dorothea ate heartily.

Dorothea finished the last bite of cake and patted her lips with her napkin. "The food is lovely. Please extend my compliments to your cook. Why aren't you eating?"

"I'm not hungry. I had an enormous breakfast."

Her sister gave her a probing look. Emma did her best to cast a pleasant, contented smile back, but it was hard to pretend that all was well. And her sharp-eyed sister was not easily fooled.

She took Emma's hand, her expression gentle and filled with concern. "My God, Emma, please tell me what's wrong."

Emma gave a soft, ironic laugh. "Everything."

Chapter Thirteen

The next few days followed a familiar routine. Jon made himself scarce. Emma knew that he spent his time at his workshop, from early morning until late evening. She understood how important his work was to him and certainly didn't expect him to neglect his project and dance attendance upon her. Neither of them had the personality to live in each other's pockets, as the saying went.

Speaking to her sister a few days earlier had greatly helped Emma. Knowing that Dorothea would never judge her, Emma had unburdened herself, telling her sister all. It had been cathartic to express her doubts and confusion, and that simple act had strengthened Emma's resolve not to be defeated by them.

Dorothea had restrained from questioning her, and most thankfully of all, had not given Emma any advice. Instead, she had sat with her, offering silent comfort and support.

In the end, Emma realized all the uncertainty about her future was not going to be miraculously settled in one afternoon. It was going to take time and patience to forge a relationship with Jon.

Her mornings were spent walking the grounds with

Sir Galahad by her side. Or rather, watching the animal racing twenty feet ahead of her. The dog bounded with energy and sheer delight at every turn, and Emma decided she would try to emulate her dog's attitude and take joy in the simple blessings of her life.

She spent the first part of her afternoons attending to household matters, which occupied a surprising amount of her time. She had not ventured out except for one brief visit to see Dorothea, Carter, and the children, needing a bit more time to bolster her courage before taking a trip to the village.

Thankfully, there were no additional surprise visits from anyone.

She had commandeered an unused upstairs chamber for an art studio, since it boasted an excellent source of natural light. She spent the second part of her afternoons there, oftentimes simply waiting for inspiration to strike. Yet even though her art supplies might sit unused for hours, it had felt good to bring a part of herself to her new home and set up her studio.

She went to bed alone, slept undisturbed, and awoke each morning alone. Jon never said why he refrained from coming to her bed and she never asked. She knew he would return, as he had promised her children, and she believed him to be a man of his word.

Yet invariably memories of their wedding night would swirl through her mind at unguarded moments, never more so than when her husband joined her for dinner each evening.

At those meals, she refused to make polite conversation about the weather, the neighbors, or household improvements she might want to make. It was just too depressing to be *that* couple. The one that led lives so separate they had nothing of interest to discuss when they happened to be together.

No, Emma was determined that she and Jon achieve some form of intimacy between them that went beyond the physical. They might not be in love, but they were capable of showing tenderness and regard for each other.

"I'm sorry I'm so late. I sent word that you should start without me," Jon muttered as he took his seat at the dining table.

His expression was guarded, as though he wondered what type of reception he would receive. Well, she intended to surprise him.

"'Twas no great sacrifice to wait," she answered lightly. She signaled to the footman standing by the door. "Please inform Cook that we are ready for the soup course. And let her know that we shall eat slowly, so the beef can be served pink in the center, as his lordship prefers."

The footman bowed and hurried away. Jon took a sip of his wine and leaned close. "Shouldn't we eat quickly so the beef isn't overcooked?"

Emma smiled. "Cook has yet to put the roast in the oven. That is the only way to ensure it will not be gray, tough, and dry."

"The three attributes my mother prefers when eating beef." Jon finished his wine and a footman poured him a second glass. "'Tis no wonder I disliked it so much as a child."

The soup arrived and they began eating.

"Did you make much progress today?" Emma asked.

"We did. Until the steam engine failed. We know that our calculations must be accurate or else the damn thing might explode. But if we can't consistently get enough power, the reaper thresher won't move and no wheat will be harvested or threshed."

"Tell me about it." He lifted a brow and Emma added, "I'm truly interested."

Jon starting speaking slowly, picking up speed and animation as the tale unfolded. His face brightened with excitement, his eyes darkened with intensity as he relayed the problems and successes that he and Mr. Norris had recently achieved.

Emma was able to follow the conversation—mostly. But she didn't mind when he lost her with some of the complicated details. She enjoyed watching his handsome face in the candlelight, his expressions thoughtful and lively.

"The machine looks very different from our original design." Jon placed his soup spoon on the rim of the bowl and cleared his throat. "I was wondering if you'd like to come to the workshop tomorrow and view our progress."

The silence between them lengthened as she absorbed his words. "I would like that very much."

"Good. Good." He smiled. "Don't forget to bring your sketchbook."

"You'll allow me to draw your machine?" Emma asked, trying to rein in her rioting emotions.

"Well, you might not be as inspired by this design as you were with its predecessor. It's very different from our first attempt."

"I'm certain I shall be transfixed by it," Emma replied.

"One can only hope."

Emma was truly surprised. She had assumed it would take a good deal of persuasion to gain permission to sketch Jon's work, as he had made his feelings on the subject crystal clear.

Delighted at the turn of events, Emma returned her

attention to her meal. A feeling coursed through her body—one she hadn't felt this strongly in days.

Hope.

Emma felt a jolt of excitement as she approached the workshop the next morning. Jon had left at his usual very early hour, but he had penned a note for her, inviting her to join him at whatever time was convenient.

Emma departed the moment she finished her breakfast. It felt strange to walk the trails of the estate without Sir Galahad by her side, but the dog had far too much energy and curiosity to bring into the workshop.

This invitation was unexpected and precious and Emma would not risk any disruptions that might jeopardize the chance to be asked back. There was no telling what sort of destruction her oversized pet could innocently cause.

She knocked briefly on the workshop door, then let herself inside. Mr. Norris was filing a section of a metal cog on a bench. He looked up when she entered, nodded in greeting and returned to his task.

Emma's pulse quickened when Jon appeared. He was casually attired in a white linen shirt, plain waistcoat, and an old pair of black breeches. His boots were dusty, lacking their usual shine, and there were dark shadows of whiskers along his jawline, indicating that he hadn't taken the time to shave this morning.

Some might label him scruffy, but Emma liked his rough persona and thought he looked especially appealing.

"Welcome, Emma." Jon smiled and swept his hand

toward the machine. "Please, come closer and take a good, long look."

Emma swallowed several times, trying to calm the sudden rush of exhilaration. As Jon had told her, this machine was indeed different from the other. It was larger in scale, boasting bigger gears, longer belts, more intricate workings.

She stepped forward, craning her neck to see all the way to the top. She fiddled anxiously with her drawing pencil as her eyes drank in every glorious detail, finding it difficult to decide where to start drawing.

"Oh, my goodness," she whispered.

"What do you think?" he asked.

"Pardon?"

"I asked your opinion of the machine."

"Sorry." Emma dipped her chin as a blush appeared on her cheeks. "I confess to being captivated by it."

She stepped forward and tentatively placed her hand on the edge of the largest wheel. The metal was cold, yet smooth to the touch. Stunning.

Decision made, Emma began sketching. She stepped back, then moved to the side for a different view. Jon watched her silently for a few moments before resuming what he was doing.

Emma was vaguely aware of his movements, but she was too consumed by her sketching to pay much attention. Her mind was blank of all other thoughts but the desire—nay, the need—to capture the essence of this glorious machine on paper.

Time passed. Eventually, her fingers began to cramp. Coming up for air, Emma scrubbed a hand over her tired eyes. Flipping through the sketch pad, she made a few notations in the margins of several of the pages.

"You'd best step back, Emma," Jon warned. "We are going to power up the steam engine."

Eyes wide, Emma did as she was bid. Mr. Norris pulled a lever and a hiss of steam escaped from a large cylinder. There was a groan from the cogs, then slowly the gears began to move. The clatter was loud, almost deafening, yet to Emma's ears it sounded almost musical.

She glanced at Jon. His face was alive, his eyes no longer weary.

Feeling the rising excitement, she yelled, "Success!"

Jon laughed. "There is quite a bit more work to be done before that can be claimed." He spoke over his shoulder, without taking his eyes from her.

A loud ping sounded as a wheel suddenly came loose and shot across the room. Cursing, Jon jumped to the side and ducked, narrowly avoiding a direct hit. Yet the object grazed him.

Mr. Norris immediately shut down the machine. Clutching his head with a groan, Jon straightened. She studied him critically, growing concerned when she saw the sizable lump forming over his left eyebrow.

"'Tis my fault for distracting you. I am sorry, Jon."

He gingerly drew his brows together. "I'm fine and darn lucky the wheel didn't roll over my foot. It would have broken it."

"Your foot or the wheel?" she teased, relieved to see he was all right.

"It will take much more than a wheel to do me in, Emma," he replied stoically.

"There's no blood, but I fear it will become a sizable bruise," she said, gently probing the area on his head with her fingertips.

Jon winced and drew back. "If anyone inquires as

to how I received it, I shall let them know you were the cause."

"I can kiss it to make it better," she offered.

"Do you think me a child, madam?"

She shrugged, taking no offense, realizing his gruffness was a reaction to his embarrassment over the injury. Men could be so foolishly prideful at times.

"'Twas merely a suggestion," she said lightly.

He leaned forward, taking her hand. "I can assure you, dear Emma, that when I crave a kiss from my wife, it's not on the top of my head."

"Do you really?" Emma asked hesitantly. "Crave my kisses?"

He licked his lips with the tip of his tongue. "More than I should."

Emma touched the front of his shirt lightly, holding a section between her fingers. His expression became distracted and she thought he might indeed take one of those kisses. But he turned away from her and went back to his work.

Tension pulsed through her. Disappointed to be denied a kiss, Emma gathered her things. She said goodbye to Mr. Norris before turning to her husband.

"I enjoyed myself today. Thank you for the invitation and for allowing me to sketch your machine." Emma tugged on her gloves. "I'll see you later this evening."

That night Emma wore her wedding gift to dinner. The diamonds felt cool against her flesh and heavy around her neck. The low-cut gown Dory had selected for Emma to wear showcased the jewels to perfection, though in truth they would have looked stunning against any backdrop.

Emma gazed at her reflection in the mirror, seeing someone new and different staring back at her. Gracious, she was *sparkling*. The high-waist gown with a low neckline revealed her bosom to advantage, the upswept hairdo with artfully arranged wisps of curls was sophisticated and stylish.

She wondered what her husband would think.

For a change, Jon was waiting upon her when she entered the dining room.

"Emma! You look beautiful."

"Thank you. Though the compliment holds greater meaning if you don't sound so shocked, Jon."

He smiled, as she had hoped, and ran a hand over his clean-shaven jaw. Emma was pleased to note that he too had made an effort with his appearance tonight.

She accepted his assistance to her chair and the first course was served. They spoke of her visit to the workshop and the progress he and Mr. Norris had made on discovering why the wheel had become dislodged. Emma was glad to note the swelling on Jon's brow was barely noticeable.

"I received a letter today from a fellow inventor," Jon said. "A Mr. George Ogdan. We have been in correspondence for several months, exchanging ideas over the design of various machinery. He is as guarded as I am in revealing his successes, but he might consider selling me the design of his latest steam engine.

"I informed him that I need to see it perform in order to assess if I can modify it for my machine, and Mr. Ogdan extended an invitation to visit him in Dorset. I plan to leave on Monday."

Disappointment streaked through Emma. She had believed they were starting to form a bond, but time apart could threaten the small progress they had made.

"Your absence will spark a new round of gossip," she

said more sharply than she intended. "I thought the purpose of our marriage was to stop the tongues from wagging."

He tilted his head, looking at her in a quizzical manner. "I never said that I intended to make the trip alone, without you."

Astonished, she pulled back. "You want me to come? Why? To silence the gossip?"

For a moment he simply looked at her. "No. I thought we could both benefit from spending time together away from this scrutiny and speculation." He smiled faintly. "It won't be an especially glamorous journey. Mr. Ogdan is a man of modest means, who lives in a somewhat remote area. Though he has assured me the village boasts a fine inn that is close to the seashore."

She looked away to give herself time to think and admitted her interest was piqued. "I do enjoy travel. How long would we stay once we arrive?"

"No more than a week. Perhaps less. I shall be working a good deal of the time, but there will be opportunities for us to explore the area."

"It's been years since I've been to the seaside." Emma grinned shyly. "I'm not easily bored and rather adept at keeping myself occupied when left to my own devices."

"Then you will come?"

"Yes."

Jon nodded. "Excellent. Do you think you could manage without your maid? Out of respect for Mr. Ogdan I prefer that we don't arrive with a caravan of servants. I won't be bringing my valet. The only servants that will accompany us are the coach driver and two footmen."

"I can travel without Dory as long as you don't object to my sporting a simpler appearance?" Emma reached up and tugged on a wisp of hair trailing down her cheek.

He cocked an eyebrow at her. "I shall struggle to endure the lack of elaborate hairstyles."

They shared a quiet laugh, then grew silent, each thinking their own thoughts. "I fear my maid has been studying the ancestral portraits in the long gallery and seems especially enamored with the intricate, over-worked, powdered hairstyles favored during the reign of Louis XV."

Jon's face lit with curiosity. "Didn't the women put bird nests and other ridiculous objects in their hair?"

"Well, that is mostly hearsay. Cartoons were published that made aristocratic women look ridiculous, wearing wigs that sported bird cages, nests filled with eggs, bows, ribbons, more flowers than a garden, even a replica of a sailing ship.

"The hairstyles in the paintings in the gallery aren't quite that absurd, but they are grandiose." Emma's brows drew together. "And Dory was rather taken with the idea of pastel-colored hair—pink, light violet, blue. Fortunately, she has no idea where to obtain the supplies needed to create such a style."

"Need I remind you that she is your maid, and a servant to boot? You can easily put a stop to all this with one word."

"And crush her spirit?" Emma shook her head. "No, 'twould be too cruel. She is young and eager, but lacking in confidence. I'm tempering her enthusiasm slowly."

A snort of laughter escaped from Jon's lips. "Your hair does look especially lovely tonight."

The smile eased the weariness from his eyes, making him look younger. Jon reached out, covering her hand with his own. Emma tingled at his touch and a pleasant warmth traveled up her arm.

"I am glad that I'm taking this journey with you," she said.

He tugged her hand to his lips and pressed a gentle kiss on her palm. 'Twas a simple, elegant gesture, made sensual by the flicker of awareness between them. Her eyes locked upon his and Emma felt her breath hitch.

Jon nuzzled his cheek against her palm and began running a line of light kisses down to the pulse at her wrist. Every place his lips touched, her flesh felt heated.

She acknowledged that despite the occasional unease between them, she desired her husband. He had the unique ability to create all sorts of restless, exciting sensations inside her.

"Will you come to my bed tonight?" she asked boldly. "Or should I come to yours?"

His eyes darkened and a number of emotions crossed his face. His thumb slowly caressed the back of her hand and she felt a flash of heat running along her skin wherever he touched her.

"I shall join you in your bed, Emma."

Her breath left her in a quick rush and Emma's heart started beating so fast she wondered if it would succeed in escaping her rib cage.

She never knew how she was able to finish her meal with such composure. As was their usual custom, they left the dining room and withdrew to the salon. A fire had been lit to chase away the spring dampness, lending an intimate, romantic air to the chamber.

They sat across from each other in matching wing-back chairs. Jon with his newspaper, Emma with her embroidery. A strange silence permeated the room, along with a rising sexual tension.

Finally, the clock struck the hour. 'Twas much earlier than her usual bedtime, but Emma seized the moment to mutter a simple good night to her husband and escape the salon before the clock hit its final chime.

If not for the footman standing at his post in the foyer, Emma would have raced up the staircase. Once in her bedchamber, she rushed to change, practically tossing Dory from the room the moment her maid had finished her duties.

Jittery with nerves, Emma arranged herself on the chair in front of the fireplace, draping her leg over the arm in what she hoped was a seductive, provocative position.

Twenty minutes later her leg started cramping.

I look like a desperate fool. Sighing, Emma gingerly readjusted herself, rubbing her upper thigh and leg vigorously until the feeling returned.

Where is he?

She sauntered to the bed, bracing her hand on the bedpost. But standing beside the bed felt even more unnatural, so she climbed in and propped herself against the pillows. The house was quiet, almost watchful. Ears straining for sounds, she was astonished to realize how many odd, creaky, and unsettling noises rattled around in the house.

Yet, to her great disappointment, there were no sounds of footsteps approaching. Miffed, Emma glared so hard at the door that connected her chambers to Jon's it nearly burst into flames.

Her head was a jumble of thoughts and emotions. Had he changed his mind? Worrying her bottom lip with her teeth, Emma reached for the book she kept at her bedside and propped it upon her lap. It took a few moments to realize that she held the tome upside down.

Straightening it with a huff, Emma leaned against the pillows and contemplated her next move. Should she go to his bed? Nay, he said he would join her here.

Perhaps she should leave the door ajar as a sign of welcome. Eagerness? Desperation? Groaning with indecision, Emma pounded the book on the coverlet.

"A disappointing ending?" a deep male voice questioned. "Books can bring such joy, but they are annoying when the plot lacks development and the characters are too one-dimensional and predictable."

Jon strode toward the bed. Emma's breath caught and for a moment all coherent thought fled her mind. He was wearing a loosely tied blue silk robe—with nothing beneath it.

Her eyes were drawn to his broad shoulders and the fine mat of visible chest hair. Her fingers itched with the desire to touch that hair and the muscled flesh beneath it.

Jon reached out and plucked the book from her fingers, then placed it on her bedside table with great care.

"I actually haven't read more than a few pages," she muttered. "'Tis too soon to tell if it will please me."

"Then we must search for something else that will please you, dear wife."

Jon sat beside her on the bed and gathered her close, his solid, warm arms encircling her. A slow, seductive smile spread across his face and she felt his hand slide to the middle of her spine. Suddenly, he rolled on top of her.

Emma squealed in surprise. Looking up, she realized

their lips were positioned in perfect alignment. Just a small dip and they would meet.

Emma licked her lips in anticipation. He did not disappoint, leaning in and brushing her mouth softly, tenderly. She sighed. His kisses were even more enticing than she remembered and she admitted that she had missed them.

Very much.

She ran her fingers gently over his cheek and jaw, then cupped his face, tilting his head so that their eyes met.

"Do you like these kisses?" he whispered, pressing his lips to the sensitive corners of her mouth.

"I do."

"Good."

He gave her another long, lingering kiss. Eagerly, Emma parted her lips and he intensified the next few kisses in a way that blanked every thought from her mind. His scent wrapped around her like a sensual cloak. She savored the passion and heat he evoked, moaning her delight.

They kissed even harder, straining together. He clamped his hands over the curves of her buttocks, pulling her sex against his hardness until they were tightly molded together. Emma's heart fluttered in her chest at the contact, alive with excitement.

She relished the warmth of his hard body pressed against hers. She wanted to pull his heat and hardness inside her, to experience the intense physical intimacy, to feel the peace and joy of sexual release.

He nuzzled his lips against her throat, kissing, licking, tasting, and her body caught fire at the sensations that streaked through her. His hands slipped down, his thumbs trailing over her nipples. She shivered.

"My beautiful, sensual wife," he muttered, his breath

hot and moist against her flesh. "Do you know how much I want you, how much I *crave* you?"

His words chased away the insecurities that had been plaguing her. Emma's fingers trembled as she ran them through his hair. Jon's arm tightened to secure her and his head moved down to capture a taut nipple between his lips.

His tongue circled, then suckled first one and then the other tender bud. Emma cried out, her whole body arching, her head falling back in restless pleasure. Shivers formed deep in her belly and raced through her.

It was a heady thought knowing how much he wanted her. Her body felt different, heavy and heated with passion, her mind free of doubts and worries.

Boldly, she slipped her fingers beneath his robe and grabbed him, wrapping her fingers around his girth, pulling and pushing. He groaned and thrust into her grip, giving her a wild sense of power.

He imitated her actions, bringing his hand between her upper thighs. The tightness and restless excitement grew as he stroked her, the sensations rising and she writhed as the pressure climbed inside her.

It crested suddenly and she shook all over when the crisis hit. Shaking, trembling, she cried out her pleasure while Jon whispered soothing words of encouragement.

Exhausted, replete, Emma collapsed into the softness of her bed, waiting for the final shudders to subside. She could feel Jon's finger stroking the dampness from her forehead and cheek.

Licking her lips, Emma raised her lids and met Jon's eyes. Under his heated gaze, a fresh wave of desire washed over her. Emma felt his knees push her thighs apart. Body quavering, she opened her arms and lifted herself toward him, a silent, sensual invitation.

Jon drew her lips into another kiss as his body took possession of hers. He filled her fully, sheathed deep inside. Reaching up, Emma grabbed his shoulders, pulling herself against him.

"Damn, that feels incredible," Jon said hoarsely, thrusting his hips forward.

He pumped harder, taking her breath away, making her forget anything but the way they moved together in perfect rhythm. Emma wrapped her arms around his back, holding him tightly.

Tears formed in her eyes as she realized that she never wanted to let him go.

Chapter Fourteen

Jon's body raged with an intensity that shocked him. His head lost all sense of reason as the pleasure built within him. He heard gasping moans of pleasure and passion, yet barely recognized them as his own.

Emma's arms were wrapped around him, holding him tight and he thrust faster and harder, again and again until she was once again writhing beneath him. They were feeding each other's needs, building the yearning deep inside with a frantic desperation that felt like madness.

Unable to hold out any longer, Jon bucked and erupted, spilling his hot seed inside her, calling her name hoarsely. He held his breath while the sensations glided over him in waves.

He felt Emma lean closer, her parted lips kissing the pulse throbbing at the base of his throat. With a final groan he collapsed upon her and they lay quietly, still joined together.

Emma's hand idly caressed his back. He nuzzled his face into the damp curve of her neck and waited for his ragged breathing to steady and return to normal.

Possessing Emma's body made him feel more emotions than he could name—or understand. It had happened on their wedding night and again tonight. After that first night together he had told himself staying out of her bed for the next few days was the decent, considerate thing to do. Her body needed time to recover from their joining.

He wasn't an animal. He could wait. Yet it had taken tremendous control to tame his desires and keep his distance. Memories of their lovemaking had haunted him nearly every waking hour.

Sitting across the table from her tonight, his body felt on fire with need. The neckline of her gown had exposed enough creamy-white flesh to remind him how truly exquisite his wife was, a sensual woman of grace and beauty.

He had been surprised and pleased when she asked if he would come to her bed—and then offered to come to his. Her willingness to expose her sexual needs had entranced him.

The wind rattled the windows, calling his wandering thoughts back to the present. Hell, he was probably crushing his poor wife! The mattress creaked as he shifted his position and moved off of Emma.

Eyes closed, she muttered something incoherent, then snuggled against him. Instinctively, he wrapped his arm around her, pulling her closer. She was warm and soft and loose-limbed, apparently suffering no ill effects from having him draped over her for so long.

The soft strands of her loose hair tickled his nose. Jon angled his head and playfully rubbed away his itch on the top of Emma's head, waiting to hear her laugh. Instead, she sighed contently and he realized she was exhausted.

He kissed her head gently, then felt the steady rise and fall of her chest and realized that she had fallen asleep. Worn out and sated, he thought with no small amount of pride.

Physically, she had given herself without reservation, as had he. Jon had stared down at her, and she had stared up at him when their bodies were joined. They had held each other's eyes throughout, while his hips lifted and fell and hers rose to meet him. It had been thrilling and intimate and yet something had been missing.

A deeper connection? A sense of complete surrender? An expression of real trust? Perhaps. Jon struggled to put a name to it, but couldn't. He just knew it was there.

Emma was a giving, generous lover, but he sensed that for all her abandonment, she was still holding a piece of herself aloft, away. He didn't believe it was done out of malice or spite or even inexperience.

Yet nevertheless, she was holding back, keeping a part of herself distant and locked away from him. Refusing to fully and completely relinquish herself.

He knew, because he was doing precisely the same thing.

Days later, on Sunday morning, Emma crawled out of bed after a restless night. They were leaving on their journey to see Mr. Ogdan tomorrow and she had been fretting over the arrangements, wanting to make certain that all would go smoothly.

In preparation for the trip, Jon had been working all hours of the day and night. He had not visited her bed again and she had seen him so infrequently she was unable to make an offer to join him in his.

Rather than dwelling on why that rankled her, Emma kept herself busy. Much was riding on the success of this trip. She felt a strong need to prove to Jon—and herself—that she could be an asset to his work, and this was the perfect opportunity.

Emma pressed her ear to the door connecting her chamber to his, listening for signs that Jon was awake. The household was preparing to leave for Sunday services in the village and she didn't want to arrive late. This was going to be their first public appearance since their hasty wedding. The gossipmongers already had plenty of fodder; Emma preferred not to give them any more.

Hearing no signs of life on the other side of the door, Emma slowly opened it. The room was bathed in darkness; the long, heavy drapes pulled tightly closed. She quietly approached the bed, getting close enough to distinguish that the shape huddled beneath the covers was her husband.

"His lordship has only been asleep for an hour," a male voice whispered behind her. "He returned to the manor very early this morning. I shall try my best to wake him, Lady Kendall."

Emma stifled a startled scream and turned to face Jon's valet. The man moved so soundlessly she had not heard him creep up behind her. Or perhaps she had been too engrossed at the sight of her husband in bed?

"No!" Emma reached out a hand to physically stop the servant. "I know he has been working very hard. Please, let him rest. He needs his sleep."

The valet frowned. "He will miss Sunday services."

"His health is more important. I shall attend and represent us both," Emma declared boldly.

It was hardly the situation Emma would have chosen for her first venture out in public. Unfortunately, there was no time to get a message to Dorothea and ask if she could ride with them. If she had to go without her husband, Emma would have preferred to have the support of her sister and brother-in-law.

The first person she saw when she arrived at the churchyard was Squire Hornsby. He didn't call out a greeting, but instead gave Emma a brisk nod, his face stern and disapproving.

Well, at least he hadn't cut her directly. The power of Jon's name and title—as well as Carter's—had offered Emma some protection from being shunned.

Emma inhaled slowly, trying to ignore the loss she felt at Jon's absence. Mindful of the scrutiny of others mingling about, she pulled her shoulders back, and focused her eyes slightly above everyone's head. She was not about to give anyone else the opportunity to snub her.

"Ah, Miss Ellingham. Or rather, Lady Kendall." Hector Winthrope's clipped voice echoed through the churchyard.

Emma was barely able to stop herself from visibly cringing as she turned to face him. Hector's eyes were narrowed, his lips thinned.

Why does he so often look as though he's just eaten something vile tasting?

Emma felt the heat rush through her as all eyes seemed to turn her way. She tilted her chin, overcoming the flash of fear that had gripped her.

"Good morning, Mr. Winthrope."

Determined to show courage, Emma approached. The crowd parted, casting curious glances in her direction. She heard—and ignored—the whispers behind her back.

"Are you all alone this morning?" Hector questioned.

"Of course not. Nearly the entire household has accompanied me," she said.

Hector tilted his head and looked pointedly down his nose. "Servants? My, you are carrying the lady of the manor role to extremes."

"These people are a valuable asset to our home and I am honored to attend services with them," Emma replied, bristling at the remark.

"How quaintly democratic of you," he chortled.

"'Tis common decency to treat others with the respect they deserve, no matter what their station in life," she said sternly.

Hector cast her a doubtful glance. "There are many who would find it distasteful, appalling even, yet I have always admired your forthright manner, Lady Kendall."

"You are too kind, Mr. Winthrope." Emma attempted a smile. It was not successful.

"Where is your husband?"

"Right here." Jon took Emma's hand and placed it on his own. "Do close your mouth, Winthrope. With it hanging open so wide you look like you've just caught a trout."

Fleeting anger sparked Hector's eyes, but then his expression narrowed, as though he sensed something was amiss yet couldn't define it. "We are honored that you decided to grace us with your presence, Lord Kendall. Yet puzzled as to why you did not accompany your new bride."

Jon shot Hector a poisonous glare. "I never knew that you were such a quizzical fellow, Winthrope."

Hector shrugged. "Oh, I have curiosities about a great many things, including how you spend your days. There have been countless rumors about what goes on in that workshop of yours, Kendall. Dire predictions, from respectable folks, that no good can come from secretive, heathen scientific experiments."

"It is not an experiment," Jon replied. "I am engaged in the pursuit of innovation for the betterment of society."

"Were we not warned of the dangers of such events in the book *The Modern Prometheus*?" Winthrope parried. "Just like you, the protagonist of that story seeks a greater understanding of the world through science. And this unnatural curiosity led to his obsession with imparting life into non-living matter."

"Are you referring to the novel by Mary Shelley?" Emma asked. "The one featuring Victor Frankenstein?"

Hector nodded. "The very same."

Emma sputtered with vindication, infuriated at the ridiculous comparison and frankly shocked to discover that Hector had in truth read an entire book.

"I read the tome years ago when it was first published under her husband's name," Jon said. "I had heard the most recent edition now identifies her as the author."

"'Twas quite shocking to discover such chilling ideas and imagery was written by a woman," Hector remarked, shaking his head in disapproval.

"I can assure you that Jon's endeavor in no way resembles the creature that is created in this novel," Emma countered. "*Frankenstein* is a work of pure fiction. Only a twisted mind would believe there are parallels to Jon's work."

Winthrope sniffed. "Your passionate defense of your husband does you credit, Lady Kendall."

Emma might have accepted the compliment if it had not been uttered in such an insincere and condescending tone. "I speak from knowledge, Mr.

Winthrope. I have seen my husband's work. I've even sketched it. 'Tis a machine that will revolutionize the farming industry and make life easier and better for all."

The doubt in Winthrope's eyes was easy to read. "When will we see it? When will he share it with the world?"

"When it's finished." Jon tugged on Emma's arm. "You must excuse us. We don't want to be late to the service."

Emma gladly allowed herself to be led away. They walked into the church and she was no longer concerned about the judgmental eyes looking their way. She was too angry with Hector Winthrope.

They took their seats and Jon handed her a hymnal.

"Winthrope seeks to paint you as a madman," Emma hissed beneath her breath. "Why?"

"He is ignorant and afraid of things he doesn't understand," Jon answered calmly. "And he is not the only one with such opinions."

Emma gripped the hymnal tightly. "You must silence him and the others from repeating such drivel."

"A waste of breath." Jon turned the pages in his book. "Try not to let it distress you."

"I can't help it."

"Try harder."

Emma's chest rose and fell in a big sigh. She didn't understand how Jon could be so calm. These attacks were petty and untrue and had the potential to cause harm. She wished she had been more forceful in her defense of her husband, but she was going to do as he asked and let it lie—for now.

The service seemed longer than usual, with a sermon laced with warnings about the grievous sin and dire retribution for men and women giving in to their baser instincts before marriage. As the reverend droned on ominously—staring directly at her and Jon—Emma clenched her teeth so tightly she feared she might break a tooth.

She forced herself not to fidget and glanced frequently over at Jon. Though he gave no outward sign of it, she knew he was tired. There were shadows beneath his eyes that attested to a lack of sleep, and a tightness about his mouth that suggested he was fighting to suppress a yawn.

Finally, the reverend stepped down from his pulpit. The congregation's voices rose together in song and the service ended. Jon smoothed his hand across his face in a weary way and escorted Emma down the aisle.

They ignored the milling crowd and went directly to the carriage. With Jon's help, Emma stepped inside and he shut the door.

"I'll return home on horseback, after a quick stop at my workshop," Jon informed her.

Emma leaned out the open window to speak with him. "I accepted an invitation to have Sunday supper with my sister and her family later. I could cancel if you are too tired," she offered. "Or go without you. Dorothea and Carter will understand."

"I've neglected you shamefully these last few days," Jon replied. "The least I can do is share a meal with your family."

"As you wish." Emma took a short breath and favored him with a contemplative glance. She would be glad to have his company, yet chafed at the notion of him attending merely because he felt it was his duty.

Jon signaled to the coachman, and the carriage lurched forward. With a sigh, Emma turned her head and watched her husband fade from view.

* * *

"Your children are accomplished riders," Jon observed, pulling his mount to a halt at the top of the hill.

Nodding, Carter drew alongside. "They both like being on horseback, though 'tis Nicole who is horse mad."

The men watched the pair race spiritedly across the flat, level ground in the valley below. Emma had been the one to suggest a ride after they had finished a delectable Sunday supper and Jon was glad to have an opportunity to speak with Carter in private.

"Has there been any news from the Bow Street runner we hired to investigate Dickenson's death?" Jon inquired.

Carter's lips tightened grimly. "He's confirmed that Lord Brayer had substantial gambling debts and apparently owed money to numerous unsavory characters."

Jon tilted his head to one side, considering. "Could one of them have killed him? Pressed Dickenson to make good on his debts and then a fight ensued?"

"It's certainly a plausible explanation," Carter replied. "Though it hardly explains why those two footmen were so adamant they saw you with him that night."

"It hardly seems to be a simple case of mistaken identity," Jon concurred. "Try as I might, I cannot understand it."

"Well, there has been a further development on that front," Carter announced. "Those two servants have suddenly disappeared."

Jon turned his head sharply. "What?"

"Vanished. No one seems to know exactly when, or has any idea where they might have gone."

"Were they dismissed?"

Carter shook his head. "Not according to the butler."

"Had they been employed long?"

"One for six, the other five years."

Jon frowned. "They gave no notice? Asked for no references?"

"The butler claims that none of the staff had an inkling they were planning on leaving. They were only discovered to be gone when they neglected to appear at their usual posts a few days ago."

"Good God. Does the runner suspect foul play?"

Carter shrugged. "He asked me if it were possible that you paid them off, so if questioned again, they could not bear witness against you."

Jon drew back, affronted at the remark. "The runner does understand that he works for me, doesn't he?"

Carter laughed. "He's honest and capable, which is what we need. I assured him that I have no doubts as to your innocence."

"You are one of the few." Jon tightened his grip on the reins, clenching his fists. "'Twas clear to me at services this morning that Emma's testimony might have saved me from the hangman's noose, yet it did not totally lift the veil of suspicion. She told the magistrates that we both fell asleep, and now the rumors are spreading that if she slept, I could have snuck out of my workshop, killed Brayer, and returned without her ever knowing I was gone."

"Christ! The gossips find it a far more gruesome tale if Lady Brayer's jilted groom went into a sudden rage and killed her husband. And the lonely Miss Ellingham turned the situation to her advantage by risking her reputation to guilt the viscount into marriage."

Jon could not contain his grimace. *Bloody hell, what a depressing thought!*

"Papa, come race with us!" the children yelled out in unison.

Smiling indulgently, Carter waved at the pair. "In a moment." He turned to Jon. "I know it's difficult, but you must be patient."

Jon reluctantly nodded, knowing his friend was right. "One thing is clear, though, we shall all rest easier once Dickenson's killer has been caught."

Dawn was just breaking the following morning when Emma and Jon's journey to visit Mr. Ogdan began. As they prepared to set off, hot bricks were placed at Emma's feet to keep her warm and chase the worst of the spring chill from the carriage. Leaning back against the leather upholstery, she settled herself comfortably for the long ride.

Jon rode out on horseback and Emma hoped he would join her inside the carriage at some point. They set a brisk pace and harnessed a fresh team of horses at the posting inn where they stopped for lunch. To Emma's delight, as they prepared to depart Jon climbed into the carriage, joking that after such a hearty meal he feared he would fall asleep in the saddle.

She fully expected him to close his eyes and doze, but instead they passed the time in pleasant conversation, discussing books they had both read, his expectations for the upcoming meeting with Mr. Ogdan, and their impressions of the scenery.

Darkness was falling when they reached their destination for the night. It was a small establishment that boasted a private parlor and a suite of rooms with two connected bedchambers. Though Emma would have preferred to have Jon sleep beside her, she was tired enough from the travel to sleep alone, soundly, in a strange bed.

The second day of travel was similar to the first. By the third day, the normalcy of their routine lent an air of familiarity to the days. Jon continued to ride out in the morning and inside the carriage after lunch. Emma looked forward to the time they spent together, and their lively conversations on a great many different topics relieved the boredom of the passing miles.

They arrived at their destination at midday on the fifth day of travel. The carriage entered a quaint village, drove past the square, and rolled down a cobblestone street. The vehicle had barely come to a halt in front of a solid building of brick, when a couple hurried out of the inn, eager smiles of welcome creasing their faces.

They proudly identified themselves as Mr. and Mrs. Jordan, the proprietors of the establishment. They seemed in awe at the notion of nobility staying at their inn and bowed so often Emma felt uncomfortable with the adulation.

Jon must have felt it too, as he was unusually extravagant in his praise when they toured their chambers. They were, in truth, a set of nicely appointed rooms. The sitting room was a good size and had a bow window which gave a view of the street below. A plush window seat made it an inviting space to sketch or read.

The bedchamber was at the back of the inn. The two windows overlooked a garden with budding trees and blooms. The furniture was dark and heavy and the tester bed was piled high with soft blankets and pillows.

Emma turned to see if there was a door leading to a second bedchamber and realized the suite contained only one. That meant they would be sharing a bed. Emma felt her cheeks prickle with warmth. And anticipation.

"My wife has traveled without her maid. Might you know of a local woman who could take over that task while we are here, Mrs. Jordon?" Jon asked the innkeeper's wife.

"I do," she responded. "My niece was employed as such before her marriage three years ago. She would be honored to serve Lady Kendall."

"Excellent."

Mr. Jordan beamed proudly at his wife and she preened with delight.

"Since we were uncertain of your exact arrival, we have prepared a cold luncheon, but can serve a hot supper at any time, my lord," Mr. Jordan said.

"If that is acceptable," Mrs. Jordan added, suddenly appearing nervous.

"That is precisely what Lady Kendall would have ordered," Jon replied graciously. "Thank you."

After several low, deep bows and fawning smiles, the couple left. Emma glanced at Jon, noting the glint of amusement in his eyes. "They appear rather eager to please."

"Painfully so. I imagine they don't often play hosts to a viscount and his lady wife."

"Well, I hope I won't disappoint them," Emma said ruefully. "I'm not particularly noble."

"Nonsense. You are a princess, my dear."

Emma grinned, enjoying this teasing, lighthearted side of her husband.

After a tasty meal, Jon and Emma explored the

village, enjoying the chance to stretch their legs. The weather was sunny, the air crisp and invigorating. They followed a footpath beside a meandering stream and crossed a stone bridge.

The tangy scent of salt air teased at their nostrils, and the squawking of birds and crashing of waves told them they must be getting closer to the sea. They turned and headed toward a cliffside field where a mass of violet-colored coastal wildflowers had recently burst into bloom.

Fighting against the stiff wind, they walked to the edge and were rewarded with their first glimpse of the ocean. The whitecaps atop the churning waves of the steel-blue water thundered and crashed upon the shoreline, leaving behind a cloud of snowy white foam on the sand.

When the ocean waves receded, puddles of turquoise-colored water formed in the lower-lying areas. Patches of golden sand stretched for miles in either direction, populated only by white birds with long, thin legs.

"It's breathtaking," Jon remarked. "You must return with your sketch pad."

"Yes."

Emma answered automatically. The sight before her was truly majestic and wondrous, teasing at her senses, uplifting her spirits. And yet she felt no urgent need to capture the images on paper or canvas. It appeared that, for now, only Jon's work had that power over her.

They walked a bit longer, debating if they should take one of the rugged pathways that led to the beach. Deciding they would return when they had more time to explore, they strode back to the inn.

Mr. and Mrs. Jordan were eagerly watching for them. After a brief rest, dinner was served in the inn's only private dining room. Jon and Emma lingered awhile, then retired to their chambers. Mrs. Jordan's niece, Deborah, arrived to assist Emma while Jon waited in the sitting room.

Deborah was a quiet woman, with plain features and a lovely smile. Her experience was obvious—she helped Emma with her toilet, took charge of her clothing, and even spread the glowing embers in the fireplace before executing a respectful curtsy and departing.

Alone and attired in her nightgown, Emma moved to the window to gaze out at the night sky. The moon was full and bright, the many stars luminous. Staring up at the endless vista made Emma feel small, almost insignificant.

She heard Jon enter the bedchamber. Emma stayed at the window, her back toward him. He moved about and she listened intently, visualizing how he looked removing his clothing. First his boots thudded to the floor, no doubt followed by his stockings. Next he would shrug off his jacket, unbutton his waistcoat, and untie his cravat.

Now that those garments were gone, he would pull his shirt up and over his head, baring his chest. Finally, he would push off his breeches and the small clothes underneath. She heard the swish of a fabric belt being tied and knew he had donned his robe.

And most likely nothing else.

Emma drew a ragged breath. She felt him draw near. Suddenly, he encircled her waist from behind, bent his head and laid a tender kiss on the exposed flesh of her collarbone.

Emma pulled in a long breath at the tingle of pleasure. She was very aware of the hardness of his body against hers. The intimacy of the moment made her glad they were sharing a chamber.

"Are you ready to come to bed?" he murmured.

An intense wave of desire ran through her at the sound of his deep, sensual voice. She tilted her head and his soft lips moved slowly up her neck to her ear. Taking the plump lobe between his teeth, he nibbled gently.

Emma released a breathy sigh and turned into his arms. Jon laughed, boyish and carefree, then bent and swept her into his arms.

Chapter Fifteen

Jon carried Emma to the bed and placed her on her back. He gathered her in his arms and for a long moment simply luxuriated in the satisfying sensations of holding her softness close to his heart.

The calm didn't last long. Jon pressed a hard kiss to her mouth and she welcomed him with a blossoming heat. She tasted sweet and luscious and his body burned brightly with desire. Instinctively, he found the curves of her buttocks and clamped his hands over them, bringing her softness against his jutting erection.

They kissed more frantically, passionately, straining together. He could hear Emma's groans of excitement as she pressed herself suggestively against him. The pleasure inside him intensified.

Jon rolled onto his back, positioning her above him. Her eyes widened in startled wonder as he grasped her hips and lifted her over his aching penis. The hard shaft teased the wet, weeping opening of her womanhood. With a cry of passion, Emma pressed down on him.

Jon penetrated her with one hard upward thrust. His breath heaved with the effort to control himself, to pleasure her in steady, even strokes. But her sheath squeezed him tightly and all reason fled. The exhilaration of having this beautiful, sensual woman *riding* him, pleasuring him with such uninhibited abandon, brought him to climax.

His shuddering release triggered Emma's. Eyes luminous with raw desire, he held her tightly as the ecstasy broke over her. When her convulsions finally ended, she collapsed against him, pressing her face against his cheek.

Jon continued to hold her tightly, breathing in the sweet scent of her, trying to understand the tenderness that was tugging at his heart.

He could do this forever, he realized. Yet, truth be told, he wasn't certain how he felt about being so uncontrollably randy around his wife. On one hand it was uncivilized, unseemly.

On the other, 'twas pure delight.

Jon trotted out to the stables the following morning, eager to finally meet with Mr. Ogdan. The one thing tempering his excitement was leaving Emma behind. He had become accustomed to having her by his side these past few days and was disappointed she wouldn't be with him. She had good instincts about people and he would have liked to hear her opinion of Mr. Ogdan.

Alas, when Jon had mentioned in his correspondence that his wife would be joining him on the journey, the bachelor Mr. Ogdan had made it very clear she was unwelcome at his laboratory and workshop.

Mr. Jordan was able to provide excellent directions,

and though located a fair distance from the village, Jon easily found his way. His knock was answered by a sour-faced woman of towering height with sharp, angular features and nervously darting eyes, who identified herself as the housekeeper.

She kept him waiting on the doorstep until confirming that he was indeed an invited guest. Only then did she bring him to the front parlor. After a few minutes, Mr. Ogdan appeared and introduced himself.

He was a short, thin, wiry fellow with tufts of gray hair that stood out from the sides of his head like a pair of wings. His voice was low and gravelly and his head had a tendency to bob and sway when he spoke.

They spent nearly an hour in guarded conversation, speaking about nothing of any real interest. Jon was just beginning to think the entire trip had been a colossal waste of time, when Mr. Ogdan finally extended the invitation to visit his laboratory and view his current project.

They left the house through the back door and followed the sloping ground to a well-worn path that led them through a thick copse of trees. Sunlight filtered through the leaves and brush, tinting everything an odd shade of green. Eventually, they arrived at a clearing. Ahead of them stood a sizeable dwelling.

"My laboratory," Mr. Ogdan announced with pride.

He removed a large ring of keys from his coat pocket and began unlocking a series of heavy iron locks. Finally done, he swung the door wide. Jon was nearly overwhelmed with the strong smell of sulfur as he stepped inside.

Mr. Ogdan scurried about, lighting lamps. Jon attempted to follow, then stopped, almost afraid to move. Books were strewn everywhere throughout the space—desk, tables, chairs, even the floor. Some were closed and stacked in tall piles, others were creased open to a specific page. Jon saw notes in the margins of many of the volumes, along with ink drawings and scribbles.

'Twas a miracle that anything could be found, much less created in so much chaos. But then Mr. Ogdan pulled a large white sheet off a structure and Jon's opinion was immediately revised.

Rubbing his hands together in glee, he picked his way through the piles of books and papers to get a closer look at the steam engine. Mr. Ogdan answered his questions and Jon was forced to admit that looks could indeed be deceiving. Mr. Ogdan's rather eccentric exterior hid a mind of scientific aptitude.

Time passed quickly. The dour housekeeper brought them a cold lunch, along with a jug of hard cider. Questions tumbled out of Jon's mouth as he ate his share of the crusty bread, sliced ham, and pungent cheese. Mr. Ogdan was guarded in his responses, revealing only partial details, but Jon understood. A petitioner was required to apply and pay fees to several different offices before a patent was granted to protect the ownership of the property.

Detailed models of the design were also submitted, making it a long and expensive process. Consequently, the specific details of most new inventions were not openly shared until such protections were in place.

When the housekeeper returned with a tea tray, Jon realized how late it had become. After securing an invitation to return on the morrow, he took his leave. Spirits buoyed, Jon mounted his horse; the foremost thought in his head was how he could hardly wait to tell Emma all.

* * *

"We've been invited to attend the annual spring dance at the assembly hall this evening," Jon announced.

Raising a brow, Emma turned from the small trunk she had been packing. "A dance?"

"Yes. I imagine this is the highlight of the social calendar for the village." He lifted the parchment aloft. "We should be honored to be included."

Emma straightened. "Well, 'tis a kindness."

Jon tapped the invitation against his knee. "I think it would be wise for us to go. Do you mind? 'Twould only delay our departure for a day."

"Will Mr. Ogdan be there?" Emma asked, intrigued at the possibility of finally meeting the elusive inventor about whom Jon spoke so often. In the three days that they had been here, she had not caught even a glimpse of the man.

Jon laughed. "No. Mr. Ogdan has more than earned his reputation as a recluse. I believe he would rather walk over hot coals with bare feet than place himself in a social setting with so many people."

Emma could understand the feeling. She had enjoyed some, but certainly not all, of the various parties, musical evenings, and balls her sisters had dragged her to over the years. The really torturous ones were dull gatherings with an assortment of shallow individuals whose sole purpose was searching for a partner with whom to either engage in an illicit affair or contract a marriage.

Emma had been interested in neither.

"Do you wish to attend?" she asked.

Jon nodded. "I hope to form a partnership with

Mr. Ogdan in the future. It wouldn't hurt to ingratiate myself with the locals." He frowned suddenly. "By any chance, did you bring something appropriate to wear?"

Emma smiled. "There are no worries on that score. Dory packed my trunk, so naturally there are several formal gowns. Deborah is a very skilled maid. She can help me get ready."

"Good. Then I'll accept the invitation." Jon shuffled through the papers on his makeshift desk, pulling out a fresh sheet of velum.

Emma turned back to her packing, removing some garments she now knew would be needed this evening. Though not overly enthused at the prospect of the dance, she was willing to attend for Jon's sake. Mainly because she was pleased that he had asked and appeared willing to include her opinion, rather than dictating what they would do.

It was a good sign of how much had changed between them.

Later that night, Emma descended the staircase at the inn, dressed in a fine gown of yellow silk. The delicate lace overskirt and elbow-length half sleeves were embroidered with tiny seed pearls arranged in the shape of a trailing vine, and that pattern was repeated on the scoop-necked bodice.

Jon awaited her at the bottom, his eyes flaring with appreciation when she reached him. Emma too felt a pang of admiration. Her husband was magnificent in his formal evening clothes. Black coat, silver brocade waistcoat, brilliantly white cravat, and diamond studs in his cuffs, he was almost princely, the picture of a nobleman.

"You look lovely," he whispered as he took her hand.

"As do you," she replied, feeling the fluttering of nerves in her stomach melt away.

The carriage ride to the hall was not long. She took Jon's hand and walked up the steps. They were greeted courteously and ushered inside. Emma felt the eyes of more than one guest turn toward them. A dark-haired woman with a double chin and an air of importance broke from the group surrounding her and eagerly approached.

She introduced herself as Mrs. Peals. When Jon took her hand in greeting, thanking her for the invitation, Emma wondered if the poor woman might faint. Her pearl earbobs danced with delight at the elegant gesture and she giggled like a schoolgirl.

While Mrs. Peals chatted away to Jon, Emma took stock of their surroundings. The assembly room was an open space, lit by numerous candles and festively decorated with garlands of greenery and flowers. There was a trio of musicians on one end and tables and chairs set up around the perimeter of what Emma assumed was the dance floor.

Men and women, dressed in their finest attire, circled about the room, while others gathered around the table of refreshments that held an assortment of cheeses, meats, breads, and cakes, along with a large silver punch bowl. The rumble of voices filled the air, broken now and again by a burst of merry laughter.

There was something rather freeing being at a party that lacked the rigidity of society's expectations. One could simply enjoy oneself, without fear of censure or criticism.

Feeling a momentary stab of guilt for abandoning Jon to the fawning Mrs. Peals, Emma turned her attention back to the pair. But she was saved from joining their conversation by the sound of the musicians tuning their instruments.

Jon's brow rose fractionally when the orchestra struck up a waltz.

"Oh, my, I do hope we haven't scandalized you with our opening dance selection, my lord." Mrs. Peals fluttered as she waved her fan vigorously in front of her flushed face.

"Quite the contrary," Jon replied, sweeping Emma into his arms. "My wife adores the waltz. If you will excuse us?"

He took them to the center of the room. Breathing deeply, Emma set her left hand on Jon's shoulder and moved a half step away, arching her spine so that she could look up at him.

"I have never done this, so please move slowly or I shall tread heavily upon your feet," she whispered.

"You've attended London balls, yet were never asked to dance?"

She laughed. "I was often partnered for a quadrille, Scotch reel, even a minuet, but I was never formally instructed on the proper form and footwork for a waltz."

"Surely you had dancing lessons?" Jon questioned, as he pulled her closer.

"I am younger than my sisters. By the time I was of age, we no longer had the funds to employ a proper dance master. Jason engaged one for me after he and Gwen married, but I grew bored after a few lessons and asked to quit before the waltz was taught."

Their bodies touched and she backed away. "However, I do know that when you waltz, 'tis improper to touch anywhere but our hands. Our right ones together, my other hand on your shoulder, and your other hand around my waist."

"I like being improper sometimes." Jon's hand caressed her waist, his fingers stroking sensually up her spine. "Especially with my wife."

The music swelled and they began to move. He pivoted and twirled her about. Emma gasped and held on tightly, feeling her body press boldly against his, her bosom against his chest. "Gracious, slow down! All this twirling about is distracting me from counting the steps."

"Your lips aren't moving."

"I count silently, so as not to embarrass myself or my partner. I'm very clever, Lord Kendall. Didn't you know that about me?"

"Well, I've learned that I should never underestimate you," he whispered, his eyes gleaming with humor.

She could not hold back a smile at his comment. "You do know that everyone is watching us?"

"Of course. Let's give them all something to remember, shall we?"

He smiled into Emma's eyes and she felt herself falling under his tantalizing spell. She lost count of her one-two-three, one-two-three steps, but it didn't matter because Jon was in control.

She could feel the warmth of his fingers as he applied greater pressure against her spine. He guided her firmly, moving proficiently, with far more grace than she would have credited for a man of his height and build.

The music flowed around them and Emma felt herself relaxing in his arms as he spun them elegantly around the floor. Trustingly, she followed as he led and soon they were dancing in perfect rhythm, gliding lightly and gracefully past the other couples.

They were close enough that she could feel the heat of his body, capture the faint smell of his cologne. The strength of his arms and firmness of his hold left her a trifle weak in the knees. She leaned back so that she could look up at him. His eyes were bright with amusement and she felt a surge of joy.

And she was suddenly very glad that she had agreed to attend the dance.

As they began the journey home the following morning, Jon elected to ride inside the carriage with Emma. They had returned to the inn late from the dance and 'twas later still before they fell asleep.

The moment they were alone in their chamber, Jon had swept Emma into his arms. She had the most tempting mouth he had ever seen and now that they were finally alone he succumbed to the temptation to possess it. Kissing her ardently, his desire had roared steadily forward, replacing rational thought.

Pressing her back against the closed door, he had pulled up the skirt of her delicate silk gown, ripping it in the process. She had gasped when he thrust his hands inside her undergarments, but was soon returning his kisses with even greater fervor.

Lost in mindless desire, Jon had fumbled with the flaps of his breeches, freeing himself. Catching her underneath her knees, he had lifted Emma high in the air, then entered her in a single, deep thrust.

She screamed with delight and her excited cries had set his already heated blood on fire. Burying his face in the hollow beneath her neck, he had breathed in Emma's intoxicating scent as his body claimed hers in primitive bliss.

She had matched him, pushing herself forward, rocking into him with the same frantic rhythm. Her hands had gripped his shoulders, and he had felt her nails digging into his flesh, even beneath the fabric of his evening coat.

He had thrust faster, harder, deeper, luxuriating in the pleasure he had hungered for the moment she walked down the staircase this evening, a vision in yellow silk and feminine allure.

He wanted her with an urgency that was almost painful, and Emma had shared that madness, wrapping her legs to his waist and arching her back to bring him closer. She had started to tremble when she was close to fulfillment and that had excited him even more.

He smothered her cries of passion when she reached her climax, burying himself farther inside her. He had growled—growled—as a haze of pleasure quickly engulfed him and his entire body shook with the power of his release.

They had remained joined together in the shuddering aftermath, breathing erratically until their senses returned. Slowly emerging from his haze of lust, Jon had carefully lowered her to her feet.

God, what had come over him? He was turning into an animal, unable to keep his sexual impulses toward his wife civilized. Of course, it was partly her fault for being so damn delectable—and thankfully neither prudish nor delicate.

He had stared down at the head cradled on his chest and fought to ease his still labored breathing. His hand stroked slowly over her hair and she had sighed contently and snuggled closer.

It felt natural to hold her so intimately when they took to their bed, to watch protectively over her as she slept. To feel a sense of peace and contentment unlike any other he had ever known before sleep had finally claimed him.

The carriage hit a deep rut and lurched, pulling Jon away from his sensual memories. Seated across from him, Emma had her nose pressed in a book, a lurid gothic novel she had confessed was filled with distressed maidens, unscrupulous villains, and supernatural occurrences.

She turned a page and he watched her brow suddenly pucker and her lips tighten together in a thin line.

"Have you reached a suspenseful section in the story?" he asked.

Startled, Emma glanced up, then grinned sheepishly. "The heroine has foolishly decided to explore a hidden passageway she discovered behind a bookcase in the library. The candle she carried has been snuffed out by a mysterious gust of wind and the secret panel door has slammed shut, trapping her inside. Bathed in darkness, her fingers are fumbling to find the latch that will release her from this damp tomb."

"Is there not a brooding hero who will—"

Jon's words were drowned out by the sudden sound of a loud crack, followed by shouts from the coachman and frightened cries from the team of horses. The coach lunged forward, then veered wildly. It shifted and fell onto its side, hitting the ground hard, sliding along the muddy road.

The frantic cries of horses, curses, and the low growl of men's voices filled the air. Jon pulled Emma to his chest, cushioning her fall. He landed on his back, the air momentarily stricken from his lungs.

"Are you hurt?" he gasped, running his hands over

her head, arms, sides, and legs, searching for any cuts or bruises.

"I'm fine," she replied. "'Twas you that took the brunt of the fall."

"I always take advantage of any excuse to hold my wife in my arms," he quipped, brushing the loosened waves of hair from her face.

Gripping his shoulder hard, Emma let out a nervous laugh. "What happened?"

Jon glanced up at the coach door above their heads. "I believe we broke a wheel. At least I hope that's the cause."

"The road is badly rutted," Emma observed.

"And our carriage has withstood far worse conditions for many miles," Jon said grimly.

"Then what else . . ." Her voice grew faint as her eyes grew wide and round. "Highwaymen?"

"Damn, I hope not."

Dusk was still several hours away. 'Twould be a brazen—and desperate—thief who would attack a carriage in broad daylight.

Jon noticed some movement outside the window. He reached into the satchel that had tumbled near his head and pulled out a pistol.

"Jon!"

"'Tis always wise to be prepared for any eventuality," he said with what he hoped was a reassuring smile.

Running footsteps approached. Jon shifted to move in front of Emma and cocked the gun. The door above them opened and a man leaned into the carriage.

"My lord, are you hurt? And Lady Kendall—?"

"We are fine," Jon replied, relieved to see his footman, Stiles. He had a cut above his brow that was bleeding profusely, but appeared to have sustained no other major injuries.

"We nearly collided with a farmer's cart," Stiles exclaimed. "Our driver didn't see him until we rounded the bend. He swerved to avoid a collision. That's when the wheel cracked and the coach overturned."

"Is anyone else hurt?" Jon asked.

"The coachman's dislocated his shoulder and possibly broke his arm," the footman responded. "The farmer's cart also tipped. 'Tis lying in a ditch on the other side of the road."

Jon tucked the pistol into the waistband of his breeches, scrambled forward, and pulled himself up and out through the open door. He turned back to look down at Emma. She was pressed against the side of the coach, her face pale, yet her eyes were calm, trusting.

"Wait here," he commanded, wanting to assess the situation before exposing her to it. "I'll return shortly."

He expected a protest, but to her credit, Emma nodded. "Please be careful."

The sight of the accident was worse than he expected and Jon was glad he had told Emma to stay inside the coach. Their trunks had broken free and smashed to the ground. One had split open and the contents were strewn over the muddy road.

He moved swiftly past the debris, shaking his head when he recognized one of his waistcoats and an extra pair of his boots lying in a puddle of dirty water.

The farmer was sitting just off the road, clutching a bloodstained cloth to his head. His cheek was bruised and beginning to swell, his body trembling, his eyes unfocused.

"The man's in shock. Bring a blanket or something else warm," Jon shouted.

Stiles ran off and returned with a slightly muddy cloak. Jon draped it over the farmer's shoulders. At the feel of the heavy fabric, the man raised his chin.

"I swear I didn't see the carriage comin', my lord," the farmer sputtered. "I tried to pull up, but 'twas too late."

"It wasn't anyone's fault," Jon concluded. "Merely bad luck for both parties."

"They said my ox is limping. Please don't let them put him down." The man grabbed Jon's arm, his words desperate. "He's the only beast I own. If I lose him, I can't plow my fields or harvest my grain. My family will starve."

"We shall examine the animal thoroughly first. If he cannot be saved, we must act humanely. But if it becomes necessary, I will compensate you for the loss."

Thankfully, the injuries to the ox were minor and after assuring the farmer that his animal would survive, Jon went to check on his coachman. As he drew near, he could see the man holding his hand against his right shoulder, which was distended at an unnatural angle. Dislocated for certain, Jon determined, knowing it must hurt like hell.

"We'll pull that shoulder back into place once you've had a few stiff drinks," Jon said.

"It all happened so fast, my lord," the coachman muttered.

"Don't fret," Jon insisted. "Your quick thinking and skill with the reins saved us all from serious injury."

"Lord Kendall!" Stiles approached. "The farmer told us there is an estate but a few miles from here."

"Are you well enough to ride, Stiles?"

"Yes, my lord."

"Good. Take my horse and go for help."

Jon returned to the carriage and helped Emma climb out, hugging her tightly when she had both feet on solid ground. Emotion tugged at his throat. *If any harm has come to her . . .*

"Is everyone all right?" she asked.

"A few bumps and bruises. Our coachman's shoulder is dislocated. Thankfully that's the worst of it. We were very lucky."

Emma went to sit with the farmer while Jon and the other footman sorted through the debris. He found one of Emma's freshly washed chemises, and she insisted upon tearing the garment and using it to bandage the farmer's bleeding head wound. Once she had performed that task, she joined the rest of them in trying to salvage what they could from the wreckage.

As the light began to fade, Stiles returned with several manservants from the nearby estate. One was driving an old-fashioned coach. 'Twas tall, boxy, and black, with a coat of arms painted distinctly on the carriage door. The gold, white, and blue crest was unfamiliar to Jon.

The driver spoke briefly with Jon and he conveyed his thanks for their assistance. One of the liveried footmen jumped down from his perch at the back of the carriage. He opened the door, pulled down the steps, and held out his hand to assist Emma inside.

Jon turned his attention toward his coachman, knowing the man was too proud to ask for the assistance he would need to climb upon the box. Predictably, the coachman protested the help, but at Jon's insistence accepted it.

"We can depart for the manor as soon as you are ready, my lord," the driver said.

Out of the corner of his eye, Jon noticed Emma had not entered the carriage. Face pale, she stood in front of the open door, so still and stiff he wondered if she even drew breath.

Jon reached out to hold on to her, fearful she might faint. 'Twas not an uncommon reaction after experiencing a trauma—the shock often hit minutes, sometimes hours, after the actual incident.

"Are you fearful of getting inside so soon after our accident?" he asked, keeping his voice low to avoid being overheard and causing her any embarrassment. "Would you prefer to be on my horse? You can ride astride, or I can ask for a sidesaddle to be sent for you."

She didn't reply. She was taking shallow breaths, as if trying to gain control of herself. He took her hand, concerned at how cold and lifeless it felt.

"Emma?"

"I recognize the coat of arms. It belongs to Sebastian Dodd, Viscount Benton," she squeaked. "Are we going to his home?"

Jon scratched his head. "No. The driver said the estate is owned by an earl. I'm sorry, in all this confusion, I didn't pay much attention to the name."

She turned to him and he was startled by the haunted, almost jittery look in her eyes. "Would you ask the driver? Please?"

Worried by her agitation, Jon did as she asked.

"The Earl of Tinsdale's lesser title is Viscount Benton," the driver explained.

Emma's face flushed red. Jon reached out, taking her hand and squeezing it tightly. "We can wait until you feel calm enough to get inside the carriage. There is no rush. The very last thing I want is to cause you any more distress."

She didn't reply, but stood, frozen in place.

"A few minutes, please," she finally muttered. "I just need a few minutes."

Chapter Sixteen

A distant ringing echoed in Emma's head. Viscount Benton. Nay, surely, she had misheard.

Sebastian Dodd, Viscount Benton, Earl of Tinsdale.

They were going to Sebastian's estate.

Fighting the trembling that shuddered through her, Emma took a deep breath, forcing herself not to panic. Perhaps she could yet devise a way to avoid seeing the man she had once loved so utterly, whose memory still had the power to twist her heart.

"Shouldn't we go directly to the village?" Emma asked, trying to keep her voice calm, to hold the distress at bay. "If our carriage cannot be immediately repaired, I'm sure we can find adequate accommodations for the night."

Jon shook his head. "The farmer told us a fire last month has closed the inn. Our only choice is to proceed to the estate. If we are lucky, they have a blacksmith in residence that can repair the wheel for us. If not, I'm hoping they have one that will fit so it can be replaced. If that also isn't possible, we will ask for the wheelwright in the village to make us a new one."

Emma glanced over at the fractured pieces of the carriage wheel. It wasn't all that bad—was it?

"Will the repairs take long?" she asked. "Surely we'll be able to depart before nightfall?"

"The sun is setting. Darkness will soon be upon us, Emma," Jon said gently. "As there is no other place for us to stay, we will have to impose upon the earl's hospitality. Hopefully only for this one night, but it might take longer."

Emma's heart began beating too hard and too fast. She smoothed the skirt of her gown in an attempt to calm herself.

"Yes, you are right of course." She gave a nervous laugh, hoping it didn't sound as hysterical as she felt. "I shall ride in the coach the earl so graciously sent for us."

She took her time climbing inside the vehicle. Jon followed her. The carriage lurched forward and Emma brought her hand to her forehead, trying to stave off the light-headedness that attacked her.

Should I put myself out of this torment and tell Jon all, before we arrive? Will that lessen the shock? But where to begin? Where to end?

This had always been a private matter between her and Sebastian. She had never spoken of it to anyone, including her sisters. And she had every reason to believe that Sebastian had also been silent.

Perhaps there was no need to say anything at all. Perhaps she could enact this charade without anyone being the wiser. Without revealing to her husband that she had been deeply, passionately in love with Sebastian for years.

The coach rounded a bend and turned down the long drive. The sun was just setting behind the rise where a structure of solid gray stone loomed. Clearly built centuries earlier, the main structure was a medieval castle that had been added to over the years.

It was stately, elegant, and traditional—three things that Sebastian worked hard at never becoming. A small smile escaped Emma's trembling lips. He always acted the carefree rogue, the flirt and charmer, the man who had the power to both tantalize women with his good looks and frighten them with the air of danger and mystery that clung to him.

Sebastian never did things by half.

And now she was about to see him, to relive the years of longing and loneliness that had driven her close to despair. Emma took a long, deep breath as she felt a fist tighten around her heart.

The carriage halted. She heard footsteps approaching, crunching loudly on the gravel stones of the drive. The blood pounded at her temples and her throat felt so constricted she could barely swallow.

I can do this. I will do this!

She swayed when she stood, her knees shaking. Jon's arm slid around her waist. His tender concern deepened her guilt and enforced her resolve to do whatever was necessary to conceal this secret from him, as she firmly believed no good would ever come from him knowing.

Emma walked forward, up the stairs, through the door, into the foyer, her eyes glued to the ground. She glanced up once from the black-and-white marble floor and caught a fleeting glimpse of a man and woman waiting to greet them.

Sebastian and his wife—a woman whom he married out of love and by all accounts still loved deeply.

Emma couldn't breathe at all. She hugged her arms around herself and raised her chin, meeting the eyes of an elegant man with silver hair. He stood proud and tall, his jawline distinctly sculpted, his eyes dark and piercing.

Her brows knit together in confusion. Who was he? She looked again, taking in his attire and realized that he was a servant, the butler. Beside him stood a woman, the housekeeper most likely. They were not the same pair that had served Sebastian years ago. The servants she knew must have retired from service, or perhaps moved with him to his new estate when he became an earl.

"Welcome to Chaswick Manor, Lord Kendall. Lady Kendall. I am Mr. Everly, the estate's butler, and this is our housekeeper, Mrs. St. Giles. We were very sorry to hear of your accident."

"Thank you, Mr. Everly. It has been a most trying afternoon," Jon replied. "We appreciate the earl coming to our rescue and opening his home to us."

Mr. Everly inclined his head. "The earl and countess are in London," he explained. "However, the household is at your disposal. Do you wish for us to send for a doctor?"

"Please. Lady Kendall and I are uninjured, but my coachman has dislocated his shoulder. I would like him placed in a physician's care," Jon replied.

Mr. Everly motioned discreetly toward one of the footmen and relayed the instructions. "Mrs. St. Giles has had rooms prepared, and we can serve dinner anytime you prefer."

"Emma?"

At the sound of her name, the fog surrounding Emma gradually lifted. *London. They are in London. My secret is safe.*

The air blew out of Emma's lungs in relief and her knees buckled. Jon's arm tightened, concern welling in his eyes as he kept her from falling.

"After the doctor has seen the coachman, please send him to my wife's chambers," Jon decided.

"I'm fine," Emma muttered, pulling back and standing on her own.

"I'm sure that you are, my dear. But it will ease my mind to have the doctor confirm it."

Having neither the strength nor the inclination to argue the point, Emma nodded. As she followed Mrs. St. Giles up the staircase, she heard Jon asking about arranging for repairs to their coach and Mr. Everly offering to bring him to the estate's forge so he could speak with the blacksmith.

Once alone in her room, Emma lay on the soft bed, doing her best to relax and rest, but it was impossible. She tried reading, but even her suspenseful gothic novel failed to keep her interest. She thought a hot bath might instill some calm, but was loath to make any additional work for the servants, who would need to heat the water and haul it to the bedchamber.

Edgy and restless, Emma paced about the room like a caged animal. Stopping, she opened one of the casement windows wide enough to allow a light breeze to circulate through the room, and smelled the sweetness of an early spring flower drifting up from the gardens.

She contemplated going down and wandering along the neatly manicured paths, but darkness was almost complete. Better to stay here.

The manor grounds were much the same as she remembered. She had not visited that often, but anytime she had been here she had meticulously cataloged every detail. Then later, she would picture Sebastian walking these corridors as a young boy, playing in the gardens, riding through the fields and woods.

She imagined him as a young man home from

university, all brash and full of himself, boasting the confident swagger of youth. Those thoughts had fueled her obsession with him and her intense desire to become an important, integral part of his life.

The doctor made an appearance. He was tall and thin, with kind eyes and a gentle touch. Emma answered his questions promptly, and after examining her arms and legs he agreed with her assessment that she had sustained only minor bruises in the accident.

Once the doctor left her, the minutes passed with unbearable slowness. At one point Emma thought she might have dozed, but when she opened her eyes, she felt no more rested than when she had first taken to her bed. Eventually Jon returned and made the announcement she feared and dreaded the most.

The carriage wheel could not be immediately replaced. At the very least, they would be staying for the night.

The news Jon received the following morning from the blacksmith was not encouraging. The wheel was unrepairable and it would take most of the day to have a new one properly made. The blacksmith also expressed concern over the strength of the other three wheels and recommended that they all be changed.

The village wheelwright was sent for and he agreed with the blacksmith's assessment. Jon offered both men a generous bonus if they could complete the work by early afternoon, and though they expressed doubts about meeting that deadline, they promised to try their best.

Jon was worried about his wife. Emma had barely eaten any of the meal they were served and took to her bed directly after. As expected, adjoining chambers had been prepared for them. Emma had not invited him to her bed, and though he wanted very much to hold her in his arms while she slept, he had not intruded upon her privacy.

She needed her rest after the shock of the accident. Her physical well-being was paramount, and even though the doctor had proclaimed her injuries minor and predicated they would heal quickly, Jon knew she was clearly not herself.

She was still restless and agitated when she joined him for breakfast this morning. When questioned, she insisted her anxious mood was a result of the carriage accident and her eagerness to return home.

Seeing her so distraught and unlike herself was troubling, and Jon was determined to resume their journey as soon as possible. And damn it, if they had to spend a second night here, he was going to do so in the same bed with his wife.

His mind on Emma, Jon entered the house through a side door and wound his way toward the center entrance foyer. The house was typical of its era—a rabbit warren of numerous chambers that one could easily mistake for another. He realized that he had made a wrong turn the moment he rounded a corner and none of the rooms or furniture looked familiar.

He started to retrace his steps, yet paused when he noticed that he had stumbled upon the family portrait gallery. Curious to learn something about their absent host, Jon strolled down the long corridor, its walls covered from floor to ceiling with framed paintings.

The first portrait he came upon was a family grouping. A father, mother, and six children of various heights and ages. They were stiffly posed and wore solemn expressions. He identified the clothing and hairstyles from the Tudor period and surmised this must be the generation that designed some of the gardens he noticed this morning.

He continued down the long corridor, noticing a resemblance of features, hair and eye color, even body size in the generations of men and women that followed.

Jon paused before the portrait of a dour-looking fellow with long, dark, flowing hair that cascaded around his face in ringlets. He wore an open-throated gold silk doublet trimmed at the collar and sleeves with lace, and matching gold silk breeches in the shape of a bellows, which were tied at the knee with cream-colored ribbons.

The tall, high-heeled boots fitted up his leg were turned down to create a wide cuff that showed off the silk lining inside. Completing the outfit was a broad-brimmed hat sporting a fluffy white feather in the brim. He was posed in a flowering garden, standing beside a stunning black horse.

Jon leaned closer to read the date on the painting, confirming this was done after the war and before the Restoration of the monarchy and the crowning of Charles II. He briefly wondered how this Royalist supporter of King Charles I was able to keep his title, property, and head after the bloody Civil War and trial and execution of the king.

Apparently, this was a family of political survivors.

He strolled farther, stopping when he reached the prominent central location in the gallery. The portrait displayed here was smaller than many of the others, but it easily dominated the room, for it depicted a man of power, prestige, and passion.

Each detail, from the wave in the man's hair to the pose of his body, was alive with an intoxicating vibrancy.

The humor in the subject's eyes glittered wickedly, the slight smile hinted at all sorts of naughty secrets. Instead of being haughty or arrogant, his confidence and sense of self-worth radiated from the canvas in an almost casual way.

And why not? He was a handsome vision of male perfection, a resplendent figure devoid of faults and weakness, yet surprisingly human.

He was not dressed as formally as his ancestors and instead wore a white shirt, simply tied cravat, single-breasted bottle-green jacket, buckskin breeches that left little to the imagination, and black Hessians.

"Lord Kendall! Oh, dear, by chance are you lost?" Mrs. St. Giles questioned.

Turning, Jon smiled charmingly at the housekeeper. "Perhaps I have made a wrong turn or two, though I refuse, on principle, to admit it. Men have a primal need to believe they possess an inherent sense of direction, you know."

"And they do like to joke about it," Mrs. St. Giles replied with a smile. "Are you enjoying the paintings?"

"They are quite remarkable. I recognize several of the artists from my brief introduction to art history at university." He spun back to the central portrait. "Though I am unfamiliar with this artist's work. The modern clothing suggests that this is the current earl?"

"Ah, yes." She nodded her head enthusiastically. "That is Lord Tinsdale. 'Tis a most extraordinary painting, is it not, filled with life and excitement. One half expects to hear him speak. I've caught many a housemaid mooning over it when they should be dusting or sweeping these floors."

"Is it an accurate likeness?" Jon had to ask. "Or did

the artist seek to improve his commission by flattering his subject?"

"The earl is an impressive-looking nobleman," Mrs. St. Giles said with a slight blush. "I've always admired the painting for its beautiful realism and the intense feelings it evokes. Though truthfully, no one is such a perfect specimen, one who can make all others appear insignificant by comparison."

"'Tis most exceptional," Jon agreed.

Mrs. St. Giles nodded, then cocked her head thoughtfully. "My personal theory is that the portrait was painted by a woman, who was deeply enamored with her subject."

"That was my first impression too." Jon stepped back and squinted at the painting. "Each brush stroke is a sonnet of love."

"I agree. Which further strengthens the theory that the artist is female."

"His wife?" Jon wondered.

"Oh, no." Mrs. St. Giles shook her head. "The countess is an accomplished lady with many talents, but I've never seen her with a brush in hand."

"Are there any other paintings by the same artist hanging anywhere in the house?" Jon asked, curious to see if the style remained the same with other subjects.

"Not that I can find," Mrs. St. Giles replied. "There is no signature on the earl's portrait, but the style is so unique, so distinct, 'twould be easy to locate any others."

"A female portrait artist is a rarity. 'Tis a shame so little is known about the painter," he muttered.

"The only hint of the artist's identity are the interlocking initials barely visible in the bottom right corner," Mrs. St. Giles said as she pointed toward the portrait.

Moving closer, Jon leaned in until his nose was almost touching the work. There, in pale cream, he saw the entwining letters. E E.

The loops on the letters had a vague familiarity, as did the way they were conjoined. Jon stood, stretching his back. His mind wandered, struggling to remember. Frowning, he bent a second time, his eyes fixating on those letters.

E. E.

E. E.

E for Emma? Second E for Ellingham?

E. E. Emma Ellingham.

No. 'Tis impossible. It couldn't be my Emma.

Yet even as he sought to convince himself that he was mistaken, Jon knew that he had stumbled upon the truth. He had never seen any of Emma's oil paintings. His only exposure to her work had been the sketches of his machine that she shared with him.

She had signed one of those sketches with her initials. The distinct looping and intertwining of the two letters were the same as those in the portrait of the earl.

Though he wished to deny it, the evidence was indisputable. Emma had painted this portrait. Emma was the artist clearly in love with her subject. For a moment he felt stunned, as though someone had landed a solid punch to his gut.

Jon looked again at the painting. What had happened between Emma and this man? According to the servants, the earl was happily married, the father of several children.

Yet clearly that had not always been the case.

"By any chance, do you know when the picture was painted, Mrs. St. Giles?" Jon asked, attempting to shake himself out of his shock. "It isn't dated."

"I'm sorry, I don't know. The portrait was hanging in place when I arrived five years ago to take up my position as housekeeper." She wrinkled her nose. "I could ask Mr. Everly. He might know."

"No need," Jon said hastily. "I was merely curious."

The thread of jealousy started as a slow burn, gradually picking up speed until it burst into flames. It riled him. He took several deep breaths, trying to achieve a very elusive calm.

She had never spoken of it, never said a word, never even hinted that she had once deeply loved a man.

Obsessively loved a man.

Still loved him?

That notion stung with far more power than Jon could ever have imagined. Emma had been a virgin on their wedding night, but there were many ways to indulge in intimacy and carnal pleasures without sacrificing a woman's virginity.

Or perhaps nothing had happened between the pair. Perhaps they barely knew each other. Perhaps they had only spent an hour or two together for a few days, while the earl posed for his portrait.

Jon knew Emma's artistic process. She sketched first, then brought those sketches to life on canvas. This painting had hung here for at least five years. As a younger, more impressionable woman, Emma might have fallen in love with her subject.

That happened to artists sometimes, didn't it?

Or this could be more serious. This love for another man could explain Emma's initial resistance to their marriage. She had only agreed to the union under pressure from her sister. She had acquiesced only after he had practically blackmailed her with the dire consequences of a scandal.

Jon's breathing grew shallow as he theorized that the earl could be the reason Emma had shown such reluctance to marry. It made sense. Awful sense. It also explained why she had gone so pale when learning the identity of their host.

The carriage accident had been a shock, but the idea of seeing the earl was the true cause of her anxiety. Why? Had they vowed to remain apart for the sake of his marriage?

For that matter, why had the earl married another woman when he had Emma's love? Was the man a blind idiot? Any fool with just an ounce of wit and judgment was able to see that Emma was truly extraordinary.

Jon gave himself a mental shake. His emotions were jumbled and disjointed—his jealousy uncontrollable and unacceptable. Taking several deep breaths, he struggled to overcome the absurd desire to land a punch on the earl's perfectly sculpted jaw.

Mrs. St. Giles would think him mad if he attacked a painting—and she wouldn't be far off the mark. He fisted his hand, seeking to understand the unfamiliar yearning that suddenly filled his chest.

Seeing the depth and breadth of Emma's capacity to love triggered something deep inside him. It was, he realized with a jolt, the piece of her that had been missing from their relationship.

They had made a bargain in their marriage to be civil, agreeable, and respectful of each other. At the time, Jon believed it would be enough to share a satisfactory life together.

Seeing this painting made him realize that he was wrong. He wanted more. Much more. He wanted what was on this canvas—for himself. He wanted Emma to love him with the fire, passion, and intensity of her whole heart, her whole being.

Just as he loved her.

Emma stood at the window in her bedchamber, admiring the symmetrical patterns of the knot garden below. She could understand why such gardens had been so popular during the Tudor age. The order and structure of having everything so neatly defined and in its place was soothing as well as beautiful.

'Twas a symbol of control and purity in an otherwise wild and disordered landscape. The plants had been carefully laid out to give a woven, almost embroidered effect, in diamonds, triangles, and rectangles. She smiled faintly, remembering Sebastian once complaining about the expense of maintaining such an intricate design.

Flowers were scarce this early in the season, but the manor gardeners had cleverly substituted herbs, sand, gravel, stones, and crushed bricks to keep the gardens' lines well defined and colorful.

Emma sighed. If only her life could be so easily compartmentalized and ordered.

The clock struck the hour. Oh, Lord, hardly half the morning gone. Jon had not yet returned from checking on the carriage. Though she desperately wished for good news, she was trying to prepare herself for spending the day—and possibly another night—in Sebastian's home.

He's in London, she told herself sternly.

He could return at any moment.
Could fate really be so cruel?

Annoyed with herself for being so melancholy, Emma left the chamber. She made her way down the stairs and across the foyer, heading for the library. 'Twas doubtful she would be able to concentrate enough to fully comprehend what she was reading, but holding a book usually brought on a sense of calm.

Memory served her well, as she found the room without having to ask for directions. The first thing she noted was that someone—most likely Sebastian's wife—had done some redecorating.

Gone were the heavy wine-colored draperies, which had lent a decidedly masculine flare to the room. Without them, the chamber was flooded with sunlight, giving it a lighter, more inviting feel. Emma grudgingly admitted 'twas an improvement.

One thing that had remained unchanged was the sideboard stocked with decanters of spirits. Giving in to the temptation, she crossed the room.

Emma lifted a crystal stopper from the decanter with the smallest amount of liquid, deciding that it must contain the best-tasting one, since it was nearly empty. Selecting a snifter from the assortment of glasses on the silver tray, Emma poured herself a small portion. She downed it in one large gulp, somehow managing not to cough as the alcohol burned its way along her throat.

It hit her empty stomach and spread, flushing her with warmth. The sensation was extreme and distracting—exactly what she sought. Sadly, it was fleeting. She contemplated the decanter for a long moment, considering a second portion, then turned away.

Using alcohol to dull her senses was hardly the answer.

Broodingly, Emma studied the titles on the spines of the leather-bound books, moving to a different shelf when she realized those were all in Latin.

The library door opened. Arms filled with several volumes, Emma peered over her shoulder. Her husband stood a few feet away.

"Jon," she said. "I thought a book might help occupy the hours. I feel all at sixes and sevens today."

"A book?"

"Well, several. 'Tis hard to choose." She set the books on a table and turned to face him. "Is our carriage repaired? Will we be able to depart soon?"

"The blacksmith and wheelwright are working on it." He tilted his head. "Though they have warned me the repairs are extensive and could take several days."

Emma blanched at the idea. There was no guarantee that Sebastian would stay in London indefinitely. Every day, nay, every hour they remained here increased the chances of seeing him.

"Several days? Goodness. Perhaps there is a carriage in the village we could hire? Or we could ask Mr. Everly if it would be possible to borrow one of the earl's coaches."

"We could." Jon propped one shoulder against the nearest bookcase and watched her.

A nervous frisson rolled through her stomach. "I don't know what I was thinking, selecting all these books. They are far too serious for my mood.

"Perhaps a stroll in the fresh air is a better idea. There is an old-fashioned knot garden on the south side of the house and a quiet footpath that leads to a small lake on the opposite side. Either would provide a lovely distraction. Will you join me?"

He settled an intent look on her. "You seem to know a good deal about the house, Emma."

A tingle of alarm ran down her spine. "Do I? Well, Mrs. St. Giles does like to talk. She is especially fond of relating the history of the manor."

She refused to address his question directly, knowing she couldn't lie to him. He deserved far better from her. Yet she could not tell him the truth either.

He trapped her in his gaze. "I've been exploring the house too."

"Oh?" She turned away and caught the ghost of her reflection in the mullioned windowpane. Was she really that pale or was it a trick of the light? "How about the grounds, Jon? Have you seen any of the grounds?"

She could sense him coming toward her, moving with deliberate slowness. Emma turned. The emotion in his eyes had deepened their color.

Panic snatched at her throat. *He knows! But that is impossible. No one knows. Stop it! 'Tis my nerves. They are causing me to be fanciful.*

"I would be delighted to see the grounds with you," Jon said softly. "Lead the way, Emma."

Her trepidation slowly receded and her breathing resumed a normal rhythm. Threading her arm through his, Emma leaned heavily against her husband as they left the library and walked outside into the sunshine.

Chapter Seventeen

They left the manor directly after luncheon in a vehicle hired from the village. It was not nearly as comfortable nor as luxurious as their own carriage, but Emma didn't care. She would have gladly ridden in an ox cart to escape that house.

To escape her past.

She leaned back against the worn cushion and sighed. Jon covered the hand resting on the seat between them with his own and squeezed gently.

"I promise we'll be home in four days, Emma."

She forced a smile. He had been especially solicitous these last few hours. She appreciated his concern and his willingness to ease her discomfort, especially since he had no real notion of why she had been so unsettled.

His caring nature was a quality she had sensed from the first time she met him, and she was grateful every time she confirmed that it was solid and true.

Jon squeezed her hand again, then began to stroke his thumb across the top of her ungloved fingers, in a slow, sensual glide. Emma felt herself blush. She glanced at him, expecting to meet a pair of heavy-lidded, passionate eyes. Yet he wasn't even looking at her. His head was angled toward the window, the expression on his handsome face intent.

Clearly his mind was preoccupied. Most likely he was working through calculations in his head for his machines. 'Twas almost as though he wasn't even aware of what he was doing, as though his need to touch her was instinctual.

Emma's heart warmed at the notion of being so needed, so necessary. One would think it would feel restricting, suffocating.

It didn't.

As Jon had predicted, they arrived home within four days. Weary from travel and being confined in the coach for so long, Emma emerged to the excited barks of Sir Galahad.

The great black beast escaped his leash and charged her, nearly knocking her off her feet. Laughing, she knelt to receive his sloppy, wet kisses.

"Only a dog can love with such unconditional devotion and enthusiasm," Emma declared, laying her cheek against the top of his large, square head.

Jon glanced down at her, his expression somewhat disconcerting. "Is that what you think?"

"Well, that's been my experience," Emma replied as she stroked the dog's ears. "Dogs are the most faithful companions; never judgmental, always eager to please and show their affections."

"You know, people can surprise you, Emma, if you just give them the chance."

Uncertain what to make of that remark, she stared up at her husband. His gaze had turned tender. She blinked.

First there was his physical affection in the carriage and now these cryptic words that seemed to carry some hidden meaning. For a moment she found it difficult to gather her thoughts, but the mood was soon shattered by the whack of an enthusiastic tail to her side.

With a small yelp, Emma gripped Sir Galahad's back to keep her balance. "I hope that he hasn't been too much trouble for the staff while I was away," she said, trying to cover the awkward moment.

"I'm sure he's been an absolute terror," Jon said in mock horror. "More than likely, I shall have to give each of the servants a gold sovereign for putting up with the mangy beast."

"He is not mangy, my lord," Emma protested with a smile. "He is a most handsome fellow, with a coat that shines like velvet."

The dog lifted his head and preened, almost as though he knew they were speaking about him. Laughing, Emma accepted Jon's outstretched hand and stood. He caught her eyes and focused on her with such searing attention she felt her senses start to expand.

The musky scent of his shaving soap filled her nostrils. She felt a glow of sensation where their hands touched, and the longing to lift herself closer and press her lips to his became a startling ache.

His eyes seemed darker and more intense than usual and his mouth boasted a hint of a sensual, devious smile. Her vision blurred as she felt the heat blazing over her flesh, imagining the pleasure she would experience from his hands and mouth.

Moments passed, but their gazes held—his filled with a raw, primal, possessive resolve, hers no doubt filled with longing and confusion.

He reached up and with the back of his fingers, skimming a tender caress slowly down her cheek. Breathing unevenly, Emma felt her body slowly dissolve into a wave of need.

This was quite peculiar. Not her reaction—she had long ago acknowledged that Jon had the power to move her swiftly to desire. Yet she could not remember ever being such an intent object of interest to her husband. Especially while they were in such a public setting.

What in the world had gotten into him?

At that moment a flash of lightning lit the darkening sky, followed by an explosion of thunder. The raindrops hit, fat and cold, snapping the mood and drenching them in short order.

Jon grabbed Emma's hand and pulled her forward. They ran the long distance to the front door, laughing like a pair of mischievous children, a barking Sir Galahad leading the way. Once inside, Emma squirmed with discomfort as she felt the cold water trickle down her back.

Her hair was thoroughly wet, the front of her gown exposed through her cloak, soaked to the point of being nearly transparent. She tried brushing some of the moisture away from her skirt just as Sir Galahad gained her side.

The dog shook himself vigorously from head to tail. Jon yelped and stepped back, but Emma was not quick enough to avoid the shower of water droplets that flew through the air.

Jon fixed the dog with a stern stare, then motioned for one of the servants. A nervous young footman stepped forward, looking momentarily perplexed at the prospect of removing the large animal without losing his dignity.

Or any of his fingers.

Inspiration must have struck, for he jammed his hand into his coat pocket and announced happily, "Would you like a treat, boy?"

Sir Galahad raised his head immediately, his eyes fixated on the footman's hand hidden inside the pocket. The clever servant wiggled his fingers and backed away. The dog eagerly followed.

Emma worried what might happen once Sir Galahad discovered there was no treat to be had, but she was confident that the dog's gentle nature would prevent him from exacting any revenge for being tricked. Of course, if the footman was truly clever, he would head straight for the kitchen and procure a morsel of bacon to toss to the dog.

Frankly, anything edible would do. Sir Galahad was not in the least bit fussy when it came to food.

"You're soaked to the skin," Jon lamented, brushing a damp tendril of hair off Emma's forehead.

"I'll be fine once I'm out of these wet clothes," Emma replied, trying unsuccessfully to keep her teeth from chattering.

"Have a hot bath prepared for Lady Kendall at once," Jon called to a footman as he lifted her off her feet and into his arms.

Emma noticed several of the servants' jaws drop upon witnessing the dashing move. She drew in a deep breath to protest that she was perfectly capable of walking up the stairs on her own, but then his arms tightened around her.

Muscles rippling, Jon held her in an iron grip. She leaned against his broad chest, hearing the steady beat of his heart beneath the layers of his clothing. He carried her with ease, up the staircase, through the long corridor to her bedchamber.

Dory was waiting and the maid's eyes nearly popped from her head when Jon burst through the door.

"Is her ladyship ill?" the maid asked in a worried tone.

"She's wet, and I don't want her catching a chill," Jon replied.

He set her on her feet and flung off her wet cloak, handing it off to a waiting Dory. The maid went to the far side of the chamber and shook the garment vigorously before hanging it outside the wardrobe to dry.

Hands on her waist, Jon swung Emma around. She blushed as she felt his hands reach to unhook the buttons down the back of her gown.

"Jon."

"Hmm."

"Jon!"

"What? I'm moving as quickly as I can, Emma, but these damn buttons are so tiny."

Emma's lips curved into a smile. "Dory can help me, Jon. Her hands are much smaller than yours."

She looked over her shoulder at him. For an instant he seemed as surprised as she was by his actions. Then he cleared his throat and lowered his chin.

"Of course. I'll leave her to it." Fidgeting with the end of his coat, he executed a short bow. "I'll see you at dinner."

And then he was gone.

Jon watched Sir Galahad cuddle beside his wife on the brocade settee and idly wondered how he could get the beast to leave Emma's side without causing a ruckus. The damn creature had been her shadow since they returned from their travels today, even going so far as to emit a low snarl when Jon had placed his arm around her waist while escorting her from the dining table.

Emma had instantly scolded the animal and the beast had succeeded in looking both chastised and contrite. However, the dog had followed them into the drawing room and settled himself comfortably on the furniture beside his mistress, his head resting in her lap.

Jon had poured himself a snifter of brandy and taken the chair opposite the pair. Emma had opened a book and began reading. She held the volume in her left hand and with the right, casually stroked the dog's ears.

Lucky beast. Jon tossed back the last sip of his drink and set the glass aside. He brooded for a few minutes, staring at his wife and her pet, finally admitting the embarrassing truth.

He was jealous of a dog. Was it possible to sink any lower?

"Have I told you how lovely you look this evening, Emma?"

She looked up from her book and touched a hand self-consciously to her hair. "Dory has been practicing with the curling tongs while we were away."

That was obvious. However, the young maid had learned some restraint, and the cascade of curls framing Emma's face in loose spirals enhanced rather than overpowered her delicate features.

"She has become quite accomplished," Jon offered.

Emma nodded, then returned her attention to her book. And the damn dog.

However, the silence wasn't uncomfortable, which made Jon feel grateful. In the short time they had been married they had managed to find a comfortable footing in their relationship, develop closeness, an easy way of talking—or remaining quiet—when they were together.

Was all that about to change now that he knew the truth about his feelings for his wife? That was a risk.

Jon steepled his hands together in front of him and considered Emma for a long minute. She was unique, special. There were no other women of his acquaintance who would have endured the most absurdly elaborate hairstyles in order to build the confidence of a young, insecure maid.

He could name no others who appreciated the simple pleasures of art and nature with the passion and reverence that Emma did, who admired his scientific achievements and showed genuine interest in his work. Who valued the reputation of her family so strongly that she had married him to avoid a scandal.

A sensation radiated through his chest like a shot, a deep, almost burning feeling that had nothing to do with the brandy he had just consumed. It was strong. True. Real.

Love.

He admitted that he had deliberately misread the signs, ignored the feelings. This was very different from what he had felt for Dianna, for the basic reason that it was mature. A love for a woman he admired, not worshiped. A real woman, with character, integrity, and heart.

He wanted to tell her, but he didn't know how Emma would react to hearing it. Love had never been a part of their original bargain. When he had proposed, he hadn't wanted to promise something that he was uncertain he could give.

Yet he knew now how much he wanted Emma to have his love. And he selfishly admitted he craved her love in return. He reasoned that since he could no longer conceal the truth from himself, why should he continue to conceal the truth from her?

Why, indeed?

Once he had admitted that he wanted her, needed

her, his mind could not stop thinking about it. He wanted their relationship to move forward and he struggled with devising the best way to make that happen.

The problem, he freely acknowledged, was that he was approaching this in his usual analytical, scientific manner. A grave mistake, as there was nothing reasonable or logical about love—it simply existed.

A discreet knock on the door pulled Jon away from his thoughts. Hopson entered, his eyes widening when he caught sight of the dog stretched out on the settee. Jon couldn't decide if his butler was amused or appalled at the notion of the animal being allowed such liberties.

"Shall I take Sir Galahad off to his bed now, my lady?" Hopson inquired.

"In the kennels?" Emma asked.

Her voice was so woeful and filled with concern that for a moment Jon feared she was going to make the absurd suggestion that the beast sleep in her chambers.

"Cook has developed a great fondness for the dog and has made a place for him in the kitchens," the butler replied, his tone conveying a hint of disapproval. "He is most content sleeping on a pile of old blankets in front of the hearth."

"And as a bonus, the dog provides excellent security should someone decide to enter the manor through the kitchens," Jon added, almost making it sound as though it was entirely his idea.

Truthfully, he had no shame and would gladly steal the credit for the arrangement, if it pleased Emma.

"That is a most satisfactory solution," Emma said. "Sir Galahad is, after all, a member of the household.

'Tis only proper that he stay inside with us through the night."

Stroking the dog's head a final time, Emma proceeded to nudge him off the settee. 'Twas no small feat to move a beast of that size, but a determined Emma managed.

Once standing, Sir Galahad's black nose began twitching. He looked toward Hopson and Jon noticed the butler held a raw piece of beef between his thumb and forefinger. His interest thoroughly captured, the dog bounded toward the butler without a second glance at Emma.

Hopson managed to back out of the room with a surprising amount of decorum and somehow remain on his feet as the animal pranced excitedly around him.

"I believe Hopson has done that before," Jon remarked, and Emma nodded her head in agreement.

She brushed the black dog hairs off the gold settee, smoothing back the fabric on the matching pillows. "I'm sure you think I am being ridiculous to fuss so much over a dog," she said.

"The great black beast makes you happy, Emma. And that, in turn, pleases me." Jon squared his shoulders. "Though you must agree that he will become completely impossible if you continue to spoil him."

"I know." Emma bit back the smile on her lips and threw him a mischievous glance. "Yet I find it difficult to stop."

"I give you fair warning, my dear, when he starts sitting in a chair and joining us at the table for meals, I will put my foot down."

Emma's musical laughter filled the room. Jon felt his heart tip. More and more this intense feeling of love was at the forefront of his thoughts and he wondered how long he could keep from speaking about it.

"Armed with the cheerful image of my beloved dog eating dinner at the table with us, I shall take myself off to bed," Emma announced, walking toward the door.

Pulled from his musings, Jon composed his features into a pleasant countenance and extended his hand. Without hesitating for a moment, Emma stopped and grasped it.

Hand in hand they climbed the staircase, turning down the corridor that led to their bedchambers when they reached the landing. Jon's door was first. Emma tried to gently disengage her hand so he could retire to his room, but he held on tightly.

Startled, she looked up. Jon's brow rose. "No need to look like a fox fleeing from a pack of barking hounds. I was merely going to suggest that you join me in my bedchamber."

"For a nightcap?"

He quirked an eyebrow at her. "If you'd like."

Her lips curled into a sheepish smile. "A glass of strong spirits will certainly put me right to sleep."

He leaned close and whispered. "Drat. That was not precisely what I had in mind."

Jon opened the door and gestured for her to enter. Blinking away the sudden surge of emotions stirring in her chest, Emma sailed inside. They had not shared a bed since the night of the spring dance, when their lovemaking had been passionate and frenzied.

In the turmoil of the past few days, Emma had not realized how much she missed their physical intimacy. The wild release never failed to leave her contented and filled with a momentary sense of peace.

The moment he spied her, Jon's valet discreetly withdrew. With effort, Emma contained her blush. She felt like a child who had just been caught snatching sweets from the tea tray. Which was foolish. She was Jon's wife—she had every right to join him in his chambers.

There was a fire blazing in the hearth and numerous lit candles. The scent of beeswax with an undertone of smoke drifted through the air, lending an almost erotic element to the room.

Feeling restless, Emma crossed the room. Her fingers glided curiously over the objects she found on the dresser. An elegant sapphire stickpin, a hairbrush and comb, an assortment of shaving implements. She lifted the pot of soft soap and dipped the tip of her little finger inside, inhaling the fresh scent of sandalwood and lemon.

She listened for the sound of liquid being poured into glasses behind her, but instead heard Jon removing his jacket and pulling off his cravat. Hastily returning the pot to its proper location, Emma whirled around.

She stilled when she noticed that he ceased undressing and was watching her. His mouth was pressed in a thin line, his expression almost blank, but his eyes told a different story. They were ringed with desire.

"I've missed you in my bed, Emma."

A quiver ran through her at the sound of his deep, husky voice, settling in a rush of warmth low in her belly. She tilted her head and offered him a shy smile.

Fire kindled in his eyes. He came quickly toward her and wrapped his arms around her in the fiercest hug she had ever been given. Frozen with surprise,

Emma stood motionless, but then she lifted her arms and hugged him back.

It was a quiet, tender moment. Her body relaxed, lulled by the strength and warmth of his familiar embrace. Emma marveled at how perfectly she fit in his arms, how safe and cherished he could make her feel. She opened her mouth to tell him, but then suddenly felt a brush of cool air on her back.

The rogue! While she had been finding comfort nuzzling into his warm strength, Jon's clever fingers had expertly unfastened the back of her gown. It gapped open from her neck to her waist.

"You are wearing too many clothes, dearest," he remarked as he easily slid the bodice of her evening gown down to her waist, then pushed it past her hips.

She said nothing as he continued to peel away her garments, his eyes growing heavier with desire as her flesh was slowly revealed. Kneeling before her, Jon cupped her ankle and lifted her foot and she obediently stepped out of her shimmering dress.

Emma gasped as he slid his hand slowly, sensually up her leg to the garter high on her thigh. Hooking it with his finger, he pulled it down, then returned to the top of her thigh and carefully rolled down her silk stockings. Flashing a wicked grin, he repeated the actions with her other leg.

Her breath was coming in short, quick pants when he finished. Jon stood, his heated eyes roaming her body. Emma knew he could see the dark circle of her nipples through the sheer fabric of her chemise and the patch of hair between her legs.

She felt a moment of embarrassment, but his eyes told her how beautiful he found her and that gave her the courage to preen before him, which seemed to delight him even further.

He unbuttoned his waistcoat and stripped off his shirt, pulling it over his head and tossing it aside. She licked her lips when his fingers went to the buttons of his breeches, her body humming with anticipation.

He removed her stays and chemise before pulling her naked body into his embrace. With a sigh, Jon pressed his lips to her neck, then moved her cascading ringlets aside to expose more of her flesh to his questing mouth. Bright sensations danced down Emma's spine at the touch of his lips and tongue, and she dug her fingers into the taut muscles of his arms.

He lifted her onto the bed, then climbed in after her. She lay down, but he didn't lie beside her. Instead, he sat in the middle of the bed and crooked his finger, beckoning her to him.

Intrigued, Emma crawled over on her hands and knees, gasping when he pulled her into a sitting position and raised her onto his lap. She lifted her chin and gazed trustingly into his eyes, then following his throaty instructions, wrapped her legs around his waist.

She momentarily blushed at being so wantonly open and exposed, but Jon's warm hands slid sensually across her body, fondling, stroking, arousing, and any embarrassment was swallowed in the heat of her arousal.

He captured her lips in small kisses, teasing her with his tongue. Squirming against his solid strength, Emma felt the hairs on his chest teasing her nipples into stiff peaks, inciting a damp, moist heat between her legs.

"Are you certain this is going to work?" she whispered, resting her arms around his neck.

"Magnificently," he answered, his eyes lighting with sensual devilry. "I promise."

She felt his penis against her belly, hot and heavy, reminding her of how glorious it felt when their bodies were joined. Cupping her buttocks, he tugged her higher, then guided her body as she slowly sank onto him.

She was shocked into stillness at the tight fullness, but then her body relaxed and took him deeper. His hands moved to her hips and he helped her find a rhythm that soon had them both straining together in frantic encouragement.

Emma whimpered as she felt him slide deeper and instinctively tightened her inner muscles. Pleasure swirled from her core, crested, then crashed as ripples of sensation tore through her, which left her shaking so hard the bed shook.

Jon matched her rhythm and then she heard his breathing suddenly stop as his climax broke. He burrowed his head against her cheek and groaned loudly. Emma curled her fingers through his hair, caressing his satiny locks while his body shook and shuddered.

He clasped her to him, pressing kisses to her breasts, neck, chin, and face. Then he raised his mouth close to her ear and whispered, "Oh, how I love you, my sweet Emma."

Hearing those words brought a rush of pure delight to her heart, followed swiftly by a pang of remorse. She angled her head and gazed into his eyes, fighting away the tears.

"My dearest," she whispered back.

Her response made him smile, as she hoped it would. But the apprehension that gripped her was impossible to ignore. She did care for him—very much. Yet while the notion of love made her heart ache with longing, she was not prepared to make a declaration until she was sure—completely certain—it was the truth.

Slowly, she uncoupled herself from him. Jon stretched out and she snuggled close, cradling her head on his chest. His steady, even breathing told her that he was starting to fall asleep and she prayed it would happen quickly. If not, Jon might be compelled to say more about his feelings and even worse, expect the same from her.

If that occurred, Emma greatly feared her composure would crack and if she spoke, her voice would betray her uncertainty. Just the thought of hurting Jon brought a sick fluttering deep in her stomach, a knot of pain to her chest. No, 'twas best to leave things unsaid, to rest and face this when her emotions and doubts were not so overwhelming.

She stretched her arm behind her, pulled the covers over them and closed her eyes. But she couldn't sleep. Those softly spoken words, the depth of emotions in Jon's eyes, haunted her.

Oh, how I love you, my sweet Emma.

His love—given so freely and completely. She wasn't worthy of it. Kind, honorable, wonderful Jon was offering to fill the empty places she always feared to acknowledge existed in her heart.

And she didn't know what to do.

He deserved more from her. She felt as though she was cheating her husband, cheating herself. She needed to fully open her heart to him or else she would lose her future. Their future.

She wanted to do it. Yearned to do it. Her chest ached, reaching for something she couldn't attain. Her past haunted her like a merciless ghost and though she tried, she was unable to get beyond it.

There has to be a way.

She closed her eyes and searched her mind and the answer sprang forth, longing and desperation pushing it forward. The very thought made her cold with fear, but she knew it was right and necessary.

She had to confront her past.

She had to see Sebastian.

Chapter Eighteen

Faint sunlight invaded the bedchamber. Jon opened his eyes, confirming what his body already knew—he was alone in bed.

Had Emma slipped away in the middle of the night? Or had she waited until first light to escape? Either notion was disheartening and a reminder of the precarious situation he had now placed himself.

Giving in to his urge last night to declare his love for Emma had not gone precisely as he had hoped. Their lovemaking had been pure pleasure, heightened by intense emotions. Fully satisfied, his mind and body feeling lax and lazy, he had spoken from the heart.

She had responded by calling him *my dearest*. A term of endearment, most assuredly. But not a clear declaration of love. A subtle, yet very important difference.

Jon slung back the covers and left the warm bed, certain he didn't want to examine that turn of events too closely.

He had just finished washing and shaving with the chilly water from the pitcher on his dresser when Gilmore arrived. The valet was horrified to discover

Jon had already attended to himself and dressed without assistance, and even further distressed to learn that he had used cold water.

Ignoring the servant's fussing, Jon made his way to the dining room. His heart sped up at the thought of seeing Emma, but there was only a footman in the room, who hastened to the kitchen and returned with a line of servants who quickly set out a selection of hot food on the sideboard.

"Has her ladyship ordered a breakfast tray for her bedchamber?" Jon asked the footman.

"No, my lord," the footman replied. "Lady Kendall has gone to call on Lady Atwood."

Jon stared at the servant, uncomprehending for a moment. "She rode to Ravenswood Manor at this hour of the morning?"

The footman looked confused. "Lady Kendall indicated that she was expected."

Surprised, Jon digested that bit of information. "Did she leave a note for me?"

"No, my lord."

What was so important that Emma had to go to her sister at such an early hour? And why hadn't she told him? Jon quashed the urge to question the servant further. It was hardly the footman's fault that Emma had neglected to tell her husband of her early morning plans.

"Did she take the beast with her?" Jon inquired, brushing the toast crumbs from his fingers.

The footman nodded. "Lady Kendall's pet was following her when she went to the stables."

The area bordering the two estates was safe, yet it gave Jon a sense of relief knowing that Emma had a protector with her.

Letting out a tight breath, Jon walked at a fast clip

to the stables. The sun had risen high enough to brighten the ground, the sky was a clear, brilliant blue. If he wasn't so out of sorts over his wife's behavior, he would have enjoyed the fine weather.

The head groom came forward, touching his hand respectfully to his cap in greeting.

"Have Hercules saddled, please," Jon requested, naming his favorite mount.

The groom bowed and disappeared into the stables. Jon tugged on his riding gloves, smiling his thanks when the horse arrived.

"He's feeling frisky this morning," the stable master warned, as Jon mounted the chestnut gelding.

"Excellent. I'm in the mood for a bruising ride," Jon replied, adjusting his hold on the reins.

He was sorely tempted to ride to Atwood's estate, but decided that trailing after his wife like a lovestruck lad was hardly an attractive image. Instead, he turned his mount in the opposite direction.

Riding hard with the horse's heavy hooves thundering beneath him, Jon urged his mount on, his heart hammering as he bolted across the fields. It was exhilarating to feel the wind in his face and the warmth of the sun on his back, to smell the freshness of the earth. He heard a rooster crow in the distance, a sleepy fellow, as the dawn was well behind them.

Birds flew from the hedgerows when he passed, squawking loudly as they took flight. He slowed only when the terrain became rougher, reluctantly pulling up on the reins. Hercules was sweating and snorting, blowing puffs of breath into the air.

Deciding they both could use a rest, Jon vaulted off the horse. Taking the reins loosely in his hand, he began walking, making certain not to exert any pressure to avoid hurting Hercules's mouth.

All was peaceful. His pensive mood continued and he slowed his strides, trying to appreciate the beauty of his surroundings.

"Jon."

Senses roused to alertness, he spun around, catching himself before uttering the curse that was on the tip of his tongue. Standing beneath a tree, the black ribbons of her bonnet flapping in the breeze, stood Dianna. Even dressed in her widow's weeds, she looked fresh, lovely, and impossibly young.

"Dianna! What are you doing so far from home?"

"Hoping to see you." She approached slowly, moving deliberately. "I spied you riding along the ridge and thought there was a good chance that you would turn in this direction."

Jon frowned incredulously. "Is there a particular reason why you didn't call at the house?"

Dianna's hand fluttered to her throat. "You might recall that my last visit was rather uncomfortable. I thought it best if we speak alone. May we walk together?"

Unease prickled over his skin as he considered her for a moment. Her eyes were ringed with a wounded sadness and an aura of loneliness hung around her like a shroud. Logic told him to move on; however, the gentleman in him found it difficult to abandon a lady in distress.

Ignoring his misgivings, he nodded in agreement.

Looking over her shoulder, Jon saw that Dianna's horse was tied to a low-hanging branch. He did the same with his own mount. The grass was high and damp along the path they walked; he could see the beads of moisture gathering on his boots. He altered his longer strides to keep pace with hers, though he did *not* offer her his arm, as that felt like a far too intimate gesture.

They crossed the bridge where as a young boy he used to stand with his father and fish. Jon's mood lightened at the pleasant memory. He had been fortunate to have grown up on this estate, a happy lad with loving parents. The good Lord willing, he would someday share it with his own children.

Dianna cried out suddenly, her boots slipping on the wet grass. Instinctively, Jon reached for her, encircling her waist to keep her steady. She stumbled into him, her hands grasping his lapels to keep from tumbling to the ground. Their gazes locked and she cast him an intimate look from beneath her lashes.

"You once said that a man would have to be blind not to love me," she said wistfully. "Do you remember?"

Damnation. Their close contact heightened his awareness of her. It was both disturbing and annoying. What game was she playing at now?

"I do remember." He gave her a cold glance. "However, these days my eyes are trained firmly upon my wife. Whom I adore."

Without missing a beat, he pried her hands off his coat and thrust her away, making certain Dianna understood he had no interest in her—at all.

She heaved a deep sigh of resignation. "I realized far too late that with you, I was loved and treasured in a way few women ever experience. You looked at me as though there was nothing in the world more important than being with me, making me happy, seeing me smile. I was a fool to throw it all so impulsively away."

A part of him knew he should simply let go of the past, yet he couldn't resist asking, "Why did you?"

She twisted her hands together. "I was young and naïve and filled with nonsensical romantic dreams. I thought Gerald was the epitome of everything I dreamt of in a man. Handsome, brash, and brave. He was exciting, a tad wicked, even scandalous. I admired his sophistication, was enchanted by his charm. He told me repeatedly that I would regret marrying for convenience and practicality instead of passion."

Jon cringed. "God, was I really that dull and boring?"

"Oh, no." She leaned closer, her eyes searching his. "You were a gentleman. My head was turned by the insincere flattery of a rake. I've spent most of this past year filled with regret and wishing with all my heart that I had been a better person and not such a shallow, silly girl."

Jon supposed he should feel a sense of triumph, even vindication at hearing those words, yet he couldn't. Not in the face of such misery. "Regrets serve no useful purpose other than inflicting further unhappiness."

"Wise words." She gave a short laugh. "Impossible to follow, though."

"If I've learned anything this past year, it is that you are responsible for your own happiness in this life."

"Tell me, Jon, do you follow your own advice?" Her tone was low and intense. "Are you happy?"

"I am," he replied emphatically, though he knew in his heart it was a partial truth. But he was hopeful and determined to achieve the happiness with Emma that he felt was within his grasp.

"I'm glad. You deserve to be happy." Dianna's eyes were downcast, but there was a sense of determination in the way she held her shoulders high and straight. "I'll be leaving soon. The title and lands have passed to the next Baron Brayer. He is expected to arrive within the month and the solicitors have told me in no uncertain terms that I must vacate the house before that time."

"Surely your parents have forgiven you by now." He narrowed his eyes at her. "Why don't you stay with them?"

Dianna's body twitched and shuddered. "They won't have me, though truthfully 'tis a blessing. Life with them would be nothing but constant lectures and reminders of how I have disappointed and disgraced them.

"I was bequeathed a very modest widow's portion," she continued, her voice softer. "I fear it shall be a miserly existence, but at least I will have my independence."

"You are young. You will marry again," he predicted, unable to imagine her alone for the rest of her life.

Dianna let out a huff of laughter. "I can assure you the very last thing I need or want is another husband."

"Your time with your husband couldn't have all been bad, Dianna," Jon countered.

"Not all. Just mostly." She settled her hands on her hips, arms akimbo. "Gerald pursued me on whim, filling my head with romantic nonsense. 'Twas all a game to him, a challenge to see if he could pull me away from you. Once he succeeded, he lost interest. Only then were my eyes open to the truth. He would have abandoned me, but he discovered he needed a wife to collect his inheritance, so he married me. It was convenient for him, nothing more."

"And you?"

Her chest heaved as she drew in a deep breath. "I had no other options. I was ruined—as he often liked to remind me—a fallen woman whose prospects for a respectable marriage were gone. Yet still I held out hope, foolishly believing that being his wife would change his attitude, alter his behavior. Sadly, I was mistaken. He enjoyed making me beg for his attention, expected me to grovel for every speck of consideration from him.

"He had a penchant for horse racing and cards, a violent temper, a taste for wenching and talent for spending coin he did not have. So, to answer your question, Jon, yes, it was that bad."

Jon was brought up short by her revelations. Her raw pain and vulnerability touched him. Yet he had no words of comfort, no way to ease this darkness from her past.

"Hearing all this almost makes me sorry that I wasn't the one who killed him," he muttered.

She looked shocked. "I know you could never do such a thing."

"Your servants claimed to have seen me at your home the night he died," Jon replied, wondering why he was reminding her of the fact. Because he needed to be certain she didn't believe it?

"Yes, about that. There's something I have to tell you. Something that I am ashamed of, something that I deeply regret." Dianna eyed him nervously. "Hector paid those footmen to say they had seen you coming from Gerald's study the night he was killed."

The shock hit him like a physical blow. "My God, what are you saying, Dianna? You wanted me to hang?"

"Never!" Dianna insisted passionately. "I didn't know what Hector had done until days later. By the time I discovered it, you were no longer in custody for the crime."

His mind rife with suspicion, Jon cast her a look of

disbelief. "What was the purpose of enacting such an odious plan?"

Dianna's lower lip trembled. "Gerald's murder was the final straw for Hector. He swore another scandal would ruin our entire family and push us to a place from which we would never recover. He thought deflecting the attention to you would save us in the short term."

"That's idiotic."

Dianna lifted her hands helplessly. "There was a second part to Hector's plan. I was to bring the footmen forth to recant their statements, to explain that upon further reflection they realized they had made a grave mistake. By saving you, I could redeem myself to you and perhaps to others in society. Yet in the end, you didn't need me. Miss Ellingham saved you."

"With the truth," Jon said bitterly. His head was reeling with the revelation and he was having difficulty making sense of it all. "Where are the footmen now?"

She cleared her throat, looking deeply uneasy. "I don't know. I swear I would tell you if I did. I believe they ran off because they were frightened when Hector changed the arrangement he had made with them. He insisted the men stand by their original statements and continue to repeat the lie about seeing you that night, whenever they were asked."

Jon swallowed. "How could you have gone along with it? Why didn't you tell the magistrates the moment you learned the truth?"

"Who would have believed me? I'm a barely respectable woman, flighty and impulsive," she said pitifully. "Hector would have denied it. The footmen were gone. I had no proof."

"Why does Hector hate me so much?"

She shrugged. "He was using you when Gerald

died, hoping the gossip would center on you and not our family. If Hector would have followed through with the plan as he originally conceived it, you would have come to no harm.

"But something changed after you wed Miss Ellingham. He was very angry. He speaks of her often, you know. I believe he had set his sights on making her his bride."

His stomach clenched, but then Jon laughed. The idea of Emma married to such a pompous windbag like Hector Winthrope was comical in the extreme.

He turned his gaze to Dianna, wondering what other tidbits she had been keeping to herself.

"Who killed your husband, Dianna?"

"I don't know. Most likely someone to whom he owed money." A slow bloom of color spread across her cheeks. "Gerald liked to gamble," Dianna continued. "Unfortunately, he was not very good at it and certainly disliked paying his debts when he lost."

Jon once again found himself not regretting the fact that Gerald was dead. For a variety of reasons, including that his death had set into motion a bizarre set of circumstances that resulted in Jon marrying Emma.

And for that he would always be grateful.

"Thank you for telling me all of this, Dianna."

"Then you forgive me?" she asked, her voice a strange mixture of equal parts hope and apprehension.

"I do." While never condoning her actions, Jon found that he could understand—and with a bit of effort, even forgive them. As for Hector, well, that was another matter entirely.

They had circled around the path, returning to where they started. Jon linked his hands together to give Dianna a foot up onto her horse, and she gazed down at him as she settled the jittery animal. A myriad of thoughts seemed to flicker behind her eyes, yet she shared none of them.

Dianna trotted away without another word and Jon watched her spring her horse into a gallop. There was no denying that she had matured from a woman who rarely considered anyone's wants or needs except her own, to one who had developed an awareness of others, and he was glad, for her sake, to see that change.

Still, as he watched her ride away, Jon's head was filled with an undeniable truth. If he had married Dianna, he could have given her a rich, full life, he could have made her happy.

But he realized that she would not have done the same for him.

When Emma reached the drive of Ravenswood Manor, her anxiety began to ease. She had always been a woman of action, and having determined that she needed to see Sebastian, she wanted to get a plan in place to accomplish that as soon as possible.

Gwen and Jason were currently in Town—it made perfect sense to tell Jon that she wanted to journey there to visit her eldest sister. Yet she needed a way to get to London without unduly arousing her husband's suspicions and she was counting on Dorothea to help her solve that problem.

Of course, it would be a challenge not revealing to her sister the true reason for a hasty London trip, but Emma was hoping Dorothea would be too intrigued and intent on solving the problem to dig beyond the surface reason for the trip.

However, the moment she stepped through the front door, Emma was surprised and delighted to learn that fate was not always unkind or unjust. Sometimes, it was perfectly marvelous.

Carter's father, the Duke of Hansborough, had arrived last night. He was preparing to return to London and had expressed his desire to bring his two oldest grandchildren, Philip and Nicole, with him. Dorothea was happy to let her children spend some time in Town with their doting grandfather, but Carter was concerned.

The children's nurse had a severe cold and sore throat and was unable to travel with them. Emma could hardly believe her luck. She immediately volunteered to accompany the children and get them settled at the duke's London residence before going to stay with Gwen and Jason.

The duke wished to leave directly, and Emma promised that she and her maid would be ready. 'Twas an ideal solution that almost seemed too good to be true. All that was left was to tell Jon her news.

Alas, her husband was out when she returned home. Nevertheless, Emma informed a wide-eyed Dory that they were leaving for London within the hour and instructed the maid to pack the trunks.

Emma was rushing through the foyer when Jon crossed over the threshold.

"I missed you at breakfast this morning," he said. "Did you enjoy your visit with your sister?"

"I have the best news." Emotion settled in her throat, making it hard to speak, but she cleared her throat and started talking rapidly, nearly tripping over the words in her haste to get them out.

"When I arrived at Dorothea's this morning, Carter's father was there preparing to return to London. He desperately wants to bring Philip and Nicole with him, but their nurse is suffering from a dreadful head cold and sore throat, poor dear, and can't travel. So I offered to accompany the children to Town and see that they are settled in their grandfather's home."

Jon stared at her for a moment in mute astonishment. "You intend to leave for London today?"

There was a puzzled tone in his voice that was hard to miss. Emma gritted her teeth as she felt the panic begin to crawl up the back of her neck. She absolutely couldn't lie outright if he probed for a deeper explanation for her urgent need to go to London.

Yet at all costs, she wanted to avoid revealing her complicated feelings about Sebastian. Especially since she didn't completely understand them herself.

"We'll depart directly so we can arrive by nightfall," Emma said breathlessly. "Dory is nearly finished packing my trunk. As you know, my sister Gwen was unable to attend our wedding and then we left for our trip to see Mr. Ogdan soon after. I miss her very much and this is the perfect opportunity for me to visit with Gwen while at the same time helping Dorothea."

"If you want to go to London so badly, then I'll take you," Jon declared, raking a hand through his hair.

"I would never ask you to leave your work at such a critical juncture," Emma exclaimed. "I'll be away for less than a fortnight. You'll barely know that I'm gone."

Emma felt the tension tighten in her shoulders as she awaited his response. What would she do if he forbade her to go?

As she fumbled to find the right words to persuade him, fate once again stepped in to grant her a reprieve. Sir Galahad came bounding through the foyer, carrying something long and black in his mouth. Running behind him was Jon's valet, shouting the dog's name loudly.

Emma and Jon exchanged confused looks.

"Galahad, Sir Galahad, what do you have, boy?" Jon called out.

At the sound of Jon's voice, the dog skidded to a stop and turned. He tossed his head from side to side, violently shaking whatever was clamped tightly in his mouth.

"Heavens, what has he caught?" Emma squeaked in alarm. "Is it a small animal?"

"'Tis his lordship's boot," Gilmore answered, his chest heaving as he sought to pull in air. "The dog's been chewing it."

Emma and Jon turned at the same time to stare at the valet.

"That looks like one of my favorite boots. How did he get ahold of it?" Jon inquired.

"Forgive me, my lord," the valet stammered. "I didn't notice the dog was in your chambers until I discovered him in the corner with it. When I tried to take it away from him, he bolted."

Emma's brow rose. One had to be half blind to miss an animal of Sir Galahad's size. What exactly had the valet been doing?

Emma glanced over at her pet. The dog was now stretched out on his belly, the boot firmly held between his two front paws as he chewed contentedly upon the heel.

Gilmore moved forward. Sir Galahad immediately stood. Boot in his mouth, he pranced away, then turned as though waiting to see if he would be followed.

"He thinks that you're playing a game," Emma remarked.

"I'm not," the valet protested with a mulish expression.

Emma narrowed her gaze, determined to win the

battle of the boot. The dog had once again resumed a prone position as he gnawed on his prize.

"Let me see what you have, Galahad," she cooed, keeping her voice soft and soothing as she moved closer.

The dog lifted his head, cocking it to one side. His tail started wagging eagerly, but just as Emma drew close enough to snatch the boot, he leapt to his feet and ran.

"He appears to be enjoying the taste of it," Jon commented wryly. "You might as well let him keep the damn thing. It's ruined beyond repair at this point."

"If you give me your bootmaker's address, I can bring back a new pair from London," Emma offered.

Jon's brows drew together in a deep frown.

She stared at him, feeling swamped by misgivings and guilt at her subterfuge.

"The trunks are packed, my lady, and I've laid out a traveling outfit for you," Dory said quietly.

Emma turned. The maid stood a respectful distance away on the bottom step of the staircase, her hands clasped together.

"I'll be right there," Emma replied, seizing the chance to take advantage of the distraction. "We must not keep the duke waiting when he arrives."

She scurried up the stairs before Jon had a chance to voice any further objections to her making this trip. But her husband was standing in almost the exact spot when she emerged a half hour later.

Emma hooked her arm in his and leaned into Jon as they walked outside to where the duke's coach-and-four stood in their drive. Philip and Nicole were literally bouncing with excitement inside the carriage and the duke was having little success in calming their enthusiasm.

"Well, this will certainly be a lively ride," Emma said brightly.

Suddenly, Jon reached for her, hauling her close, his body pressing hard and taut against her softness. Emma lifted her mouth and stood on her toes to get closer, awaiting his kiss. His arms locked around her and he kissed her hard and fierce, as though he were afraid she might forget the feel of him.

When he finally pulled away, Emma gazed up at him blindly, her heart twisting with confusion.

"Hurry back to me," he said gruffly, and then he turned on his heel and swiftly walked away.

Chapter Nineteen

Emma awoke early and sat by the window in the guest bedchamber of Gwen and Jason's London townhome, watching the sunrise. As the rays of light slowly appeared, they glittered off the still waters of the ornamental garden pond, casting a golden glow over the plants surrounding it.

She pushed open the window, catching a whiff of the morning air, fresh and clean and full of promise. It bolstered her mood and helped to chase some of the cobwebs from her head.

Today was the day.

She and Dory had both been tired and travel weary last night when the duke's carriage had driven to the most fashionable section of Mayfair and deposited them at Gwen's front door. It was an impressive residence and Emma had noticed Dory staring up at the façade of the imposing home with awe.

The maid's eyes grew rounder as they were ushered inside and graciously attended to by the staff. Having no advance notice of her arrival, it was a relief for Emma to discover that her sister and Jason were out for the evening. That meant that she had been temporarily spared the need to make explanations for this unexpected, unannounced visit.

Thankfully, Emma was well-known to the household staff and they soon had her settled in one of the guest bedchambers. After a soothing bath and a light supper served in her room, she sat at the writing desk and penned a note to Sebastian.

It was answered within the hour. He had accepted her invitation and would come to call later this morning. Emma sighed, hoping that would give her enough time to find some mastery over her emotions.

She had spent a sleepless night concocting, reviewing, and casting aside what she was going to say to him. Her thoughts had been so consumed with it that she had given barely any consideration to how she was going to explain to Gwen the reason she had summoned Sebastian.

She had spent so many years never giving away her thoughts or feelings for him, hiding it so expertly from those she loved, that she wasn't certain where to begin.

There was a light knock on the door just before it opened and Gwen swept into the room. She was still in her nightclothes, and the train of her white India muslin robe glided quietly across the floor.

"Well, isn't this a lovely surprise."

Smiling fondly, Emma crossed the chamber and gave her sister a hug. "I hope you don't mind my unannounced visit, but when the opportunity arose I seized the chance to come to Town."

"I am delighted to see you," Gwen replied, beaming with pleasure. "Though I confess to being vastly disappointed when I discovered that your husband isn't with you."

Managing a sheepish grin, Emma attempted to offer her sister an excuse. "Jon regrets it also. He is very busy at the moment, but has promised to come the next time."

"Splendid. Both Jason and I would like to get to know him better."

Emma sat in the chair at the dressing table while Gwen settled on the silk-covered chaise opposite her. The casual, cozy atmosphere was comforting, reminding Emma of their childhood and the many confidences they had shared over the years.

Yet despite that familiarity, Emma was still uncertain how to broach the real reason she had come to London.

Unable to stand the quiet, she finally asked, "Where did you and Jason go last evening?"

"The Duke of Havenshire's ball," Gwen replied. "It was a mad crush, as usual, but Jason and I enjoyed the dancing and taking a private late-night stroll together in the duke's gardens. They are magnificent."

"So I've heard."

"Do you have any specific plans for your visit, or will I be able to have you all to myself?" Gwen asked.

It was the perfect opening, yet for some reason her sister's curious, penetrating stare set Emma's nerves skittering. "Actually, I don't plan on staying long."

"Oh? But you've only just arrived. I do hope there will be time for you to visit my new modiste while you are in Town. She has a rare talent for simple design and an eye for making her clients look their best. She's in great demand, but I'm sure with some encouragement she will be able to fit you into her busy schedule."

Emma sighed heavily, then forced herself to smile at Gwen. "That sounds delightful."

"Does it?" Gwen raised an elegant brow. "Then why do you sound like I am proposing a long hike through a muddy field during a rain storm?"

"Sorry." Emma felt the blush creeping up her neck and into her cheeks. "I'm still rather fatigued from the journey yesterday. Philip and Nicole are so inquisitive and energetic. I can understand why Carter did not want them to travel with only his father caring for them. The little scamps would have certainly exhausted the poor duke by the end of the first hour."

The subject of children had always been a favorite of Gwen's and she easily launched into several amusing tales about her own youngsters, though she lamented more than once that they were growing up too quickly.

"Jason cannot bear to be separated from our brood, so naturally they are with us," Gwen said. "I haven't yet told them that you are here, but they will soon find out. I shall try to hold them off until you've eaten a fortifying breakfast, but then you must brace yourself for an assault."

Emma smiled. "I'd like that very much, but it will have to wait for a bit. I've invited Sebastian to call upon me later this morning," she replied, holding her sister's gaze. "I hope that you don't mind."

"Sebastian? Are you referring to Sebastian Dodd?"

Emma nodded vigorously.

"Why?"

"I need to see him. 'Tis the reason that I've come to London."

Gwen stared back at her, confusion glinting in her eyes. "Emma, what is going on?"

A cold, fragile feeling wrapped itself around Emma's heart. She nervously twirled the ends of a loose strand of hair and stared back at her sister.

"There are several things that you don't know about Sebastian. Things I've never told you. Things I've never told anyone, really," Emma said, licking her suddenly dry lips.

Gwen's expression turned grave. "I'm listening."

Emma nodded and took a deep breath. She started, stumbled, started again, and then suddenly it was as though the floodgates had opened and her words were the water rushing through them.

She told Gwen about the years of depression and despair she had experienced from Sebastian's rejection of her love, the searing pain that had stabbed at her heart and eroded her confidence.

How she had tried to convince herself that it was her pride that had been wounded, but the hurt had gone much deeper than the feelings of a young woman scorned by an older, more experienced man.

She also spoke about Jon and her confused feelings over a marriage that she had never sought and her deep desire to overcome the hurt and wariness of her past to somehow make it succeed.

To learn how to expose her vulnerability, to accept the love that her husband had bestowed upon her and return it to him in equal measure.

An almost eerie silence filled the room when she was done. Drained and exhausted, Emma slumped back in her chair, shutting her eyes. She felt a single tear roll down her cheek, but didn't bother brushing it away, as no more fell.

Gradually, Emma lifted her eyelids, fearing her older, wiser sister would have a great deal to say that Emma lacked the strength to hear at the moment. But Gwen had the perfect response. She merely opened her arms and offered Emma a comforting, greatly needed hug.

The front door of Ravenswood Manor swung open before Jon even had the chance to knock, making him wonder if Atwood's butler had exceptional hearing or a driving ambition to do his job better than any others in his position.

"Good afternoon, my lord," the butler said as he took his hat and greatcoat. "The marquess is awaiting you in his study."

"Very good." Jon straightened the cuffs beneath his jacket and followed the servant through the familiar hallways.

"Lord Kendall," the butler announced.

Atwood closed the ledger he had been reading and rose from behind his desk. After shaking hands and accepting a glass of wine, Jon sat across from his host, relishing the warmth of the blaze in the fireplace.

"There's been news from the Bow Street runner," Atwood announced. He shifted several stacks of correspondence on his desk, pulling a parchment from the bottom of a pile.

"Has he located the missing footmen?" Jon asked.

"He has." Atwood raised his glass in a silent salute before taking a sip.

Jon joined him, allowing the smooth, robust flavor of the wine to settle on his tongue before swallowing. "Have they told him of the payment Hector Winthrope made to them in exchange for their false accusations against me?"

Atwood frowned and rubbed the back of his neck. "Did you also receive a report from the runner?"

"No. I saw Dianna yesterday morning. She told me everything." Jon kept his gaze steady as he fielded a speculative glance from the marquess.

"Christ, she's a part of this too?"

"Not exactly."

Atwood stared at him a moment longer, but let the cryptic answer stand without further questions.

"The runner reports that there are few leads as to the identity of Brayer's killer and reiterates what you and I have already concluded—he might never be found. Not surprisingly, the baron had plenty of enemies, leaving a wide number of suspects.

"In order to ensure that you shall always remain off that list, Kendall, I recommend that we have the runner bring the footmen back here to tell their tale to the magistrates and obliterate any suspicions against you once and for all."

It was a prudent, sound plan and precisely what Jon had also concluded needed to be done. Yet he hesitated, remembering how hearing the dullness of Dianna's voice and witnessing the pain in her eyes had flooded him with feelings of empathy.

"Since there is no urgent need, I want to wait to reveal this information," Jon said firmly. "Dianna will be leaving within a few weeks and I would spare her this additional humiliation. She has suffered enough. None of this was her doing. Hector bears this burden alone."

"Are you certain?"

Jon nodded, aware that Atwood didn't know what to make of this strange request. "I'll deal with Hector later," Jon assured him. "Though I'll admit that ever since I learned of his treachery, anytime I hear Winthrope's name I imagine myself wrapping my hands around his neck and choking the life out of him."

Atwood grinned. "An understandable sentiment, but please do try to restrain yourself. We have only recently found the means to fully clear your name of one murder charge. I don't relish the challenge of having to get you out of another."

A deep chortle escaped from Jon's lips. "I too have

had my fill of criminal accusations and am more than ready to resume the simple life of a boring country gentleman."

"Country life is hardly ever simple or boring." The marquess's look turned considering. "Are you still working on that farming machine of yours? The reverend has Squire Hornsby and half the congregation convinced 'tis an unnatural calling to be building such contraptions."

Jon gave a snort of exasperation. "Small-minded men have difficulty accepting the concept of progress and innovation. But I will not be deterred."

The marquess's face lit with curiosity. "I'd like to see it. I might even want to purchase one or two for my estate."

"When it performs as I expect, I will gladly give you a demonstration."

"Has anyone seen it?"

"Only Mr. Norris, my assistant, and Emma. She's made several sketches of it and plans on doing a painting once the design is refined and complete. Honestly, I don't understand how a lifeless machine of metal and gears can inspire her, but as long as it makes her happy . . ."

Jon shrugged. Most people wouldn't understand that he was risking the secrecy and integrity of his designs by allowing his wife to sketch them. Especially while the work was in progress. But it brought her joy and that in turn delighted him because, above all, he wanted Emma to be happy.

"Emma is drawing again?" Atwood quirked a smile. "That's splendid! Dorothea will be pleased to hear it, though she has chosen a most unusual subject. I've seen her still lifes and landscapes, but she has always insisted that her favorite subjects are people."

Jealousy reared and Jon tightened his jaw at the memory of the emotional portrait of the Earl of Tinsdale. "Has she accepted a lot of commissions for portraits over the years?"

Atwood looked pensive for a moment. "As far as I know, she's never earned any commissions. Her subjects have all been known to her—family members or close friends. I believe the last portrait that she completed was one of my father. She presented it to him at Christmas two years ago. It was quite magnificent. Slightly flattering, while at the same time, true to life. He adored it."

Jon's gut lurched. *Emma only paints family and close friends? Which is the earl?*

"We stayed overnight at the Earl of Tinsdale's home after our carriage wheel accident," Jon probed, apprehensive at clarifying the relationship between his wife and the mysterious earl. "Emma never mentioned that she was related to him."

"Tinsdale? Oh, you mean Viscount Benton. Or rather, Sebastian. I always forget that he is now an earl. It takes me a moment to make the connection between his older title and new one." Atwood took a sip of wine. "But no matter what he's called, Sebastian is not related to Gwen, Dorothea, and Emma. He's one of my oldest and closest friends. We were at Eaton and later Oxford together, getting into more trouble than we ought, especially when we were bachelors. Sebastian is a capital fellow, with a wicked sense of humor. He caught the bouquet at my wedding. Ah, well, that's another story entirely."

The marquess chuckled. "Emma has known him for years. I'm surprised she didn't say anything about it."

This was hardly the news that Jon was hoping to hear. He shifted in his seat, feigning a casual indifference that he was far from feeling. The portrait had revealed Emma's deep emotional connection to her subject. Though a part of him had doubted it was true, he had clung to the hope that her contact with the earl had been limited to the time she painted his portrait.

'Twas a blow to discover the pair had known each other for many years—and even more disheartening to find that Emma had felt the need to hide this relationship from him.

"Thankfully, Emma wasn't injured in the carriage accident, but she was rattled," Jon revealed. "I'm sure telling me about the earl slipped her mind in all the confusion. Besides, we didn't see him as he wasn't in residence."

Atwood nodded. "His earldom came with a large estate located in the wilds of Yorkshire. I still find it hard to imagine Sebastian flourishing in such a rural environment, but he has assured me it suits him very well."

"He wasn't in Yorkshire," Jon replied. "The servants informed us that he was in London."

London. Where Emma had rushed off to in such haste yesterday. Coincidence? Or was this the perfect opportunity for them to meet in secret?

A prickly tingle ran down Jon's spine and a rushing noise roared between his ears as Emma's sudden, unplanned trip took on a sinister bent.

What is she hiding?

The possibilities swirled through his brain, all of them hurtful, all of them messy, all of them unacceptable.

Stop it!

Jon tried to tell himself that he was being illogical, jumping to conclusions that had little or no facts to support them. It was the Season—there were hundreds of nobles in the city right now.

Trust. He had to trust her. He had to take her at her word that she had gone to London because her niece and nephew needed a chaperone for the trip. He had to believe that she was with her sister, enjoying a long-overdue visit.

He had to do that, or else he would rush to Town like a lovesick fool, too blinded by his own jealousy to act in a rational, civilized manner.

His breathing gradually slowed. They would talk when she returned. He would ask her for the truth about her relationship with the earl—past and present. Wondering, speculating, assuming, would eat at him, wound him, and jeopardize the love that he had for her.

"You have a visitor, Lady Kendall."

Emma looked up from the book that she had been pretending to read and stared down at the silver tray Gwen's butler held out to her. A white card, facedown, rested in the middle.

Though she knew the name that was engraved on the other side, she did as the butler expected, lifting and then turning it over. Her breath squeezed in her lungs, her fingers trembled, and the letters seemed to swim together before her eyes, yet somehow she kept her composure.

Barely.

"Please let the earl know that I am at home," Emma commanded.

The butler inclined his head respectfully and withdrew. Left alone, Emma had several agonizing moments to question her sanity and brace herself for a torturous ordeal. Fortunately, before she could crowd her mind with any additional upsetting thoughts, the drawing room door opened and Sebastian stepped through.

She stood, swallowed hard, and linked her fingers together. He had aged, of course, but magnificently. His hair was still thick and dark, with but a few streaks of silver at the temples that gave him a mature, distinguished air.

Small lines fanned out from the corners of his eyes, but they sparkled with the same life and humor she remembered. His shoulders were as broad, his legs firm and muscular, his stomach flat. The power and strength within him had not diminished with age, nor had the rakish swagger she always admired.

"Hello, Emma."

He smiled and Emma felt her heart melt. She opened her mouth to greet him, but found that she was too choked with emotion to say anything.

"Shall we sit?" Sebastian finally suggested.

Emma bobbed her head and wordlessly led him to the matched set of settees. He waited politely for her to sit and then took a seat opposite.

"Thank you for agreeing to meet with me," Emma said, looking down at her still clasped hands.

"Nothing could have kept me away," he replied. "I've been waiting many years for this summons."

"I behaved rather badly the last time we were together," Emma said softly, wincing at the scalding memory.

"You were in pain," he said gently. "And for that I

blame myself. Hurting you has been the biggest regret of my life. It has torn at me for years. Through my friendship with Carter I was able to find out where you were, what you were doing, and it eased my guilt a tad knowing that you were safe and with your loving family. But I was never able to discover if you were happy."

Emma's heart began to beat rapidly. He had thought of her. Worried about her. Hoped for her happiness. She had meant something to him.

There was another long pause.

Emma crossed her arms and stared at the carpet. "What happened between us was not entirely your fault, Sebastian. You never encouraged me, you were never forward or inappropriate, you never gave me any reason to expect more from you.

"You didn't flirt—well, perhaps a bit, but I've come to understand that is so ingrained in your character you don't even realize that you are doing it."

He shook his head vigorously. "I confided in you, came to you when I needed comfort, teased and joked with you. I treated you as a grown woman, but you were a young, impressionable girl. That was wrong."

"You thought of me as your friend. What we shared was uniquely ours. But then I spoiled it all by falling madly in love with you," she said sadly.

"God, Emma, it hurts me now to hear you say it. I never deserved such devotion," Sebastian replied, the pain behind the words easily heard.

"I shouldn't have said anything," Emma lamented. "Yet I was determined not to take my unrequited love to the grave without speaking of it. Of course, the scenes I played out in my mind ended in a very different way than the reality."

A muscle pulsed in Sebastian's jaw. "I was an arse to you that day."

"You were hungover and nursing a broken heart. My timing was not the best."

He looked skeptical. "I should have handled it with more finesse, more compassion."

Emma felt the edges of a smile tug at the corner of her mouth. "I'm not sure that's possible under those circumstances."

"I would have spared you this pain if it had been within my power."

"I realize that now." Emma raised her chin. "The worst part was that you were the one I needed, you were the one that I wanted to turn to for comfort. And I couldn't. 'Twas an impossible situation that I unwittingly allowed to fester for years. Thinking of your rejection made my insides ache, so I tried to ignore the pain, to run from it. It was my form of protection.

"Over time it made the scars around my heart tough, nearly impenetrable. However, I have come to understand that refusing to confront it made it grow larger in my mind, in my life. I allowed it to control me, to overshadow any feelings that might have blossomed for other men."

Sebastian leaned forward, resting his wrists on his knees. "And now?"

Emma released her breath with a small sigh. "I've broken through those scars. I can't change the past, but I want the future to hold no fears."

"How can I help you?"

Emma smiled ironically. "You just did. Seeing you was the final piece that I needed to complete the journey. There will always be a very small corner of my heart that belongs to you, Sebastian. But all the rest, the biggest part, the best part, I will entrust to my husband."

Sebastian's expression grew fierce. "I hope that he deserves it."

Emma felt a smug clap of joy. "Jon is a remarkable man. I am indeed a fortunate woman to be his wife."

They stood. Sebastian brought her hand to his lips and kissed it tenderly. It was a sweet gesture that brought a comfortable warmth to her heart. However, it was a far cry from the breath-catching tingle she felt when Jon did the same.

For the first time, her past and future blended together in sharp clarity. She had loved Sebastian as a girl. Jon, she loved as a woman.

It was past time to tell him.

Chapter Twenty

A week later, Jon was glowering out the window and debating yet again if he should leave for London. Ever since he had learned that the earl—Sebastian— had been a part of Emma's life for many years, the memory of that portrait had crawled beneath his skin and pricked at him.

He had no definite proof that Emma had gone to London specifically to meet the man, but the coincidence made it too real, too disturbing a possibility. And Jon's heart felt like it was tightening in his chest every time he thought of it.

The remedy to retain his sanity, he believed, was to keep busy. Yet, no matter how hard he tried to occupy his mind with other matters, images of Emma invaded. Walking through the solarium the other day, he was certain he heard the soft tread of her feet on the stone floor.

When he entered the drawing room he could picture her sitting on the settee, book in hand. He ventured to the third floor and roamed about her studio, gazing at her sketches, imagining her slender hands creating the images.

Late at night he would toss and turn restlessly in his

bed. Closing his eyes, Jon swore he could smell her perfume, feel the soft silk of her tender flesh, hear the sound of her voice.

His longing for her was a constant pressure in his chest, made worse by his uncertainty of her affections. Jon scowled. The intolerability of the situation was taking a toll on him. He felt constantly on edge, the speculations as to why Emma had kept this a secret from him nearly driving him mad. There were moments when he wanted to hit something, to strike out physically in hopes that would ease the tension hammering through his body.

Seven days. Emma had been gone for seven days and would not return for another seven. It felt like an eternity. Even her dog had been so forlorn that in an attempt to cheer him up, Jon had tossed the beast the mate to the boot Sir Galahad had destroyed the morning Emma had left for London.

Chewing and ripping the footwear into small pieces had kept the animal contented and entertained for a few hours, but eventually the dog had also returned to his desolate state. He was now a fixture at Jon's side, trailing after him day and night. The animal's presence was an odd form of comfort, easing some of Jon's loneliness, though the relief was always temporary and far too short.

The sheet of plans laid out on his desk beckoned, and Jon forced himself to look at them. The modified designs Mr. Ogdan had sent of a steam engine seemed promising, yet Jon failed to summon any enthusiasm for them.

He could go to the workshop, but in his current state of distraction he might cause a serious accident. 'Twould be safer for all if he tried working with paper and pencil rather than machinery.

Sir Galahad lifted his large head and let out a single bark. The sound of carriage wheels brought Jon out of his chair and closer to the window. A flash of bright blue appeared as a woman stepped down from the coach.

Emma!

His first instinct was to rush to the foyer like Sir Galahad to greet her, but Jon held back. He would wait for her to come to him. The sound of her voice floated to his ears. She was speaking to the dog, her voice happy and amused. No doubt the animal was preening for her, basking in the attention and affection.

Ears straining, Jon tried to determine where she was headed next. The door to his study swung open and he got his answer. Emma strode into the room, Sir Galahad attached to her side as though he were glued to her. They made a fetching pair, the pretty, slender woman and the large, hulking beast.

Jon snapped his fingers and directed the dog to lie down near the fireplace. Sir Galahad gazed at Emma adoringly, his mouth curved up in a doggie grin, and after few gentle strokes on his head from his mistress, the animal obeyed the order.

"Good afternoon, Jon."

"Emma." He was relieved to see the warm look in her eyes, yet trepidation made him nod his head, stiffly, formally, politely. "Welcome home. You look lovely. Is that a new frock?"

Emma blinked, looking down at her gown in confusion, as though she was amazed he would notice. "Gwen insisted that I patronize her modiste. I ordered several new gowns. I hope that you don't mind."

"You look beautiful in everything you wear." He felt a wave of possessiveness that nearly stole the breath from his lungs. She had become the center of his world. He couldn't lose her. "Are your sister and her family well?"

"They are all fine. It was wonderful to see them, but well, 'tis good to be home."

"Is it?" he asked softly. "I'm delighted that you returned far sooner than you said, but I truly don't understand why you went to London in the first place."

Emma glanced about the room, looking everywhere but directly at him. Jon watched her fidget with her hands. She looked more nervous than he had ever seen her. His heart sank, but he had to stay calm, in control. Let her speak at her own pace, reveal her feelings to him as she needed.

He had to be prepared to hear anything—including how the earl still held her heart. Even though the very thought brought a pain so sharp it nearly brought Jon to his knees.

He gestured toward a chair facing his desk. He poured her a drink, brought it to her, then crouched at her feet.

"There's so much that I want to say to you, but I hardly know where to begin," Emma said uneasily, setting her untouched drink aside.

"Why don't you start with the portrait you painted of the earl?" Jon took her hand in his, giving it a light squeeze. "I saw it when we were stranded at his estate."

She made a strangled noise in the back of her throat. "Why do you assume the portrait is one of my paintings?"

"Your initials are on it—they are most distinct."

"Ah, caught out by my youthful vanity. That was the last portrait that I signed." She smiled ironically. "I've often wondered what happened to it. Secretly, I hoped it had been destroyed. Or at the very least, left to rot in an attic somewhere."

"That would be a crime," Jon replied. "'Tis an extraordinary piece."

"'Tis an embarrassment of emotion." Emma's voice grew quiet. "Sebastian's grandmother, the Countess of Marchdale, commissioned it. She died before I finished it."

"How did it come to be in the earl's possession?"

Emma's eyes darkened. "I presented it to him a few months after his grandmother's death. He was very hungover that afternoon, drinking cup after cup of hot coffee, squinting his eyes and holding on to his aching head."

"How did he react?"

"He was horrified," she replied with a soft, exhausted sigh. "He had no inkling of how deeply I loved him. He had always thought of me as a dear friend, a sister. Never a woman he would love romantically."

Jon winced, feeling Emma's pain. Wishing there was some way he could take it away. "Why have you never spoken of him to me?"

Emma responded with a sharp shake of her head. "I couldn't. It was too painful to remember, let alone talk about."

"Did you see him when you were in London?"

"Yes," she whispered.

Jon's stomach dropped and his limbs grew cold. "Do you still love him?"

"No. I love another." Her eyes shut briefly and then they opened, focusing on him intently. "I love you, Jon."

A sharp stab of joy pierced his heart and twisted his breath. He was struck by the resolve in her voice, humbled by the vulnerability he saw in her eyes. He understood the pain of lost love, the difficulty of learning to trust and hope again. For them to have this second chance made the moment even sweeter, more precious.

Jon had to clear his throat before he spoke. "I love you, Emma. You mean the world to me. Words are inadequate to express the feelings that encompass my heart. When I suspected that you might be going to London to see the earl, it tore a hole through me. I can't lose you, Emma."

"I'm not going anywhere, Jon. I'm sorry I didn't tell you about meeting Sebastian. It was something I had to do on my own. I had to put the past behind me once and for all."

"And have you?"

Leaning forward, she pressed her lips to his. Her kiss was possessive and demanding, miraculously imprinting her even more firmly in his heart. He returned the kiss soundly, taking and giving, hiding nothing from her. When he finally took his mouth from hers and looked up at her, he felt vibrantly alive.

"Oh, Jon, I'm so happy. I've known for several weeks that my feelings for you were intensifying, yet I had to know that I had finally let go of my past. Then, and only then, could I fully commit myself to you, allow myself to love you as I wanted. To love you as you deserve."

She was looking at him in a way he'd never seen before, her eyes gleaming with joy and love, her mouth twisted in a trembling smile.

"I know you were afraid of this feeling," he whispered. "I was too. But, Emma, when I saw that painting, saw the power of your love, I knew that was what I wanted from you. And I would do anything and everything to get it."

She smiled. "I am yours, Jon. As you are mine. Please, don't ever forget it."

Emma looked at the gentleness in Jon's eyes, and the walls around her heart that had started crumbling the moment she became his wife, completely broke apart.

She felt whole, renewed. She had been adrift for years, fearful and alone. She didn't feel alone with Jon. She felt connected on a level that went beyond herself. In his eyes she saw the reflection of her secret desires, the same wants and needs.

To be accepted. To be loved. Fearing with all your being that it might not come to pass, yet finding the courage to reach for it. She was beyond lucky to be married to such an amazing man. She ran her hand slowly over his chest, over his heart.

"I am honored and humbled by your love for me and intend to return it tenfold. I want to spend my days and nights with you, experience life with you, grow old with you. I want to hear your ideas for inventions and watch them come to life. I want to dance with you and ride with you, share your bed, give birth to and raise your children. And I vow to forever safeguard the heart you have bestowed upon me."

"You had better," he replied gruffly, pulling her down and into his arms. "For I shall never give it to another."

The next few days were idyllic. Emma and Jon spent nearly every waking hour together—in bed and out of it. They were equally matched in passion, and to her blushing delight, she found herself in an exhausted and satisfied state at the most shocking times of the day and night.

Yet it wasn't only bedsport that they so passionately shared. Jon discussed his work with her, encouraging her to offer her opinions and suggestions. Emma allowed him to view her sketches, which in addition to his amazing machine included a few drawings of her newest portrait subject—Sir Galahad.

They even managed to entertain Dorothea and Carter, Squire Hornsby and Mrs. Hornsby, and the reverend and his wife for dinner one evening and make it a tolerable affair. Emma was determined to ease them into local society and erase any of the lingering rumors of suspicion surrounding Jon's eccentricities as an inventor and his possible involvement in Baron Brayer's murder.

"Will you be joining me and Mr. Norris at the workshop this morning, Emma?"

She placed her coffee cup on its matching saucer and gazed across the table at her husband. "The weather is so lovely this morning, I thought I'd bring my easel and paints outside on the patio."

Jon nodded approvingly. "I'll be back in time to share luncheon with you."

She lifted her face to receive his kiss. He kissed her long and deep, until she was nearly squirming in her chair and wondering if there was time to slip back upstairs to the bedchamber.

Jon's carefree laugh let Emma know her thoughts were easily read. But instead of succumbing to her maidenly blushes, she slapped his shoulder playfully.

"If you are very nice to me, Lord Kendall, we shall take an extra-long lunch today. Abovestairs."

His eyes flared with sensual heat, letting Emma know he approved of her plan. After a second, far more sedate kiss, Jon departed.

Emma finished breakfast and rang for one of the footmen to help her with her art supplies. She felt energized with the sun casting a warm glow on the canvas, and had a productive morning, bringing her latest artistic vision to life.

She reached a natural stopping point after several hours and decided it was time for a break. Setting her brushes down, Emma leaned back to assess her work with a critical eye, approving of the proportions and colors of her subject, yet not entirely pleased with the size perspective.

Knowing it was best to leave the work instead of continuing to fuss with it, she stood and stretched. As there was enough time before lunch for a brisk walk, she headed through the gardens, and across the lawn.

Deciding she would like some company, Emma gazed about, hoping to catch a glimpse of Sir Galahad. But the faithful dog was nowhere in sight and she realized he must have gone with Jon to the workshop.

Though she knew the dog was devoted to her, he had apparently switched his strongest allegiance to Jon while she was away. The circumstance might have caused her a bit of distress, had she not so thoroughly approved of her pet's choice.

She reached the folly and decided to rest for a moment before starting back. Sitting on the stone bench inside the structure, Emma gazed up at the vaulted ceiling, admiring the intricate tile pattern.

"Lady Kendall! How fortuitous to have encountered you on this fine day!"

Emma's heart sank as Hector Winthrope emerged

from the edge of the woodlands and approached. *Drat!* An encounter with him was certain to ruin her good mood.

"You are trespassing, Mr. Winthrope," Emma stated firmly. "I recommend that you turn tail and run before my husband discovers that you are on his property."

Winthrope stopped short, his expression surprised and hurt. "You sound so hostile, my lady. I don't understand why. Are we not friends?"

"No, we are not friends," she replied as she rose to her feet. "Jon told me all about the footmen and the lies you paid them to tell the night Lord Brayer was killed."

"I'm sure that your husband twisted the intent of my actions to showcase himself in a better light." Hector entered the folly and stood in front of her.

"He told me the truth. Make no mistake, Mr. Winthrope, you will have to answer for the crimes that you committed."

"Crimes? What crimes? Those servants did not give testimony under oath. They merely told the authorities what they *believed* they saw," Hector replied smugly. "That is not a crime."

Fearing that he might be right, Emma clenched her fists in frustration. "You are truly an odious man."

Hector's face darkened with confusion. "You must know that I did all this for us, sweet Emma."

"Us?" Emma heard her voice rise in a squeak of disbelief.

"There's no need to be coy," he said, placing his hands on her arms. "I can see how unhappy Kendall has made you. Everyone can."

What? "I am most happy married to Jon," Emma insisted, twisting out of his grasp.

"You mustn't pretend with me, my dear, though I admire how brave you are in the face of such disappointment." Hector gave her another smug, knowing glance. "Kendall's been seeing my sister, you know. Alone. She met him in the woods while you were away in London. It won't be long until they renew their romance and begin a torrid affair."

"That's another lie," Emma insisted, feeling a momentary pang of jealousy. Jon and Dianna? No! It wasn't true and she wasn't about to allow such falsehoods to shake her faith in the husband she loved.

Still, the image of Jon with Dianna momentarily distracted Emma and Hector seized the advantage, leaning forward in an attempt to kiss her. She recoiled and managed to turn her head in time for his lips to brush sloppily against her cheek.

Undeterred, Hector lunged at her again. "Come, my dear, that wasn't a proper kiss," he protested, his fingers biting into the tender flesh of her upper arm as he pulled her closer.

"Release me at once!" Emma commanded, stunned and repulsed by his behavior.

Winthrope ignored her cries and continued trying to haul her body closer to his. She bounced against the softness of his rounded belly, arching her back as she struggled to break his grasp.

"Get your filthy hands off my wife, Winthrope! This instant!"

Hector pulled back from her in surprise at Jon's roar of rage and Emma cried out as the viscount's fist struck Hector's jaw with a loud crack.

Hector flew backward, waving his arms frantically in an attempt to keep his balance. It failed. He fell on his rump on the hard marble floor of the folly. Grunting in anger, Winthrope scrambled to his feet and raised his fists.

Emma glanced at her husband, but Jon was smiling, apparently pleased with the opportunity to continue his pummeling.

"You have obviously misunderstood the situation," Hector shouted as he swung wide, missing Jon completely.

"I don't think so," Jon countered, jabbing a punch to Hector's midsection. Winthrope let out another loud grunt and doubled over in pain.

Gasping for air, he gestured toward Emma. "Tell your husband that you are unharmed."

Emma shrugged and crossed her arms. Hector was bleeding from the nose and lip and she felt a primitive sense of satisfaction at the sight.

"You were hardly willing to release me when I asked," Emma said. "In fact, you held my arm rather tightly."

Jon's expression darkened further. "Are you hurt, Emma?"

Emma hesitated in replying just long enough for Hector to receive another well-placed blow. He pitched forward and this time when he hit the hard floor, he didn't rise again.

Jon came to Emma's side and wrapped his arms around her. She gratefully pressed herself against his chest, sinking her face into the curve of his neck. Then they both turned and stared down at Winthrope.

Hector winced and gingerly ran his fingers over his jaw as though testing it. Emma could see a large bruise forming under the streak of blood that had dripped down to his chin from his split lip.

Grunting in pain, Hector labored to gain his feet, a look of frustration shining in his eyes. His breathing was loud and harsh. In contrast, Emma noticed that Jon scarcely appeared winded.

"Lady Kendall and I have shared a mutual affection for over a year." Hector sniffled loudly, pulling away the handkerchief he had pressed to his nose. His color paled when he saw the amount of bright red blood on it.

"She was forced to marry you after you ruined her," Hector continued, his face twisted with overblown arrogance. "If not for your interference, she would have happily married me!"

"Never!" Emma shouted, outraged at that ludicrous notion.

"You don't mean that," Winthrope said, stepping forward, his swollen lips meshed together.

Apparently having heard more than his fill from Hector, Jon reached out and grabbed him by the cravat, lifting him off the floor. "It's over, Winthrope. If you ever approach my wife again, I will make you sorry for the rest of your days in ways that you can only imagine."

Winthrope's eyes bulged. Jon opened his hands, and Hector dropped to the floor, barely managing to stay on his feet. Without another word, he hurried away, glancing back several times as though he expected he would be followed and further thrashed.

Emma sighed and leaned against her husband. "I always thought he was a pompous windbag, but this behavior was beyond anything I could have predicted. Carter used to tease me that Winthrope was enamored of me, but I never suspected that his delusions ran this deep, especially since I never once encouraged him."

"I would make a quip about your irresistible allure to all men, my love, if I were not still so damn angry. I fear I quite lost my mind when I caught sight of you struggling to get out of Winthrope's embrace."

"My hero." Emma placed her hand on his.

Jon dropped a kiss on the tip of her nose. "I shudder to think what might have happened if I hadn't come looking for you."

"I don't believe that I was in any real danger. Well, except for having to endure one of Hector's kisses." Emma did shudder at that possibility.

"I must erase that horror from your mind immediately."

Jon captured her lips with a series of light, almost lazy kisses. Emma strained upward to deepen the contact and he gladly obliged.

There was something different about his kisses, she realized. True, they were still passionate, still had the power to weaken her knees and flutter her stomach with excitement.

But there was more. They were filled with love and hope and dreams. They meant forever.

To both of them.

Two months later

The August sun crept up in the sky as the crowd gathered at the edge of the field where the stalks of wheat were full and bursting. After instructing everyone to stand clear, Jon and Mr. Norris positioned the reaper on the opposite side.

Emma and Lady Sybil, hands tightly clasped, took several steps back. There was a loud bang when Jon started the steam engine at the rear of the apparatus. Slowly, the gears of the reaper began to move. When they were spinning at a consistent rate, Jon stepped onto the platform and carefully steered the machine into the field.

The noise grew louder as the sharp, heavy blades swung back and forth, slicing through the thick, high stalks. By the time Jon reached the end of the field, the machine had cut a swath of wheat twelve feet wide. The stalks were piled neatly in a row, waiting to be gathered and threshed.

"Five minutes!" Squire Hornsby shouted excitedly. "It would take a skilled worker with a sickle half the day to cut the same amount by hand."

The machine chugged closer and Emma could see Jon's eyes narrowing with concentration as he made a wide turn. She held her breath, releasing it only after he had successfully completed it. His face broke into a wide grin when the reaper headed back to the field to make another pass and harvest the next section.

The turning mechanism was one of the gears Jon insisted needed further refinement and she was so relieved that it had cooperated during this all-important demonstration.

He was disappointed that he had not been able to successfully incorporate the thresher section of the machine and it had taken her and Mr. Norris over a week to convince him that a steam-powered reaper alone would still be of great value.

And they were right! Jon cut the engine when he arrived at the end of the field and jumped down from his driving perch to the near deafening sounds of cheers and applause.

Everyone ran forward to congratulate him and Mr. Norris and ask an endless stream of questions.

"I don't know why you have been so anxious," Lady

Sybil admonished when she and Emma joined the crowd. "Your machine worked flawlessly, Jon."

"It's extraordinary," Carter exclaimed. "I want to know how soon you can build one for me."

Dorothea reached over and gave Emma a big hug. "You must be so proud."

"I am," Emma replied, her cheeks almost hurting from the width of her smile.

Looking over the heads in the group, Emma met her husband's eyes. It made her heart sing to see him so pleased and happy.

That night, after the celebrations had ended, Emma carried a cloth-covered canvas into Jon's bedchamber. Curious, he knotted the belt of his robe and followed behind her.

She brought it to the brightest spot in the room, propped it in the middle of a chair, then turned to him anxiously. "I have something for you."

"So I see."

"I hope that you like it."

Without further ceremony, she yanked the cloth away. Jon's breath caught and for a moment he was utterly speechless as he beheld his wife's painting.

The machine was beautifully majestic, almost poetic. The shafts and gears vibrated with life, evoking a sense of power and dominance. But it was the likeness of the man standing beside the metal that robbed Jon of speech.

'Twas him.

Not precisely the man Jon saw when he looked in a mirror. Emma's version of him showcased a man spectacularly self-assured and striking. There was more than a hint of sensuality in the strong hand braced on the largest iron wheel and a captivating sense of mystery and allure in his secretive stare.

The connection between subject and artist was palpable—Emma's love and admiration of him was immediately obvious. A childish grin stole across Jon's face. This painting made the portrait she did of the earl seem pale and weak by comparison.

He cleared his throat. "I confess to feeling rather godlike when I gaze upon it. Is this truly how you see me?"

"No. It captures but a small part of my feelings and admiration." A nervous uncertainty glinted in her eyes. "Do you like it?"

"How could I not."

Emma let out a long sigh of relief. Jon put his arms around her and held her tight. He felt a tide of elation flood through him. The success of the reaper today had been the realization of a dream, but the love and devotion of his wife—

Ah, now that was a miracle.

Epilogue

Four years later

The sweet scent of lilacs drifted through the garden, twitching Emma's nose. She paused as a sudden wave of nausea overcame her. Clutching her middle, she abruptly sat on the nearby stone bench, anxiously waiting for it to pass.

Sir Galahad lifted his head from the bush he was exploring, and looked at her curiously. Face contorting in discomfort, Emma somehow managed to swallow back the rising bile. Sensing her distress, the dog came quickly to her side, sympathetically nuzzling her hand with his snout.

"No worries, boy," she said, pressing her hand over her flat stomach. "I'm not ill. Just in an *interesting condition*, as they say."

She pulled in a deep breath and felt a silly grin bloom across her face. A babe. She had confirmed it with the doctor this very morning and promptly burst into happy tears at the news. After four years of marriage, what she had feared would never happen was finally a reality.

She and Jon were going to be parents!

Thankfully, he had been so consumed with his latest project that she had been able to hide from him her lethargy, retching in the mornings—and evenings—and sudden exhaustion. Fearing to raise and then dash his hopes, she had not wanted to say anything until she was absolutely certain.

Sir Galahad's tail started wagging and he emitted a friendly bark. Emma raised her head and watched the loyal beast make a mad dash toward the man walking their way.

Jon.

Even after all this time, the sudden sight of him still managed to take her breath away. He bent and gave her a kiss on the cheek, then touched the corner of her mouth tenderly with his thumb.

"Mother told me that I would find you here. I have come to escort my lovely wife to luncheon."

Emma's stomach lurched at the notion of food or drink. Swallowing hard, she closed her eyes briefly, then felt Jon's hand on her back.

"Are you ill?"

Her gaze flew upward. "Yes—well, no. I'm feeling a tad nauseous, that's all."

His brows knit together in worry. "You should have told me sooner that you weren't feeling well. I'll have Hopson send for the doctor immediately."

"No." Emma wrapped her fingers around Jon's arm to restrain him from hurrying away. "I've already seen the doctor this morning."

"Why wasn't I told?" Jon asked, his voice rising with concern.

Emma grimaced. This was not the way she had intended to share her news. "I'm with child."

Jon blanched. "What?"

"You heard me correctly, my love," Emma whispered, a tear sliding down her cheek. "We are going to have a baby."

The lines of concern vanished and Jon's face filled with such tenderness that she had trouble controlling her emotional sobs. The tears tickling the back of her eyes began falling freely. Jon folded her into his arms and Emma cried against his shoulder.

A moment later, he pulled far enough away to allow his eyes to skim excitedly over her frame. "Oh, Lord, Emma, you should have told me sooner. Last night in bed . . ." His voice faded away.

"Are you embarrassed about something, my lord?" she teased through watery eyes.

"Damn it, Emma, I was too rough. I should have been more careful. Trust me, from now on I shall be. Unless we should cease marital relations entirely until the child arrives? I'll have to consult with the physician."

"You will do no such thing!" Emma cried, slapping his shoulder. "Besides, I already asked the physician and, uhm . . . he said it was, uhm . . . fine."

"Who is embarrassed now, Lady Kendall?"

"Oh, Jon, we are a well matched pair." She met his eyes and they gleamed with an underlying intensity of emotion. "I've never felt this happy in my life. It almost scares me, for I fear it shall vanish."

"There are no difficulties in life that we cannot conquer if we face them together, my love."

Comforted by the strength of his words and the conviction in his voice, Emma captured his face between her hands. "I love you, Jon. Very, very much."

"And I adore you." His expression turned reflective. "I can't help but wonder, what would I do without you?"

"Lead a dull, reclusive life as a brilliant inventor?" she ventured with a smile.

"Most likely."

Thomas Gabriel Edward Burwell arrived in this world on a snowy winter afternoon, a week later than the physician had predicted.

His grandmother's eyes filled with tears of happiness, his aunts and uncles cheered, and the servants smiled when his lusty cries were heard belowstairs. But it was his parents who shared the greatest euphoria, over the moon to have a healthy child of their own to love and cherish.

Four weeks later they all gathered together in the village church to celebrate Thomas's next milestone. The future viscount slept through his baptismal ceremony, barely opening his eyes when the holy water was gently poured over his head.

His proud grandmother carried him out of the church and his two aunts hovered.

"Your sisters and my mother are in yet another scuffle over whose turn it is to hold our son," Jon observed as they prepared to enter the carriages.

"I'm rather impressed with how righteously indignant your mother can get whenever Gwen or Dorothea tries to take the baby away from her," Emma said with a grin. "Though I'm sure they know she is exaggerating her ire, my sisters have difficulty denying her."

"I find Gwen's strategy of constantly reminding everyone that she'll be returning home soon, so she should be allowed more time with him than the others, rather brilliant," Jon commented. "And it appears to be working."

Emma grinned as she noticed her eldest sister had prevailed and was now cradling the babe in her arms. "I fear that young Thomas will be spoiled rotten well before his first birthday."

"No doubt."

They paused together, hand in hand, to take in the picture of their son surrounded by such a loving family. Emma's eyes suddenly welled with tears.

"I love him so much, Jon. He is, without question, my greatest accomplishment."

"Our greatest," Jon said tenderly. "And he has already brought us more happiness than we ever dared to dream."

Connect with U s

Visit us online at
KensingtonBooks.com
to read more from your favorite authors, see books
by series, view reading group guides, and more.

(Join us on social media)

for sneak peeks, chances to win books and prize packs,
and to share your thoughts with other readers.

facebook.com/kensingtonpublishing
twitter.com/kensingtonbooks

Tell us what you think!

To share your thoughts, submit a review,
or sign up for our eNewsletters, please visit:
KensingtonBooks.com/TellUs.

Books by Bestselling Author
Fern Michaels

___The Jury	0-8217-7878-1	$6.99US/$9.99CAN
___Sweet Revenge	0-8217-7879-X	$6.99US/$9.99CAN
___Lethal Justice	0-8217-7880-3	$6.99US/$9.99CAN
___Free Fall	0-8217-7881-1	$6.99US/$9.99CAN
___Fool Me Once	0-8217-8071-9	$7.99US/$10.99CAN
___Vegas Rich	0-8217-8112-X	$7.99US/$10.99CAN
___Hide and Seek	1-4201-0184-6	$6.99US/$9.99CAN
___Hokus Pokus	1-4201-0185-4	$6.99US/$9.99CAN
___Fast Track	1-4201-0186-2	$6.99US/$9.99CAN
___Collateral Damage	1-4201-0187-0	$6.99US/$9.99CAN
___Final Justice	1-4201-0188-9	$6.99US/$9.99CAN
___Up Close and Personal	0-8217-7956-7	$7.99US/$9.99CAN
___Under the Radar	1-4201-0683-X	$6.99US/$9.99CAN
___Razor Sharp	1-4201-0684-8	$7.99US/$10.99CAN
___Yesterday	1-4201-1494-8	$5.99US/$6.99CAN
___Vanishing Act	1-4201-0685-6	$7.99US/$10.99CAN
___Sara's Song	1-4201-1493-X	$5.99US/$6.99CAN
___Deadly Deals	1-4201-0686-4	$7.99US/$10.99CAN
___Game Over	1-4201-0687-2	$7.99US/$10.99CAN
___Sins of Omission	1-4201-1153-1	$7.99US/$10.99CAN
___Sins of the Flesh	1-4201-1154-X	$7.99US/$10.99CAN
___Cross Roads	1-4201-1192-2	$7.99US/$10.99CAN

More by Bestselling Author
Hannah Howell

Available Wherever Books Are Sold!

Check out our website at
http://www.kensingtonbooks.com